A Life Unraveled

JILL HANNAH ANDERSON

Jill Hannah Anderson

A Life Unraveled
Red Adept Publishing, LLC
104 Bugenfield Court
Garner, NC 27529
https://RedAdeptPublishing.com/

Cover Art by Streetlight Graphics[1]

1. http://StreetlightGraphics.com

In memory of my friend Donna K.

And for everyone dealing with invisible wounds.

Chapter 1

August 2011

NERVES CUT MY STOMACH as if I'd swallowed the circular razor wire gleaming above the chain-link fence. Across the Faribault Correctional Facility parking lot, I turned off the SUV and rolled down the windows. The typical summer morning Minnesota humidity drifted in. As I stepped out of the vehicle, the only noise came from my knees knocking, my teeth chattering. I counted the minutes until eight o'clock, the time listed on the letter.

I fixed my binoculars on the side door where freed prisoners would walk out any minute. Time squeezed my heart like a vise until I spotted him, carrying a cardboard box that likely contained personal items. I waited to see who would pick him up, hoping for a link to the hell I'd been living in the past year. Anything to prove I wasn't losing my mind.

Someone hurried toward him, arms opened wide. Once they broke apart and walked through the parking lot, I had a decent view of their faces. That's when the binoculars slipped from my shaking hands and shock robbed me of my next breath. The answer to so many questions strolled in my direction, arm in arm with him.

July 2010

IN OUR MASTER BATHROOM, I hummed Alicia Keys's "Try Sleeping with a Broken Heart" as I pulled my hair into a ponytail. I passed through our bedroom and stopped to plant a kiss on Luke, stretched out in our bed below the Always Kiss Me Goodnight sign. His scruffy cheek tickled my nose.

"Don't run, Lily. Let's snuggle instead." He reached for my arm to pull me back into bed. A grin spread across the face I fell in love with eighteen years ago. I didn't believe for a second that we'd stop at just snuggling.

"Nope. You know I didn't get any running in on our anniversary trip last weekend." I wagged my finger at him as if he was to blame. He was. After dropping off our three daughters at his parents' home in Chicago for a few days, we had spent most of our free time on bedroom activities at the hotel. We'd even missed a Cubs game.

"I'll be back by seven." I ruffled his hair, revealing a few flecks of stark gray amid the black.

"Love you," we whispered in unison before he closed his eyes and stretched.

I headed down the hall and stopped to check on Codi and Ali, curled up like two little commas in their bedroom, which smelled of sunscreen. Ali's covers lay smooth and neat over her thin body. Behind her, each purple stuffed animal was lined up by size against the wall. Meanwhile, Codi and her covers resembled an EF1 tornado.

I blew them each a kiss before walking past Pria's room. Pria, in that typical teenage give-me-privacy phase, kept her bedroom door closed. Pria had been born two years into our marriage, and I'd assumed getting pregnant again would be easy. Instead, eight years had passed before we'd had Ali. Codi had followed two years later.

In our kitchen downstairs, I downed a glass of water and half a protein bar while I set out Ali and Codi's cereal and bowls. They would likely be up by the time I got back from my run, neither of them late sleepers like their fifteen-year-old sister. Blueberry Mini-

Wheats for Ali—ten, to be exact. Any more or less could derail her for hours. And something laced with sugar—and plenty of it—for Codi to start her day with a smile.

I set my running watch and headed out into our quiet neighborhood, the humid air heavy with the scent of mowed grass and blooming flowers. I started along the paved trail through the woods. As a kindergarten teacher, summers were my time to recharge. Our small town of Lakeview, located forty miles north of the Twin Cities, reminded me of the farming community in Wisconsin where I'd grown up. Slower paced with plenty of fresh air.

As much as I missed farm life, our sprawling neighborhood on the outskirts of town was a wonderful substitute. Most of the neighbors were comfortable enough to ask a favor, friendly enough to stop by unannounced for a visit, and reliable enough to offer help in a pinch. A perfect place to raise children.

Twenty minutes into my route, chatty banter between two oncoming runners interrupted the peace. Runners were creatures of habit. I usually met those women before I passed the halfway mark on my Friday run. Next up would be the tall teenage boy who would give me a silent nod as we passed each other on the trail.

I'd missed my morning run yesterday thanks to Codi, who had turned off my alarm Wednesday night as I cleaned finger paint out of Ali's hair—also thanks to Codi. Last night, we'd hung out with neighbors at the local park for "Thirsty Thursday," a weekly summer event for several of us with young children. While the kids explored the playground or played in the ball field, the parents caught up over drinks or joined in on a game. That meant my butt usually dragged on Friday mornings during the bursts of speed in my fartlek run. It was worth it.

Luke would be tired too. Summers were busy in our lakes area, swelling the customer base at the communications company where he worked as a central office technician. Sometimes, he left early for work to get a jump on his workload. If I didn't make it back home before Luke left, he would wake Pria to watch her sisters, which meant spunky Codi would put Pria through the wringer by the time I arrived home.

During my final sprint, I contemplated our family's weekend plans. Everyone except Pria had voted to take our boat out on the lake north of town tomorrow. She wanted to go to her friend's family cabin. Luke and I would need to decide that morning before he left for work. I wanted Pria to spend time with us, but I remembered what it was like to be a teenager.

My brother and I had been raised to work hard and reap the benefits, one of them being time away from the farm to hang out with our friends. Friends were everything, and Pria had plenty. Things were different for Ali and Codi. Codi would be in kindergarten this year. Most of her friends at the moment were neighborhood children. Ali's social skills had improved last year thanks to an after-school program, one she would attend again in September.

She'd done well last week at his parents' home while Luke and I celebrated our seventeenth wedding anniversary. We'd met on the seventeenth and married on the seventeenth. Luke, ever the romantic, had put our wedding picture in the local newspaper two weeks ago with a short poem he'd written of seventeen things he loved about me. Hopefully, anyone reading the morning newspaper hadn't gagged on their breakfast.

I was so lost in reminiscing that I barely registered passing the teen male I often met on my Friday route. Then my ponytail was yanked backward. I stumbled, and a hand clasped over my face, forcing my stifled breaths into a sweaty palm. Another hand clenched around my waist, pinning my arms. As I was jerked off the trail, I worked an arm free and pushed myself around until I faced the teenage runner. My instincts screamed danger when I caught the steel glare in his eyes as he pulled me into the woods.

His clammy hand suppressed my screams, clenched so tight against my face that I fought to breathe. Fatigue from my sprint run added to my fight for air.

"Get your hands off me!" My command was muffled by his palm. I kicked at his legs but stumbled as he dragged me farther into the woods, brush scratching my bare skin. My eyes scanned the area wildly, and I registered that we were heading in the direction of a ravine. I prayed someone would come by the trail soon and notice me in those dense woods. Luke's warnings over the years for me to stay on well-traveled trails rang like an alarm in my head. I'd considered my route safe.

I tried to bite his palm but couldn't find any loose skin. He was lean and young, about half my age. *What could he want with me?*

He looped a hairy leg over mine, pinning my legs. Hysteria exploded in my chest from the constricted hold he had on me. *Oh, God, don't let him rape me!*

His hand left my mouth for a millisecond, giving me time to scream before material covered my mouth and nose. He wrapped something—*a shirt?*—around my face, pulling it tight against the back of my head. The knot ripped at my hair as it tangled with the tie in the back.

Was he wearing a shirt? Sometimes he ran shirtless depending on the weather. I'd been so engrossed in my thoughts that I hadn't noticed. He pinned my arms to my sides again, and I thrust my left fist into his thigh. I pinched the inside of his leg and clawed at him. He let out a stifled yowl, covering his mouth with his shoulder, but didn't let go.

Somewhere in my brain, I recognized I might not be able to overpower him. I dug into his damp skin so I'd have as much of his DNA under my short fingernails as possible. He'd either let go of me or yell loud enough for someone to hear. I grabbed his crotch and squeezed.

"You bitch! I hate you!" Spit dampened my already sweaty neck. He dragged me deeper into the woods, branches scratching my face and legs.

He hates me? But I had no idea who the teen was. Maybe he'd mistaken me for someone else. I struggled to get my bearings. The trickle of water running in the rock gulley was to my left. I wondered if he planned to leave me there to die.

I lost my footing as he jerked back my ponytail then swung me around again. His foot came up and kicked my right knee so hard it buckled. He wielded a thick tree branch and swung it at my leg. When it connected with my right ankle, my whole leg jolted with pain. I pushed up off the ground, but his fist slammed into my jaw, landing me flat on my back.

He straddled my chest, pinning my arms with his knees as he dug into a side pocket for something in his running shorts. It was substantial, pulling the elastic of his shorts down with weight. His exposed lower abdomen was mere inches away from my face. I spotted small, round burn marks there.

As I tucked those telling marks in my memory, my fingers fumbled for anything I could use as a weapon. I grasped a small stick between the fingers I could still bend and then thrust my arm up. It was enough to gouge the skin on his stomach, enough to draw blood, enough to make a long, deep scratch.

He yanked my feeble weapon from my grip then tossed it aside before he pulled a folding knife from his pocket. He pushed a button that flipped open the knife, revealing a six-inch blade. With one swift move, his arm came toward my chest, aiming for my neck. In a desperate motion, I rammed my uninjured knee into his groin.

His knife missed my neck thanks to the direct hit to his crotch, but pain seared through my left shoulder instead. The searing wound took my focus away from other injuries.

He staggered off of me, cupping his groin.

He dropped the knife! I dragged myself toward it as he struggled to stand behind me. I lunged for the blade then threw it as far as I could. It landed in the gulley nearby, the steel ting echoing against rocks as it fell. It was pointless to use it on him. He was twice my size.

I attempted to rise on my left leg when he caught me.

"I hate you!"

But he gave me no time to think about why he despised me. A blow from behind knocked me to the ground. My skull felt as if it had been hit by a grenade.

I had so much to fight for. But I never got the chance. He bashed my head against the ground. I got a good look at him then, his face mere inches from mine. Green eyes, lighter than Luke's, bushy eyebrows, a cleft chin, and chin-length blond hair. I added every detail to my memory.

It was then that I noticed a faint scar running from below his right ear to under his jaw— it would stand out in a lineup. Something about it niggled at my brain. I struggled to keep my eyes open. Grit and dirt irritated them and filled my nose.

Sticky moisture matted my hair. I pushed against the ground, struggling to stand. My arm collapsed beneath me as he continued to beat me. The metallic taste of blood filled my mouth, my right eye was swollen shut, and my attempts at self-defense left my fingers throbbing in agony.

I no longer feared rape. I feared for my life.

Chapter 2

Someone was feeding me through a wood chipper, like in the movie *Fargo*. My body throbbed. I tried screaming for help, but nobody heard me above the incessant beeping. *What kind of wood chipper beeps?*

A young man, one I recognized but couldn't seem to place, lashed out at me, tortured me. In between the pain, someone would ask me to open my eyes or touch their hand like some cruel joke before they went back to abusing me. And then, the beeping wood chipper.

My panic lessened when Luke's voice penetrated the noise. "I'm here, Lily. I'm here."

Someone glued my eyes shut! I put as much effort into opening them as I did convincing Codi to eat her Brussels sprouts. No luck.

Wait. There he is! Through a sliver of bright light, Luke's face came into focus. Bags pulled at his beautiful eyes. *What's wrong with him?*

"Lily, honey. Nod if you can hear me!" Luke shouted.

Does he think I've gone deaf? Where am I?

He answered my nonverbal question. "You're in the hospital."

In the hospital? So all that racket wasn't a wood chipper.

"Your mom is here, too, at the cafeteria right now. Your dad went back to check on the farm for the day, and my mom has been staying with our girls. Nod if you understand, okay?"

My parents left the farm? They wouldn't leave in the summer. Something must be horribly wrong. I gave a small nod.

"Do you remember what happened? Just nod yes or no. Don't try to speak."

I shook my head. My throat and jaw throbbed like they had been used in a drum solo. Same with the rest of my body, even the inside of my nose.

"You've been through the fight of your life. I'm so thankful you're awake now."

I had a thin line of vision in my left eye and focused it on Luke's beautiful cat-green eyes. Whatever happened to me had made him cry. It was tempting to say I did *not* want to hear what happened. My jaw felt like it needed a shot of oil like the Tin Man in *The Wizard of Oz*.

Luke's jaw quivered as he blinked unshed tears away. "I'll let the doctor explain your injuries. Before I get Dr. Kathy, I'll tell you what's happened the past four days."

"Huh?" I managed. *Four days in the hospital?*

"Yes, it's Monday night. Do you remember going for your run on Friday morning?"

I nodded.

"Do you remember getting attacked during your run?" He covered his mouth with a fist as if it would keep the awful words from spilling out. "Someone dragged you into the woods by Timber Park and left you in the rocky ravine."

Even as my mind raced to deny such an outrageous claim, remembering seeped in like a Kool-Aid stain spreading on a white tablecloth. Yes, yes, I remembered bits and pieces. Things I thought had been part of my nightmare. Instead, they were my reality. The reason I had been out of it in a hospital for four days. I nodded, remembering my morning run near Timber Park—"Thirsty Park," where we'd hung out the night before.

Luke leaned forward. "Do you know the person who did this to you?"

A sharp pain reverberated down my left shoulder as I moved my head. "No."

"A retired Minneapolis cop and his wife were walking his police dog along the trail. The dog caught your scent and led them to the ravine. They called Lakeview Hospital, and an ambulance transferred you here, the Level 1 Trauma Center in Minneapolis."

Hot tears slid down my cheeks, which felt swollen like I'd gained ten pounds in my face. My right eye hurt too much to keep open, so I closed it and focused my left eye on Luke. He grabbed a nearby box of Kleenex then dabbed at my face.

"When I got the call, I woke Pria up, ran next door to ask Irene to help her if needed, then called and left a message on your parents' landline. I called my mom, and she was on the road within the hour. She arrived before supper Friday and has stayed at our house ever since. Your parents got my message when they came in from their morning chores and were here at the hospital by noon." He pinched the bridge of his nose and used a tissue to dry his eyes.

"I spoke with the couple who found you, and also met Detective Doyle Boyle, who is assigned to your case." Luke sat back down next to the bed and gently put his hand on mine. "He interrogated me to make sure I wasn't behind your attack. I had no scratches or marks on me, not to mention I had Codi and Ali as an alibi if needed." He shook his head as if the notion of him hurting me was ridiculous. It was. He'd never laid a hand on me in our eighteen years together, never shown anything but love and respect for me.

"You had plenty of skin under your fingernails, so they know you fought like hell. Someone out there has marks on them thanks to you." He leaned over my bandaged hand and kissed it. "Now, I better get the doctor and your mom. I'll call the detective. He's been waiting to meet with you. I'll be back in a few minutes." He stopped for a second to stare at me with a silly grin as if I'd thrilled him by waking up. As if I'd come back from the dead. Maybe I had.

A minute later, Mom scurried into the room. The tough farm lady who never cried slobbered all over me, doing her best not to hurt me while covering me in kisses and hugs, dodging wires, bandages, and whatever other booby traps surrounded me.

"Oh, Lily, I'm so glad to see you awake!" Mom's face, inches from mine, radiated relief and joy. She pushed her faded-blond hair away from a face that didn't reflect her sixty-four years or decades spent working in the sun. Mom credited Noxzema and a wide-brimmed hat. I'd done my best to protect my skin over the years. I wondered then if I would forever carry wounds from the attack, feeling and looking much older than my almost-forty years.

Mom stepped back from the bed, apologizing for getting so emotional.

Luke walked back in and put his arm around her. "It's okay, Patricia. I feel the same way." He kissed Mom's cheek.

"You can call Jerome first, and then I'll call the detective." He handed his cell phone to Mom—my parents didn't own cell phones. "Doctor Kathy, the trauma surgeon, will be here in a few minutes," he said, blinking away tears.

My mind put up a road block as if in preparation for an onslaught of bad news. My mom and Luke rarely cried, and if I'd been sedated for four days and a trauma surgeon was on her way to speak with me, something horrendous must have happened to me.

Luke and Mom left the room to make calls, and Doctor Kathy, tall with dark-brown hair and eyes, arrived. Her steady smile worked magic in calming my fear of the unknown. As if handling fine china, she stepped forward and touched the bare skin on my arm.

"I'm Dr. Kathy, one of the trauma surgeons who operated on you. We hope to manage your pain but also need you to feel enough to let us know what is working and what isn't. Your husband said he explained what happened to you?"

I nodded.

"You had a brain bleed—a hematoma from an epidural hemorrhage. We performed a unilateral craniotomy and inserted a ventriculostomy tube, which is a temporary external ventricular drain or EVD." Dr. Kathy paused, allowing me to digest her words. "You'll have a small curved scar on the right side of your head. Also, you had a scalp laceration on your head that needed sutures. We had to shave your head."

I didn't care about my hair. Hair grew back. But my brain was another matter. I cared a lot about *that.*

"Once we relieved the pressure around your brain, an orthopedic surgeon did a washout on your patella fracture since it was an open wound. The surgeon stabilized the kneecap with screws and wire cerclage. The knife wound was also attended to on Friday since it was an open wound." The doctor softly touched my upper shoulder, which burned with pain.

"You had a muscle laceration from the knife. It missed your brachial artery"—her finger traced my upper arm—"and missed nerves, thankfully."

I closed my eyes, sure I was stuck in a nightmare. At any moment, I would wake up in our bed, and life would go back to normal. And the incessant pain would go away.

Dr. Kathy interrupted my wishing. "Your jaw was fractured, so they placed a breathing tube in your nose. This morning, a surgeon inserted titanium plates and screws in your jaw, and an orthopedic surgeon inserted pins in your broken fingers."

I'd mentally traveled through my body as she described each injury, flashes of the attack coming back with each wound mentioned, making me flinch.

"We've kept you sedated to keep the pressure and swelling down. After your jaw and finger surgeries this morning, we removed the ventriculostomy and took you off the ventilator." She cleared her throat. "A CT scan was performed Friday morning and again eight hours later to check for any post-surgical complications. I'm happy to report all went well. The epidural hematoma should have no lasting effects on your brain."

I let out the breath I'd been holding, one that pained my ribs.

Dr. Kathy must've seen me wince. "You have a few cracked ribs too. They'll heal on their own. We will have you do deep breathing exercises to ward off possible pneumonia."

She stood at the foot of my bed and gestured toward my foot. "You've got a lateral malleolar fracture in your ankle. The good news is that we didn't need to do surgery. You'll have a walking boot once the swelling goes down."

This woman, and the rest of the Level 1 Trauma team, had my back. They would put that humpty-dumpty body of mine back together again. And to think I'd been ticked off in high school over two broken toes.

"For now, you need rest." Dr. Kathy came to stand by my shoulder. "You've made it through the most difficult period. I'm not saying it will be easy. You'll have extensive therapy." Her smile reached her dark eyes. "But you're tough and otherwise healthy. I've given strict orders that no more visitors are allowed until tomorrow."

I nodded as she turned to leave. She didn't need to convince me. All I wanted to do was sleep. I vaguely remembered Luke, Mom, then my dad entering the room later on. As much as I wanted to wake up and talk to them, a cloud of exhaustion pushed me back into a mind-numbing escape.

Chapter 3

When I awoke, sunlight formed a halo around Mom. She sat next to the bed, her gaze focused to my left, where a whispered conversation took place. I recognized Dad's deep voice and Luke talking with an unfamiliar man. The room held an aromatic combination of black licorice and peppermint. *Is the hospital drugstore nearby?* Slowly, I moved my head to the left.

I'd been awake off and on for the past few hours ever since a nurse checked my vitals at 6:03 a.m. Most of the night was a blur thanks to the medication pumping through my body.

Luke stood next to a man older and taller than him. He wore a wrinkled dress shirt with a handful of black licorice sticking out of the pocket. Dad, in jeans and a denim work shirt, held a Green Bay Packers baseball cap and stood on the other side of Luke. *Dad!*

They were so intent on their conversation, nobody noticed my movement. "We need the sketch artist in here ASAP. Lily's attacker could be thousands of miles away by now," the man said.

I couldn't let that happen. "Skechd ard... ist!" I slurred and tried again. Once I told them what he looked like, they could arrest him, and then maybe my nightmares would stop. He could've killed me. People killed for no reason. Nobody went running with a knife. Yet I sensed he'd held back. *Why?*

The monitor beeped faster as I remembered the glint of the knife and the shirt suffocating me, pulling at my hair. His distinctive marks, vivid in my memory, expanded like an octopus inside me.

Markings I'd worried I'd never get a chance to describe. I struggled for words again.

Dad's deep-blue eyes lit up at my slurring, and he took a step toward me as Mom rose from the chair and moved aside.

"Aw, baby girl!" He crouched to meet my eyes, bracing his beefy arms on the side of the hospital bed. He smelled of hay and fresh air. My one good eye caught the rapid movement of his Adam's apple as he swallowed several times.

"The farm..." My jaw pain had lessened overnight.

"Gus has been milking our cows, feeding the livestock." His face crumpled. Dad rarely asked for help ever since my younger brother, Jacob, left the farm after being kicked out of college. Years later, our long-time farmhand, Earl, had up and deserted Dad. Gus, who owned a farm down the road from my parents, had to be seventy-five or more.

Dad stepped back and took Mom's hand as they joined Luke, allowing the man with black licorice to take a seat next to me.

"Hello, Lily. I'm Detective Doyle Boyle."

I blinked at the name, wondering if my hearing had been damaged too.

"I am so sorry for everything you've gone through. I work for Wright County and have been assigned to your case. Before I bother you for details, I'll try to fill in some information for you, okay?" Freckles surrounded his pale-blue eyes, etched in wrinkles.

"I understand you spoke with Dr. Kathy, so you are aware of the extent of your injuries. Since you were unconscious when they brought you here, they did a rape kit test on you, which is standard procedure in cases like yours." He paused. "Did he rape you, Lily?"

Though his voice remained calm, I felt everyone perch like vultures, ready to feed off my answer, hoping it tasted like reassurance and not despair.

"No... rape." I reaffirmed my words by attempting to shake my head.

The detective nodded. "Good, good. You had your underwear and shorts on. Rapists don't typically re-dress their victims. We won't rush the test results, then." He leaned back for a second to loosen the light-blue tie that matched his eyes. "Jiminy, it's already hotter than a two-dollar pistol out there." He mopped his brow with a handkerchief. "Sorry, I rushed to get here."

His short hair was more white than red and had a curl to it, probably from the heat and humidity. People were going on with their lives outside. Time had stopped for me, and I pretended I could crawl out of the hospital bed, get dressed, and go on with my life as if nothing had changed since Friday morning.

"Luke probably told you I questioned him first, and I had to ask about the status of your marriage, if he thought you were seeing someone." The detective turned to glance at Luke, a half smile on his face. "He informed me he was positive you weren't meeting another guy, that if you 'knew' your attacker, it wasn't in the biblical sense."

"Don't... know him." I closed my eyes at the pain of talking and the pain of remembering. Yet something had seemed familiar about him. I assumed it was just that I often spotted him on my Friday running route.

"I had to ask Luke so we could clear his name. I'd be a half-ass detective if I didn't follow all leads." He chewed on a peppermint. "I used to be a CHP officer in California before leaving my motorcycle behind for detective work. My wife and I moved here to get away from all the crime. We've had no recent attacks in the area, so nothing suggests this is a serial attacker. We've submitted tissue found under your fingernails for DNA testing, but results can take months, much like the rape kit test. I'm hoping that, with your help and a sketch artist, we won't need to rely on the DNA results. They'll come in handy at the trial though."

Trial? The thought of enduring a trial was one more thing I couldn't think about.

"We've interviewed others who came forward, people who run the trail where you were attacked. Nobody saw anything unusual. Same with the people who live around there. Did he put something over your mouth?" He leaned forward, clasping his freckled hands. "I'm assuming you couldn't scream, or eventually, someone would've heard you. There was nothing over your mouth when we found you, but you had indentations on your cheeks and the back of your neck when you were discovered. We didn't locate anything in the area."

"Shirt?" I wished I could have remembered if he'd been wearing a shirt when he'd stopped me. If he had, he wouldn't have had time to take it off without freeing his hand from my mouth. He must have been holding it as he ran.

"Good to know. Did you see the shirt? Was he wearing one when he attacked you?"

I hated to admit I hadn't been paying attention, hadn't been aware of my surroundings—something I'd preached to our daughters and my students more than once. I shook my head no.

"That's okay." He changed the subject. "So, are you up for a sketch artist?"

"Yes!" My body vibrated in anticipation. If I could, I'd sketch the man myself.

"We found a large pocket knife in the ravine near the area of your attack and believe that's what he used to cut your shoulder. I'll need you to identify that later." Machines beeped in sync with his words before he stepped into the hall to call the sketch artist.

"She'll be here shortly," he informed me a few minutes later.

Luke, Mom, and Dad stood like soldiers waiting for the next command. Waiting to see what my attacker looked like.

"Thanks, Detective Doyle. Boyle?" I croaked. "Sorry. Your name..."

He chuckled. "It's okay. Believe me, you aren't the first person confused. It's Doyle Boyle. My Irish parents had some twisted humor. I'm named after my mother's father, Doyle."

I attempted a smile for him then rested until the sketch artist arrived. The young woman went to work, beginning with the suspect's approximate age group. I chose fifteen to twenty-five.

Luke, standing next to the sketch artist, raised his eyebrows. I'd been just as surprised that someone so young would attack me.

"Have you seen him before?" the artist asked.

"Yes. He runs."

She wrote various hair colors on the sketch pad below the face. I grunted when her pencil touched "blond," then I did the same with eye color, "green."

From there, I tried to use as few words as possible or nodded as his face took shape. Longer, wavy hair, full mouth, darker eyebrows, thin face, around six feet tall. The sketch looked enough like the face that had haunted my dreams. It could also have been a hundred different teens, the description too general. But finally, luck ran in my favor thanks to his unique marks.

"Scar." I fought off the panic that clawed like a tiger. I remembered that face, that scar, inches above mine as I fought to stay alive.

"Where, Mrs. Gallo?" The artist's pencil hovered above the drawing until she landed on his right ear. I indicated the scar ran from the bottom of his ear down the side of his neck.

That was a game-changer. Not many guys around there had a telltale scar like that. As she worked down the torso of the man, I said, "Stop. Small burns."

"Like cigarette burns?" Boyle asked from behind me.

I nodded. I wanted to explain how I saw his lower stomach when he hadn't sexually assaulted me, but it took too many words. I would explain later. For the moment, I zeroed in on the detective, who sucked in a gulp of air behind me.

"Son of a bitch!" he muttered under his breath. He rounded my bed and stood in front of the sketch, rubbing a freckled hand over his lined face.

"Son of a bitch" was right. Detective Boyle recognized the guy. I read it in his slouched shoulders, in the frustration slicing his words, and in the way he pinched the bridge of his nose. My gut churned, sensing this wouldn't be an easy arrest.

"I need to make a call," Detective Boyle announced before turning to stroll out the door, whistling as if he didn't have a care in the world. I'd only just met him, and I didn't buy his happy-go-lucky demeanor for a second. Luke followed, likely determined to get answers, leaving me stuck in a hospital bed, clueless.

Chapter 4

After Luke came back in the room, swearing Detective Boyle hadn't told him who he believed the attacker was, Mom wisely suggested I take a nap. The emotional exhaustion from reliving and relaying the attack had sapped all my energy. As soon as the next round of my pain meds kicked in, I zonked.

I would fade in and out, certain a man who resembled Dr. McDreamy came to visit. *What is this,* Grey's Anatomy*?* When I woke up, I asked Luke about him.

"He's the orthopedic surgeon who operated on your fingers."

Luke's face was close enough for me to smell the soap on his skin. He and Mom had been taking turns going home to sleep, shower, and eat a decent meal—thanks to Luke's mom, Rita, and her fabulous cooking.

Rita was the opposite of the dreaded mother-in-law. She'd retired two years ago and had been pacing like a caged tiger ever since, waiting for Luke's dad, Louis, to retire so they could travel. She was like an overgrown kid herself, and our daughters loved Grandma Rita. And her cooking. She'd grown up in Puerto Rico but embraced Luke's father's Italian heritage. She made a mean ravioli that stood up to Luke's Nona's approval, which said a lot from a mother who didn't want her son to marry a woman from "someplace else." As if Nona hadn't come all the way from Italy herself. Our girls loved Rita's energy and the made-up stories she would tell. I treasured her for all of those things and more. Mostly for giving me such a loving husband.

"Your parents went back to our house for supper and to get some rest. Pria would like to see you, but I think Ali and Codi are too young to visit you yet. It might upset them, especially Ali. If you can wait, it might be for the best."

As much as I missed the girls, I probably looked like Frankenstein. "Okay." Ali handled change better this past year, but my physical appearance went way beyond the realms of her comfort zone.

"What about Pria coming to visit?"

Pria was responsible, smart, and level-headed. And in her volatile-hormone years. The way she'd been acting, it surprised me that Pria *wanted* to see me. Anything that went wrong seemed to be my fault. She might look at my attack the same way.

"Up to you," I mumbled. "Boyle back yet?"

"Any minute," Luke said.

The sketch artist had left with the detective. Boyle informed Luke that he would be back with photos of possible suspects for me to look through.

Luke paced beside my bed until Detective Boyle walked into the room with six enlarged driver's license photos.

"These men loosely fit your description. I'll show them to you one at a time so you can study them. Your attacker may not be one of the six, but we'd like to rule out these possibilities, okay?" His voice was as smooth as butter.

I focused with my uninjured eye as he slid the first photo in front of me. "Nope." The man was too old.

The teen in the next photo was too husky. The one after that had freckles, and his teeth were crooked. I worried my assailant wasn't in the stack. And none of them had a scar on their neck. Until the fifth photo.

"That's him!" Spit flew as I did my best to enunciate.

"Are you sure?" Boyle's clenched jaw led me to believe that was the guy he'd pegged as my attacker too. If nothing else, the end of a scar showing below his short blond hair would've been a telltale sign. He presented the last photo to me as if I'd change my mind. I shook my head no.

I focused back on the fifth photo. "Who is he?"

"Dalton Digg. He'll be a senior in high school. I'm sure you've heard of him." Boyle sighed as if the discovery exhausted him.

My eyes darted back and forth between Dalton's smiling face in the photo and Luke's contorted face as the name registered. "Huh?"

"You mean the football star?" Luke raised his voice as if scolding Boyle for saying something so ridiculous. Dalton Digg was the star quarterback of the high school football team. "I've seen his picture several times in the local newspaper, but the photo is in black and white, and his hair looks darker and super short compared to Lily's description."

Anxiety thrummed through me. There had to be some mistake. *Why would the star quarterback attack me?* I then understood Boyle's concern. High school football fans would be one step away from a riot with the news.

"Yes, that's him. He's on the track team too, so I'm not surprised that you've seen Dalton running on the trail." Boyle pushed his chair back and stood. "I appreciate your help, Lily. I'm sure it was difficult to look at him again, but we needed positive confirmation."

"Why in the hell would the star quarterback attack Lily?" Luke asked.

Boyle shrugged. "That's a question I hope to get answered. Dalton's been in and out of foster homes most of his life. I believe the scar and burns are from his younger years at home—that tells you what his home life was like before. This is a surprise for me and will shock the socks off the community. He's only lived in Lakeview a few years." Boyle pointed to his neck. "That scar and the burn marks on his stomach are as common knowledge as his impressive football stats."

"I don't get it. It's not like Lily was ever his teacher." Luke ran a hand through his hair, making it stick up. "Hell, we haven't even attended football games in the past couple of years. Our oldest daughter has had junior high soccer games on Friday nights."

"I don't know what to tell you," the detective said. "He's in a decent foster home now with stable, loving parents, has been since he moved here. His life was a shitshow before that." He frowned. "Unless he's got a twin with the same markings, we've got our man."

I took in a deep breath, which spiked pain through my ribs. Anger clearly still flowed under the surface for him. Sad to say, many children had a horrible upbringing. But most didn't beat the hell out of a total stranger. "What now?"

"I contact Prosecutor Katz, and he issues a criminal complaint showing probable cause to support the charges. Then a judge signs it, and we issue a warrant for Dalton's arrest." Boyle blew out a long sigh. "After that, he's jailed until his arraignment, which may tick off some football fans. As you know, he's got an enormous fan base, not only because of his outstanding athletic ability but because it's well known about his troubled past. They cheer him on for rising out of a difficult situation."

Luke scoffed. "It doesn't seem like he conquered his troubled past. Something is wrong with him to attack Lily like this."

"You're right. I don't think Dalton's shaken the demons like everyone thought." Boyle turned to me. "It doesn't help that football season is right around the corner."

Luke was back to pacing. "Pria will be a sophomore this fall, which means she'll attend the senior high with Dalton—if he's free on bail."

I cringed at that. The team had made it to the state tournament the last two years with the monster as their quarterback. That year the team—and town—were counting on him to lead them to a state championship. Not if Luke and I had anything to say about it.

After the detective left, Luke pulled up a chair next to me. His hand felt like a whisper under my three fingers in splints. We sat in silence, deep in our thoughts. I reflected on the suburb we'd lived in for most of our married life. We loved our neighborhood, our jobs, and the convenience of most everything nearby without the congestion of city life.

We'd agreed Lakeview was the right size for us—city boy and farm girl. But our perfect-sized town's high school students might take Dalton's arrest out on Pria. Ali and Codi weren't at the finger-pointing age yet, but teenagers could be real jerks. And Pria would be on the bottom rung of the ladder in the high school.

PHYSICAL THERAPY BEGAN the following day, and soon, counseling would follow—according to my doctor. *That's what they think.* Farm kids were raised to suck it up. Jacob, my brother, followed that rule until around the time he graduated from high school. I hadn't seen him in years and wondered if he followed any rules now, or if every day was a struggle for him. After almost twenty years, we had something in common again.

I slept off and on that late Tuesday afternoon. While I visited with my parents and Luke, Detective Boyle and a woman walked in and announced my attacker's arrest.

The woman placed herself in my line of vision. "Hello, Lily. I'm Brook Henry, your crime victim advocate, or CVA for short." Her dark, shiny hair was pulled back from her olive skin and dark-brown eyes, her voice soft yet professional. "I'm sorry that we meet under these circumstances."

I nodded slightly since I couldn't muster a handshake.

"Now that you have a case, I'll be here to help in any way I can. Dalton turned eighteen in June. They'll try him as an adult, which is a plus for you. My job is to help you with your legal rights, provide you with information, and offer emotional support through this process."

I felt like I'd just been pulled from the brink of death and was suddenly expected to fight another battle. I pictured Dalton going back to his foster family after attacking me. I'd fought like hell. They had to have seen his wounds. *Evidence!*

"What about... his scratches?" I asked, my jaw throbbing.

Detective Boyle flipped open a small notepad. "Dalton's been helping his grandparents. He stays there often in the summer. They live in a town nearby. That's where they arrested Dalton. With their health problems, they may not have noticed his scratches and bruises. If they did, who knows what story Dalton fed them?"

"What matters is that he's behind bars now," Brook added, reassuring me.

"I need to ask a few questions," Detective Boyle said. "Did you often see Dalton on the running trails? Recently or for several months?"

I tried to do the math in my head. When I'd crossed paths with him on those trails, I considered whether I'd seen him in running tights, a winter cap, or gloves. "Months?"

"Like since last winter or so? We're trying to determine what may have triggered him now. It's clear he planned the attack."

"Maybe since winter," I said. *What triggered him? Was he in pain?* I doubted it.

After Brook and Detective Boyle left, I rested. Mom and Pria arrived at the hospital at five.

"We brought you supper." Mom handed Luke Tupperware containing Rita's ravioli. My mouth watered. I wondered how long it would be before I could eat anything.

Pria stiffened when she saw me even though Luke said he'd warned her about my physical injuries. For the moment, we could ignore my emotional wounds. In fact, I wanted to bury them forever.

Last night, I'd insisted Luke hold a mirror up so I could see myself. The bruised and swollen face and a shaved head with stitches had jolted me. No wonder I'd shocked my daughter.

Mom put her arm around Pria's shoulders. "It may not look like it, but she's doing okay." She gave me an encouraging smile before stepping forward to kiss my cheek.

Then slowly, Pria walked toward me, reaching for my hand where pins were placed in some of my broken fingers. She caressed the top of my hand with one of hers as the other covered her trembling mouth. "I'm so sorry, Mommy!" She pulled her hand from mine, dabbing her eyes with her wrist.

Mommy? She hadn't called me that in years. *And what is she sorry for?*

"Don't be sorry. Not your fault."

Luke stepped in. "It's scary to see your mom like this, but—"

"That's not it." Pria cut him off before grabbing a handful of tissues.

"What is it?" I asked.

Pria turned back to me but kept her distance. "Oh, Mommy, are you mad at me? Please don't be mad at me."

Mad? I couldn't imagine she knew the monster. Even if she did, his attack had nothing to do with Pria. She thumbed away tears.

"You did nothing wrong." I wasn't 100 percent sure of that. Pria was a teenager. I guessed there were plenty of things she did that I didn't know about.

Pria fiddled with the fray on her jean shorts. "Remember last week when you asked for your running shorts with the pockets?" She hiccupped through sobs. "I pretended I forgot you asked so I could keep wearing them to soccer practice. If I'd have given them back to you, you could've carried Dad's cell phone with you, and then n-n-nothing c-c-could've h-h-happened."

Luke pulled Pria in for a hug. Something I wished I could do. "Aw, Pria, a cell phone wouldn't have saved her in this case. Your mom has run for twenty years without a cell phone, and nothing has happened. The shorts wouldn't have changed a thing."

He cast a look at me over Pria's head. He'd tried pushing a cell phone and pepper spray on me before, preaching about staying safe while running. The line he'd fed Pria was the response I'd told him more than once. He didn't like my answer then but now used it as a balm to soothe our daughter. And make a point with me.

I moved my broken fingers above the blanket, attempting to reach for her. She noticed the gesture. "Love you, Pria. It's okay."

She stepped forward and gently took my hand, smiling through her tears. And I felt a sense of peace for the first time in days.

Chapter 5

A nurse had me hobbling around again that morning, my second day out of bed. The clunky boot on my right ankle and a cast from my crotch to the ankle boot made it a challenge, along with maneuvering crutches with splints immobilizing some of my fingers.

Physical therapy had started yesterday. First up was learning to use crutches with my shoulder and finger injuries.

"The longer you veg out in bed, the more muscle strength you lose," the day nurse said.

Her words hit home. I wanted to run again, *needed* to run. I tightened my grip and finished my lap.

"You're lucky he didn't break your thumbs. At least this way, you can use crutches."

Yes, lucky, lucky me.

They'd moved me out of intensive care yesterday and into a step-down unit where I had a nice view of downtown Minneapolis from my bed. I had to use the bathroom on my own—one of many goals that week before I could transfer to a mainstream room.

During one of my shuffles around the step-down room with Luke on one side supporting me and a crutch on the other, Brook knocked on the door and peeked in. Luke waved her in then helped me back into bed, my body aching from that bit of exercise jostling my injuries.

"I wanted to fill you in on what's happening. At today's arraignment, the public defender representing Dalton informed Prosecutor Katz that Dalton said he had nothing to do with your attack. They're arguing that you picked him out of the photos because he looked familiar—that you see him while running and his photo is often in the newspaper." Brook's eyebrows arched in an "isn't that a line of bull?" look. "Detective Doyle may have more details for you."

"He's lying!" The pain in my jaw limited the rant I wished to unleash. Right now, it was my word against his. They may need to rush the DNA tests after all.

"Dalton also pointed out that you two don't know each other, which you've backed up in your statement. So why would he go after you?" Brook took a deep breath. "And as far as the scar on his neck and the burn marks on Dalton's stomach, his argument is that they're common knowledge." Brook and Luke exchanged a look as if they'd been force-fed dog poop.

I'd done my best to explain how the knife in his shorts pocket had pulled down the elastic waist so that when he leaned over me, his lower stomach was eye level as he pinned me to the ground. I hoped they could envision what'd happened and understood my mumbling.

"We get it, and we've seen your extensive injuries firsthand. But some of the football community may want to downplay your injuries once word gets out about Dalton's arrest—which will happen soon." Brook took a sip of Diet Coke.

"The newspaper ran the story about Lily's injuries after the attack, how she could have died. Isn't that enough for the public?" Luke folded his arms across his chest, tucking his hands under his arms—one of his go-to ways to keep from cracking his knuckles.

"People have short memories. If Dalton sits in jail for the next few months, some of the football community that's been relying on him to carry the team to a state win might choose to forget what they read," Brook said.

My stomach roiled at the way my world continued to spiral.

"They may not know the truth, but the law does. That's what matters." Luke kissed my cheek. I inhaled his scent, which reminded me of fresh sheets on the clothesline after they'd hung in the sunshine all day. He'd used the same deodorant and aftershave since I'd met him. I could pick him out of a crowded room blindfolded.

I wished for a legal system that wouldn't allow the accused to roam free while the victim struggled to recover. The football team winning shouldn't be so all-consuming for people. I thought of the students who would start high school soon. I'd taught some of those football players when they'd been in kindergarten. I wondered where their loyalties would lie. *And why should I need anyone's loyalty?* The truth should persevere. Even as I thought it, I knew it wasn't always the case. A squeaky cry escaped my throat. Me, a previously rare crier like Mom.

"Luke's right," Brook said, trying to comfort me. "We've got detailed statements from the couple who found you. Having a retired police officer be the first on the scene will be a big plus if this goes to trial. It doesn't point fingers at Dalton, but it backs up the extent of your injuries. They'll go over Dalton with a fine-tooth comb, looking for any scratches or injuries from you, like the mark you left on his stomach. He'll have to explain that."

I closed my eyes, wondering how the football community would react. I shouldn't have to care, but there was Pria. I could handle their wrath. She shouldn't have to. She would be a sophomore soon, surrounded by avid football fans. *How will they treat her in school?*

As soon as everyone left the room, that fear pushed me to reach for my savior and new best friend—the patient-controlled analgesia IV pain pump.

I THOUGHT OF MY CHILDREN every night, worrying how Pria's first year in high school would go with my attacker's arrest, how Ali was handling the chaos with her need for structure, and if spunky Codi was wearing out Grandma Rita. My parents had gone back to the farm for a day or so. Mom would return so Rita could go back to Chicago for a few days. They would continue tag team helping Luke with the girls even once I arrived home.

And every night, I had nightmares. Sometimes horrible, realistic nightmares that began after they moved me out of ICU. Nightmares so vivid, I swore I felt warm breath on my neck with whispered threats. "I could easily smother you with a pillow, finish off the job."

The words cut me like a scythe as I fought to wake up, certain someone was there. I had to remind myself that they'd arrested my attacker. There was no way he could sneak into my room. No, no, they were just bad dreams, much like the wood chipper nightmare.

I blamed the meds for messing with my head. I'd never been a pill popper, never felt the need to cushion pain with alcohol or drugs. But I'd never been in that condition before. *Was this what Jacob felt like?* In college, he'd fallen down an entire staircase. The extreme pain had made him reach for the bottle with one hand and push our parents and me away with the other.

I promised myself I would manage without medication once I was home with my family. After two long weeks in the hospital, I was antsy to leave. They'd taken X-rays to monitor the healing of my bones, I had no signs of pneumonia from my cracked ribs, and PT was going well. Once they removed the pins from my fingers—hopefully within the next few weeks—I could start occupational therapy. They would remove my leg cast within a month, and I could begin rehab and range-of-motion exercises for my knee. I didn't care if I had to perform in a circus when I got out of the hospital. I just wanted to be home again.

My spirits lifted when Rita and Luke brought Ali and Codi to visit. I wore a soft-green hat Mom had knitted for me. The swelling and discoloration in my cheeks and right eye had lessened, and I beamed when they ran into the room.

"Mommy, Mommy! I bringded you some chocolate chip cookies!" Codi bounced on her heels next to the bed, clutching the container close to her rounded tummy. I guessed she'd been told I couldn't eat anything solid yet and was certain she hoped to eat every single cookie herself.

Luke took the container then set it on the window ledge.

"That was thoughtful of you." My heart felt as light as a butterfly.

Ali stood quietly behind Codi, her hands clasped behind her back.

"And do you have something, Ali?" I asked.

"Yes." She revealed a bouquet of wildflowers. Daisies, purple thistle, and black-eyed Susan, all arranged in a quart Mason jar.

"Thank you both." I enveloped their small bodies that offered hope. Their visit inspired me to work harder with the physical therapist so I could move back home.

After Rita left with the girls, Luke stayed. "What's wrong?" he asked, noticing sadness pull at my face. "Are you worried about Ali? I know she seemed pretty solemn tonight, but I promise you, she's doing okay."

"That's not it. Well, that's part of it." I shook my head. "Don't think I'm losing it, but I've had horrible nightmares where I swear someone was in my room, whispering threats." I understood how silly it sounded to someone whose life wasn't being threatened.

"They've been since I was transferred out of ICU. It felt as if someone was in the room during the night, whispering how they could hold a pillow over my face, stifle my breathing, snuff me out for everything I've done. I swore I felt their warm breath on my cheek, sensed their presence, yet I couldn't seem to wake up." I closed my eyes, my body thrumming in pain.

"Honey, people can't wander around the halls here at night. The staff would nail them. It's probably flashbacks of the attack haunting you. Maybe too much of your pain meds?"

I opened my eyes at his words. Yes, I'd questioned myself. I didn't need him jumping on the bandwagon. But what could I say? Reason told me—and Luke—that the well-monitored hospital wouldn't allow such a breach of security.

My family and the medical staff suggested I meet with a counselor at the hospital. I used my jaw pain as an excuse for not wanting to talk too much and promised I'd schedule counseling once it healed. Honestly, I wanted to forget the monster existed. I couldn't understand why in the hell people thought I should revisit the horror.

THE SUN SET OUTSIDE the hospital windows, reminding me that our too-short Minnesota summer was passing me by outside. Luke left for home to get a decent night's sleep. I dreaded the nighttime, the darkness. Being alone. And if I was honest, I was a little upset at Luke's reaction when I'd told him about someone sneaking in my room at night. Doubt had never been a part of our marriage. Once we were under the same roof again, things would be better.

And I would be off my pain meds. The days coated with mind-dulling meds from my patient-controlled analgesia pump were over, although if I belly-ached at all, pain medication was freely given. I fought the urge so I wouldn't follow my brother's path.

I stared out the window, lucky to have a beautiful view from my room. Tonight's sunset brushed orange and amber hues over the skyline. The Metro Light Rail moved between buildings, the sun's light gleaming on its white-and-yellow fiberglass top.

Seeing the Light Rail reminded me of another summer day, back in 1992, when a long train had changed my life. It was the summer before my senior year of college, and I was living back home at our family farm in Wisconsin. I had the day off from my two waitressing jobs and was caught in a line of cars waiting for the train to pass through our small town. Roxette's "It Must Have Been Love" played on the radio as I drummed impatience on the steering wheel. My best friend, Kara, was waiting for me to pick her up so we could head to the beach for the day.

That's when I'd sensed it—that feeling of being watched. The driver of the battered pickup in front of me stared at me via his side mirror, sunglasses perched on top of his dark hair. His light-colored eyes stood out against his bronze skin and gleaming smile, which I returned with one of my own. I didn't recognize him, and I knew most everyone in our town. Once the train passed, I might never see him again.

When the cars ahead of us pulled away to cross the tracks, I hit the gas and lightly bumped into the back of his low-riding beater of a pickup.

He turned around and grinned before pulling off to the side of the road. I parked behind him, turned off my car, then used my beach towel to wipe the sweat from my face, neck, and armpits. I stepped out of the car, pulling at the bottom of my jean shorts, which had ridden up my butt. I didn't want him to think I was coming on to him. I was totally coming on to him.

He hopped out of his pickup, the rest of him as cute as his face. "That's a darn shame you accidentally rear-ended me." He pretended to inspect the rusted and dented tailgate. "Now we will have to exchange names, phone numbers... all sorts of personal information." He put his hand out to shake mine. "Luke Gallo. Nice to meet you." His grin was so bright, I expected stars sparkling on his teeth like in chewing gum commercials.

"I'm sorry. My foot must have slipped onto the gas pedal instead of the brake. I'm Lily Connor. Are you from around here?" I needed to gather as much information as possible in case he was in a hurry to go somewhere. Like, God forbid, a girlfriend's house.

"Nope. Chicago. My aunt and uncle own a farm near here. I've worked for them every summer during college. I graduated from the University of Minnesota in May. How about you? What do you do when you're not intentionally ramming into vehicles?"

I blushed. Busted. "I'll be a senior this fall at the University of LaCrosse."

He nodded toward the tailgate. "Should we pretend to inspect the damage or skip ahead to exchanging phone numbers?"

"To be clear, I've never done that before. Do you want my phone number and insurance card in case you find some major damage to your tailgate?" I could've taken a crowbar to it, and it wouldn't have made a difference to the rusty rattletrap.

His mouth twitched. "Good idea. Your phone number, address, and also when you're free. You know, to discuss the accident in further detail." He followed me back to my car, and I wrote on a scrap of paper every way he could contact me.

He tucked the paper inside his wallet. "I better get your information, too, in case..." I struggled to come up with a feeble excuse for why I would need to contact him.

"In case I develop amnesia?" Luke helped me out. I handed him the pen and the small notebook I'd used. He scribbled his information on a page before giving it back to me. He leaned in closer to me, smiling. "I'd hate to forget you," he whispered.

After we'd parted ways, I picked up Kara and recited in excruciating detail every word Luke had said. And like the best friend Kara was, she had let me blather on. When I'd arrived home that night, Mom said a young man named Luke had called for me. Twice.

A nurse interrupted my happy reminiscing when she entered the room to get me ready for bed. As I settled in for the night, I had one goal—to get out of the hospital and be home with Luke and our girls. Eighteen years after our chance meeting, I still craved being with him, the pull even stronger than my desire for pain pills.

Chapter 6

Pria and Luke sat in my room after I'd been given the thumbs-up to leave the hospital by the end of the week—three weeks after the attack. I shared the good news, but Pria didn't acknowledge it. She was in a pissy mood.

"I don't want to go to soccer practice next week."

"Why?" She'd been looking forward to high school soccer since she first began playing in fifth grade. I thought soccer would help take her mind off things.

She rolled her eyes. She was almost a miniature version of me, her coloring and attitude so similar to mine at that age, but I'd done a better job of hiding my assertiveness. Ali and Codi had more of Luke's Puerto Rican and Italian genes, their hair and skin a little darker and their eyes brown, even though Luke had green eyes—the only one in his family other than Rita's sister.

"Ugh, Mom. Do you know what it's going to be like with the star football player accused of attacking you? What if he has to go back to jail? They'll blame *me.* And the football team starts practice next week too. I'm going to have to see him and the other football players!"

He was out on bail, and Luke had done his best to keep any rumors away. I had no idea what people were saying about me. I didn't want to endure a trial. I wanted him thrown in the slammer and for me and my family to get on with our lives and forget it ever happened.

Detective Boyle had called earlier and said he would stop to speak with Luke and me later that day. The man was stoic, never giving away if the news was good or bad. All he said was he had a "Dalton update," and as I looked at Pria's downturned demeanor then, my primary concern was how it would affect her.

"Keep your chin up, Pria. People don't have all the facts, and hopefully, most people will keep their opinions to themselves," Luke said.

Our eyes met over Pria's head as she leaned her elbows on her tanned legs. Teens could be cruel.

"They're saying that even if Dalton gets off, he might lose any chance at a college scholarship," Pria whispered at the floor.

"Too. Damn. Bad." I'd spend the next several months fighting to become even close to "normal" again. It was a wait-and-see process. Physically, there was a chance. But the verdict was out on the emotional damage. I didn't give a flying monkey whether he nabbed a football scholarship.

Detective Boyle said they'd held back some information from the press. I wanted to steal the megaphone from the head football coach and shout the facts to our community. Like the fact that other runners verified seeing him on the trail that morning. Or the fact that I'd given details of a long scratch he should have on his stomach from the stick I'd used as he leaned over me—a mark they found after his arrest. He'd claimed it had come from cleaning up the brush in his grandparents' yard. He'd said I'd have noticed it since he'd run shirtless that morning.

Luke and Pria left soon afterward. He would drop her off at home, put a few hours in at work, and be back later. Until then, I had physical therapy followed by a nap on my schedule.

That afternoon, Boyle arrived and got right to the point as he pulled up a chair next to my bed, dabbing at the perspiration on his neck from the August humidity. Luke, who'd been doing work on his laptop, shut it and stood, listening like a tiger ready to pounce.

"As you well know, Dalton has had an excuse for every scratch, every accusation, and everything we've thrown at him. As his attorney points out, it's nothing concrete. So I've asked for a rush on the DNA testing. And I let Dalton and the public defender know it. Make them sweat a little, put an annoying itch in their underwear." Boyle sat back in the chair.

Luke cracked his knuckles, pacing behind Boyle. "How long will the results take?"

"Could be a month. Hard to say. The BCA is the only DNA lab in Minnesota, and since this isn't for a murder or sexual assault—thank heavens for that—I can only ask so much." Boyle shrugged. "Prosecutor Katz and Dalton's public defender have mutually agreed to delay the omnibus hearing until DNA results are in."

"It would be nice to get the results before football and school starts." I'd hoped once the public found out his DNA was a match, it would help smooth the way for Pria at school. Nobody could harass her once we had concrete proof. At least, that was my wish.

THREE DAYS LATER, THREE weeks to the day since I'd entered the hospital, I was officially given the stamp of approval to go home.

The ride home felt like ice cream on a hot summer day, like breathing in a bouquet of peonies and lilacs, like driving the tractor on the farm, sunshine warming me as I breathed in the heady scent of hay. It felt damn good.

I'd dodged a rehab center with the promise of a quiet transition and plenty of help at home. Luke's mother brought Ali and Codi back to Chicago with her while Luke, my mother, and I adjusted to the rigors of caretaking away from the hospital. Codi had too much energy for me right then, and Ali didn't need more upheaval in her life. Pria stayed home with us. Her soccer, and the high school football team's practice, started next Monday.

One of the obvious changes I noticed during my first few days at home was how much Pria sat in her room. Not biking to the beach with her girlfriends, not chatting on the phone, not on social media—the new lifeline for teens. We had one computer, and it sat in the corner of our family room. I didn't know what she was doing in her bedroom and sure as hell would not get the truth from her. All our bedrooms were upstairs, and I had to sleep in a hospital bed in the corner of our living room until I could maneuver the stairs.

TWO DAYS INTO HER SOCCER practice, I sat with Pria and my mom at the kitchen table. Pria picked at her half-eaten peanut-butter-and-honey sandwich. Luke was back at work, and Mom had just picked Pria up from practice.

"Soccer isn't any fun at the senior high." She glared at her sandwich as if it was at fault. "Everyone blames me, well, *you*, for Dalton getting into trouble."

I flinched. "Everyone?" I didn't imagine that was the case, but even a few people would be a few too many for Pria.

She nodded.

"It will be hard, especially for you, but we all need to let the nasty comments roll off our backs. Easy for me to say, I know." Other than doctor appointments, I wouldn't be going anywhere soon. I could stay cushioned in our home, away from the public, making it easy to pop an extra pain pill. The DNA results couldn't come fast enough for me. For my family.

"This would all be different if he was still a tough kid struggling at his mom's house, getting into trouble." I paused, choosing my words. "People often ignore the facts when it comes to a sports hero. Like OJ Simpson, for example."

Pria looked at me. "Who?"

Mom and I chuckled. "OJ was arrested for killing his ex-wife and another man the year you were born. He was a famous football player, a movie star. And many people refused to consider he might commit such a horrific crime."

Pria pushed her plate aside, digesting my words instead.

"People believe what they want. Right now he has some football fans on his side who feel sorry for him because of his crappy upbringing. Not knowing why he attacked me makes it harder to defend. Once we get the DNA results and he's proven guilty, things should improve." Until then, the he said, she said was ugly for everyone, especially Pria.

THE FOLLOWING MORNING, Luke walked into the living room after showering when his cell phone rang. It was Brook Henry. He sat at the edge of my bed and put her on speakerphone.

"I didn't want to call your landline and possibly wake Lily and the girls. Are you leaving for work soon?" It was almost seven o'clock.

"In about half an hour. Why? Did something happen?"

"Doyle and I will stop by your house soon. Dalton's left town." She hung up.

Luke and I stared at each other in surprise.

Brook and Boyle knocked on our front door ten minutes later, and Luke led them into the living room.

"What's going on?" I bypassed any pleasantries.

"Dalton jumped bail. As you know, one requirement is that he doesn't leave town," Brook said. "His birth mom had been lurking around his foster home last spring. They haven't seen her since June and figured she'd left town." She smirked. "She did, but apparently, she's back now. She picked him up after football practice last night."

Luke reached for my hand, well on its way to healing.

"And...?" I asked.

"We have witnesses. A few players described a rusted brown four-door sedan. They didn't recognize her but saw a petite woman with blond hair arguing with Dalton before he got in the passenger seat. She slid back into the driver seat and sped off," Detective Boyle said.

I gripped Luke's hand. It could be the break we needed.

"His foster mom reported him missing when he didn't show up after practice," he continued. "The foster parents gave police the make of Dalton's mother's car. They had her license plate number. The description of the vehicle sounds similar to the one the football players observed. Throw the arguing in, and it sounds like his mother was trying to convince Dalton to leave with her and succeeded."

"She has 'issues,' otherwise he'd never have been put in foster care over the years," Brook said. "Guess she got the motherly bug right before his eighteenth birthday, about eighteen years too late for him."

Realization spread relief through me. "When they catch him, they'll throw him in the slammer, right? Bail violation?"

"Bingo," Boyle said.

Luke and I smiled at each other. One more reason for him to be behind bars.

Chapter 7

A few days after I'd returned home, depression set in, and with it, my craving for pain medication. As a farm girl, I'd never been afraid of hard physical work, but the internal pain and guilt at everything my family was going through was incessant torture.

Mom and I were in the kitchen when Detective Boyle called our landline with some good news. Two days after the monster left town, they'd arrested him and his mother in Ely, Minnesota, sneaking out of a café without paying.

"So now what happens?" Hope perked me up.

"Now he's back in jail for violating his bail conditions. His mom will be extradited back to Iowa, where she was out on bail for drug charges. Seems like she has a problem staying in her town too."

After I hung up, Mom asked, "What's wrong?"

I relayed Boyle's message to her while she blended a green smoothie for me.

We sat at the kitchen table, and she sipped her morning coffee while I stirred my smoothie. "This may make things worse for Pria once the hard-headed football fans find out he's back in jail."

"Maybe the team will do okay without him," Mom said.

The football team's season would begin in two weeks—a team that had made it to state on the monster's shoulders. Without him, they would need a miracle. I no longer believed in miracles. I doubted my family did either.

ONE WEEK AFTER COMING home, I still felt as unsettled as I had in the hospital. My attacker's second arrest that morning helped calm my nerves somewhat, but the knowledge our fight was far from over only tempted me to pop another pill. Instead, Mom drove me to my doctor appointment, where they took X-rays of my ankle and fingers to make sure my bones were healing according to schedule.

If only everything else in my life would heal as it should. Later that afternoon, while I rested in the living room, our phone rang. Mom answered, and her voice carried down the hall from the kitchen to the living room so I could catch bits and pieces of the conversation. I assumed it was Dad, checking to see what time she would be home tomorrow.

Rita would arrive back from Chicago with Ali and Codi tomorrow, and Luke would be home for the weekend. I overheard Mom laughing. "Rita said when she took Ali and Codi to the grocery store, Ali insisted on buying two containers of the green tea that only Lily drinks to bring home from Chicago so Lily will get 'quickly healthily.' Isn't that sweet?" I could hear the smile in Mom's voice, and I smiled too, nestling into my pillow.

My happiness vanished when Mom continued. "Luke is sugarcoating how things are going for Pria to Lily. I've picked her up fighting back tears more than once from soccer practice. A few of the juniors and seniors have said some nasty things to her. As if this is somehow her fault!" There was an edge to Mom's words, and my heart ached imagining it all.

"Pria told me she wants to quit. Yesterday, when I picked her up, I got there early and caught some of their practice. When they walked off the field, I gave several of the older-looking girls the stink eye."

I silently thanked Mom for sticking up for Pria but gave up any hope of sleeping now that I had another thing to worry about.

A few hours later, Luke arrived home before supper. He sat on the edge of my bed. "The peach fuzz around your stitches is growing out nice."

Luke reached out to touch my hair, but I pulled away. "I don't want to talk about my hair. Tell me what's going on with Pria at soccer."

He sighed. "I didn't want to worry you about her 'issues.' She isn't going to quit. I told her quitting is the easy way out, and she'd only hurt herself." Luke rubbed my forearm. "I reminded her we need to keep talking about this, not ignore our problems."

"Please stop leaving me out of everything. I'm here, and I deserve to know what's going on. I'm not some weakling that can't handle the truth." The lie pinched my conscience. *If you weren't weak, Lily, you wouldn't be snacking on opioids.*

MOM LEFT FOR THE FARM the following morning. "Remember, I'm just a phone call away." She waved the new cell phone she'd purchased so I could contact her at any time.

"Thanks, Mom. I'll keep you updated." She'd pressed me to make my first counseling appointment for early September. Physical and occupational therapy were fine. But dredging up and dissecting the attack was the last thing I wanted to do.

Mom had used Jacob as an example. He'd never sought treatment for his problem with alcohol or counseling to figure out why he'd allowed his once-steady life to derail. I wasn't proud to admit that the summer before he'd left the farm, I'd told Jacob he was weak.

Back then, I'd scolded him for not trying harder. Now, every time I swallowed a mind-numbing pill, I couldn't help but wonder if I was trying hard enough. *Would he judge me now?*

After Mom left, Luke cleaned the garage, and I read, both of us awaiting Ali and Codi's return. Pria holed up in her room. When Rita pulled into the driveway Saturday afternoon, she'd barely turned off the car when Ali and Codi flew through the front door.

"Guess what, Mommy?" they said in unison, smiling and bouncing around as if Rita gave them each an IV of sugar on the way home.

"What?" I motioned them both to come give me a hug, somewhat surprised at Ali's excitement. It usually took a lot to get her amped up about anything. A smile from Ali wasn't as unusual as it had been a few years ago. But with each year of help—especially the new program she was in this past year—Ali was learning to adjust to the chaos of life.

Ali turned to Codi. "You can go first." She folded her hands behind her back and patiently waited while Codi snickered behind her hands. Neither had stepped up to hug me.

"I lost something at Grandma Rita's," Codi mumbled through her hands.

I raised my eyebrows. "Whatever could it be? A toe?"

She shook her head.

"Was it an ear or your belly button?"

More giggles from Codi as she shook her head.

"Well, then, what?"

She stepped forward, pulling her hands away from her smile and displaying a gap in the front of her mouth.

My mouth dropped open. "Oh, my goodness! Where did your tooth go?"

In great detail with theatrical gestures, Codi told me the perils of her tooth coming out in a peanut butter sandwich. All the while, Ali stood still, waiting. I had to cut into Codi's retelling or Ali would turn a year older before she had a chance to share her news.

"And how about you, Ali? Did *you* lose a tooth in Chicago?"

"Nope." She stepped toward me while Codi ran off to find Luke. Ali dug in the pocket of her shorts and pulled out a sandwich bag with several Cheerios. "Grandma said I could paint her fingernails any color I wanted if I tried a new cereal. I chose orange and pink. And Cheerios." Pride pulled back her slim shoulders. "And guess what, Mom? They're so tiny. I didn't even count how many I had in the bowl!"

"Aw, Ali, I am so, so, so proud of you!" I pulled her in and held her tight, firm enough to know my fingers would ache later. "They're good, aren't they?"

"Yes. Grandma said I could sprinkle sugar on them if I wanted, but I didn't. And I ate Cheerios two days in a row." She leaned her warm cheek onto my good shoulder, where I could feel her eyelashes flutter against my bare skin, sticky from sitting outside on our deck earlier.

All will be fine. My heart beat as one with Ali's. As long as I had my family, we would make it through together.

DETECTIVE BOYLE CALLED Monday morning. "Any chance Luke can take a break from work for an hour? I'd like to stop by your house this morning and speak with you two." Boyle often kept any emotion out of his voice, but it sounded like his jaw was clenched.

Great. What now?

Luke had missed work the last week of July and half of August, accomplishing little from his laptop at the hospital.

"I'm a big girl, Detective. You can talk to me, and I promise I'll share it with Luke."

"I know you can handle it. Just wanted to save you from having to repeat everything. I'll contact Brook to see if she's available. I'll be there by ten."

After we hung up, I hobbled to our backyard, where Rita played in the sandbox with Ali and Codi.

"Hey, Rita, Detective Boyle and Brook are coming over in a bit!" I called to her from our deck.

She stood and walked to me. "Good news or bad?" Rita's short dark hair—thanks to a little color maintenance from her stylist—was pulled back in a headband. A smudge of dirt graced her forehead.

"I've got a feeling it's not good." I relayed our brief conversation.

"I'll take Ali and Codi with me when we drop Pria off at soccer practice at nine thirty, and then we'll go to the park so you have privacy."

"Thank you. I appreciate it." Rita had not only tireless energy but a brain that solved problems a mile a minute. If I owned a company, I would have hired her to run it.

I changed my clothes. Lately, I spent most of my time in sweat shorts and a button-up sleeveless top—easy to dress and undress, easy to stay cool. For Boyle and Brook, I opted for a button-up sundress.

After Rita left with the girls, Brook arrived. I hobbled to the door to let her in. Lucky for me, my temporary bedroom and former living room was close to the front door. Today marked one month since the attack. The doctors projected it would be another few weeks before I could test out my ankle and knee on the stairs once the cast and ankle boot were off. The sooner I could sleep in our bed next to Luke, the sooner our lives would be on their way to normal again. That and having the monster convicted and behind bars.

Brook saluted me in greeting with her usual can of Diet Coke. She tilted her head. "You getting enough rest?" Brook, adopted from Korea as an infant, was a few years older than me and had ten times the energy I did since the attack.

"Nobody lets me do anything around here *but* rest." I waved her toward my makeshift bedroom. "I haven't slept this much since I was a child." *Thanks to sleeping pills.*

Shhhh, Lily.

I was about to shut the front door when Detective Boyle pulled into our driveway.

"Have you met with a counselor yet?" Brook stared as if we were in a last-to-blink contest.

"I made an appointment. It's the first week in September after the girls go back to school. But really, I'm fine." It was a statement I recited on repeat.

Detective Boyle whistled as he jogged up our sidewalk. I let him and the cool late-August morning air inside our house. It was the first day I'd been able to have the windows open since the air conditioning was off, and I loved having the fresh breeze inside the house.

We all took a seat in the living room. "No update on the DNA results yet," Boyle said, looking fresh and unrumpled for the first time since we'd met.

I closed my eyes and took a deep breath, my cracked ribs healed.

"So, what's the bomb you're going to drop, Doyle?" Brook asked. She knew him well enough to know this wasn't a celebration visit.

"I met with Prosecutor Katz this morning. As you know, they've deferred the omnibus hearing until the DNA results are in. Katz met with Dalton's attorney. Seems Dalton has changed his tune and is tapping his feet to another song after being tossed back in the slammer for violating a condition of his release." Boyle chewed on a peppermint, no licorice in his dress shirt pocket that day. "I don't know what scat Dalton's birth mom tossed at him to convince him leaving town was a good idea. The DNA results will come in any day now, and I'm guessing he feels like a caged tiger."

"Just tell me. I can handle it." I sounded like the old Lily, the tough farm girl who wasn't afraid of anything. If only I felt as tough.

"Dalton's new defense is that yes, he was there, initially, defending himself against your sexual advances." Boyle pressed his lips together, leaned forward on his knees, then shot me an apologetic shrug. "But that he just fought you off and left. Never had a knife.

Never beat you to within an inch of your life. Just defended himself against you coming onto him as if he's got a shiny halo on his head." He scoffed.

My blood pressure shot skyward. "Are you freaking kidding me?" I aimed for a yell, but even four weeks after jaw surgery, I still couldn't accomplish it.

Brook's long hair, curled in big loops, could've stood on end from his news. "Oh, Doyle. Don't feed us such bullshi—"

"I'm only serving it, not cooking it, Brook. It's all they have to go on." He shrugged.

Brook rolled her eyes. "Dalton's fast enough to have run away in three seconds flat if Lily had made an unwanted move on him."

"I'd been two steps away from dying when they'd brought me to the hospital by ambulance. He walked away with a handful of scratches and a few bruises. Attempted sexual assault? What a crock."

"There's another reason he's admitting to being at the scene now. I was going to tell you and Brook before she copped an attitude." Boyle winced then grinned when Brook leaned forward and feigned a face slap to his face.

"Cough it up, Doyle. We're getting old waiting."

"Dalton Digg has a juvenile record. When he was twelve, he cut up an adult 'friend' of his mother. Really messed up the guy. That's how Dalton ended up with the knife wound on his neck. I'm guessing it was in self-defense, but he went overboard. Way overboard." Boyle shook his head. "The fact he has a prior record of juvenile violence, along with his skipping town and the upcoming DNA results, will show proof he was there, not to mention your extensive injuries. Those go far beyond him fending off an unwanted advance. It's their ludicrous attempt to blame you."

"Oh, criminy." Brook snorted. "He admits to being there now, but says he left, and then some other guy mysteriously showed up and beat the daylights out of Lily?"

"Then I'd have another man's DNA under my skin too, right?" Boyle nodded at my question. "Do you think they'll eventually accept a plea bargain?" I learned more about the judicial system each day. Up to 95 percent of felonies ended in a plea bargain. If they accepted one, I could avoid court. As much as I wanted to nail him to the wall, I didn't want to drag out what had happened in front of everybody in our small town. Court could take months. I wanted closure. I wanted to get back to teaching, back to running, and back to a normal life.

"Prosecutor Katz will meet with the public defender soon. With the DNA results showing only Dalton's DNA and hopefully a little reasoning sprinkled in—possibly from his foster parents—he may change his tune. If you want to avoid a trial and are willing to accept a plea bargain, that's your call. Either way, Dalton needs some fire and brimstone under his posterior to help him pull his head out of it. The DNA results will help."

After they left, I closed my eyes and whispered the Serenity Prayer. I'd never been good about accepting things I couldn't change. I had courage and wisdom. I hoped that would be enough.

Chapter 8

September brought more adjustments to our family. Codi started kindergarten, and Ali began a new after-school art program that focused on creativity and not control. The football team played—and lost—their first two games, and Pria played in her first two soccer games with an invisible barrier of steel around her to defuse jabs about her "crazy mom."

I don't know how she did it without clawing their eyes out. Her friends had disintegrated like the wicked witch in *The Wizard of Oz.* In this case, the bucket of water was me—the off-her-rocker mom. In Pria's corner stood her coach, two teammates whose parents were fellow teachers in our school district, and her friends, Erin and Sylvie. It wasn't a crowded corner, but at least Pria wasn't in it alone.

September also brought me one step closer to freedom after they removed the pins from my fingers, along with my leg cast and ankle boot. With only a hinged-knee immobilizer, I began rehab and range-of-motion exercises for my leg and continued hand therapy.

And counseling, which I'd sidestepped for six weeks in a tremendous feat. If I wasn't at physical therapy, I was at occupational therapy, and then, lucky me, I sat my butt in the counselor's office, where everyone assumed I would slay the emotional dragons clawing at me.

The first session with Dr. Arlene reminded me of a polite parent-teacher conference. "Please tell me about yourself, how you're feeling, what goals you'd like to accomplish, and how we can wipe July twenty-third from your memory."

Okay, she didn't really ask that last one. But the session felt stiff, impossible. Maybe that was just me. I wanted to point out there were millions of people who'd lived through worse. POWs, abused children, parents who'd lost a child. The list was long. I didn't need to waste a counselor's time when others needed her more. Didn't need to vent the perpetual simmer of anger inside me.

But she wouldn't have listened, much like my parents and Luke hadn't listened to me. They should have known the last thing I needed was to drag up the stench of that day. The fact I hadn't been aware of my surroundings at the time of my attack was one I wouldn't share with anyone. The "stop, look, and listen" motto I'd driven into our daughters and my kindergarten students every year played like a song on repeat. I'd been daydreaming, caught off guard. I'd screwed up. Pills diffused the guilt.

Every time I caved and popped a painkiller, a voice, sounding like my long-lost brother's, whispered in my thoughts, "See how easy it is?"

Once life got back to normal, I would toss them. I was a better liar than I'd thought. Rita minded her own business, but my mom was like a crime scene dog, more than once scolding me for keeping the pills within reach of our children.

"Isn't that what childproof caps are for?" I'd pointed out.

"*You've* managed to open them, and your fingers barely function." Mom raised an eyebrow and folded her arms over her chest.

"Only from sheer determination." I tried to make light of it, but it wasn't Mom's first merry-go-round with parenting a child with a penchant for mind-altering help. I still wasn't sure if they'd booted Jacob to the curb or if he had left on his own. It was one of those family subjects we never brought up—a subject Jacob might answer. I needed to reach out to him again.

Home after my first counseling session, I danced around Mom bringing up my ability to open the childproof prescriptions. It was another step toward my future freedom without the revolving door of Rita or Mom babysitting me during the week and Luke on the weekends.

I couldn't wait to drive again. Apparently, it wasn't safe to maneuver the gas pedal with a hinged knee brace. "Two to three months" was the projection I heard every time I asked the physical therapist or doctor, which meant the end of September at the earliest. Once I could drive, Mom and Rita would be off duty. And I could have my privacy back.

A WEEK AFTER LABOR Day, my best friend, Kara, came to visit. The girls were in school, Luke was at work, and since it was a Monday, Mom wouldn't arrive until late afternoon. I had no doctor appointments that day. It would be Kara's and my first visit alone since the attack.

While I'd been busy with our children these past several years, Kara had focused on her Italian restaurant, Pizzorno's. She'd inherited her German father's blond hair and pale skin but her Italian mother's brown eyes and flair for cooking family recipes.

Other than her hairstyle, Kara's appearance had changed little since our teens. I would like to say it was because she didn't have children. Maybe it was all that Italian cooking. It seemed to keep my mother-in-law looking young. Kara's hair, lighter than mine, fell to her shoulders and curled around her petite face. Her white capris and striped shirt were crisp and fitting.

I felt like a slug. Inch-long, fine newborn hair surrounded my scar, capping off my style with the sweatpants and zip-up hoodie that were essential to getting dressed on my own. "When I look like hell, a true friend would've shown up without showering and wearing stained clothing."

"Next time, I'll baptize myself with spaghetti sauce." She grinned. "Does it help that I brought stuffed rigatoni for our lunch?" She waved the insulated container at me before she set it on the kitchen counter. I was past the soft-food stage for my jaw but hadn't ventured into eating anything crunchy. The flavorful meal from Pizzorno's would be easy to chew.

We sat at the kitchen table, me with my green tea, Kara with espresso and cream.

"I don't know how you stand that green stuff. You're going to end up as green as Kermit the Frog."

"I'm trying to get healthy again after these past several weeks. I sure won't be running anytime soon." Green tea and smoothies would help offset any damage my pill fetish caused. "And in case you didn't notice, Kermit doesn't have a nose. I do."

"Thanks for pointing that out." Kara leaned over the table. "Okay, since nobody else is here, I want to know how things are going. Give me the soul-baring, don't-shit-me real version."

"Well, I'm being treated like a young child. I hear things they don't want me to hear, and nobody wants to address the fact I might never be emotionally or physically the same again. There's haunting guilt pulling down Luke's face every damn day as if this was his fault. As if he should've been running next to me, my knight in shining armor."

I caught my breath, surprised at how good it felt to unload. I kept going. "Pria wanted to drop out of soccer. Some of her so-called friends are treating her like she's got the bubonic plague. Mom hovers, Luke worries, and I'm bored for the first time in my life. Dr. Arlene, my counselor, wants me to dig deep and purge my fear and anger, and I want to pour a cement slab over it. Other than that, I'm doing fine." There was no need to mention my penchant for painkillers and worry Kara.

"So better than I expected." Kara winked. "Seriously, though. Are you okay?" Her dark eyes were steady on my face. After decades of friendship, she understood me. I could lie to her, but only so much.

I shrugged. "I'm alive and recovering. I'll take that as a win for now."

"I'm worried about your emotional recovery. At least you're finally meeting with the counselor now." She reached for my hand. "You need to get that anger out, be pissed off at the asshole, at the world. Hell, you can clock me one if that helps."

We both chuckled at the idea of me ever hurting my best friend. "Not after you brought lunch." I sniffed the air, and my tummy did a happy dance.

Kara dug into the large bag she'd brought, pulled out a wrapped package, and handed it to me. "I made you a few things to cheer you up. Hey, don't act so shocked." She feigned injury when my jaw dropped in surprise. "I may not be Sewing Sally, but when my friend has her head shaved, I'm not above whipping out my grandma's sewing machine to make some super cool head scarves for her."

I ran my fingers over the silky, stretchy material. "These are so cute! I'm impressed by your talent." I held each one, admiring the fun prints she'd chosen for the fabric.

"One for each day. They're two triangles sewn together. Even I can manage that." She had me select one for her to tie around my head. "You'll be the most stylin' chick in town." She wrapped a scarf decorated with Rosie-the-Riveter material around my head.

I thought of women with cancer who had blazed the trails for fun and stylish headwear. Mom had been busy knitting soft caps for me, ones I would keep wearing after my hair grew back in.

"These remind me of scarves Mom and I wore when I was young and helped her in the garden." I held a scarf, rubbing it between my hands as if to unearth the memories. "When I was about seven,

Mom assigned me a small section of the garden, instructing me how I needed to care for it every day." I would kneel on a vinyl boat cushion, planting and weeding my corner of the garden, breathing in the freshly tilled soil, a soothing scent I still craved.

"I remember learning how some plants are strong, some are weak. Before that, I'd assumed that every seed planted would grow and produce. That first summer, when some of my plants—and Mom's—failed to thrive, I'd asked her why. Know what she said? 'Only the weak fail.'" I looked over at Kara, blinking away the painful reminder.

"Oh, Lily, what's wrong?" She hugged my shoulder.

I swallowed hard. "I'm afraid I'm failing, that I'm weak." My nose tingled. I reached for a Kleenex to wipe away the emotion threatening to explode in me.

"Don't be silly! You are the opposite of weak. Look at you, tough as nails. Just like you've been since I met you in grade school." She leaned in for a hug, her tummy growling. "And when you don't feel strong, call me. I mean it," Kara whispered in my ear.

This would've been the perfect time to come clean about my weakness for pills, but the words stuck in my throat. If I could kill my desire for them, I would never have to tell Kara about my crutch. I changed the subject. "Sounds like we better feed your stomach." I pulled back.

She stared at me, unblinking, and I pasted on the best "I've got this" smile I could muster before we dished up our lunch.

The aroma of garlic, oregano, and rosemary followed us to the porch, where we ate under the warmth of the sunshine, even though the temperature didn't hit sixty degrees. Our talk turned to hairstyles.

"I'm keeping my hair short when it grows back." Maybe it would wipe out the phantom feeling of the monster yanking on my ponytail, a sense that still haunted my hair follicles.

"Short hair is liberating," Kara said.

After we finished lunch, she packed up the leftovers and brought them to the kitchen. I followed with our plates.

"You up for a walk to the lake?"

Other than car trips to medical appointments, I hadn't left our yard. "As long as you're prepared to pick up my sorry ass if I fall."

The small lake by our house was several hundred steps, yet it took five minutes for me to maneuver them with the help of Kara and one crutch. We sat on a bench in the grass and spoke of dreams and plans like friends do when they pretend everything will work out. Never once, in the thirty years of friendship, had I imagined lying to Kara. It was a lie of omission but a lie nonetheless. I'd convinced myself it was to protect her from worrying about me. Luke's eyes, permanently etched with concern, weighed enough on my conscience.

An hour later, we made our way back to the house before school let out. Kara and I were in the backyard when we heard Codi and Ali in the house fresh off the school bus.

"Hellooo... who's there?" Kara called out through the open windows to our kitchen.

"Barbie!" Codi shouted, giggles echoing inside our home.

That was a new one for me. Luke loved to teach our girls knock-knock jokes. Their little minds were sponges, remembering ones I'd soon forget. "Barbie who?"

"Barbie-Q-Chicken!" The screen door slid open as Codi tumbled outside. "I missed you, Auntie Kara!"

Codi's chubby legs carried her full speed to Kara's lap. A minute later, Ali joined us, and both girls hugged me as if I was made of glass. They were aware of where my "boo-boos" were. They smelled of sunshine and ChapStick.

Codi's cheeks had some sort of food on them. The girl ate nonstop. "Guess what book my teacher let me pick out today?" Codi said to Kara. "She has lots of books in our classroom. Even more than Mommy!"

Ali looked at me in awe at Codi's comment, amazed that someone would have more books than me. It was a joke between Luke and me that if we were ever in dire straits, I could sell the books—both mine and the many children's books I'd accumulated for our girls.

"What book did you pick?" Kara asked.

"*Scaredy Squirrel.* He's afraid to leave his nut tree. He has to be brave, but he doesn't want to. He's supposed to go out into the unknown. Know what that is?" Codi's eyebrows rose as if she expected to have to explain "unknown" to us.

"No. What is it?" Kara played along.

The Italian in Codi came out as she waved her arms. "The unknown is stuff you don't know about yet. Like if your mom stays in the hospital for a long time, and then you have to get tucked into bed every night by your dad or grandma. They read you bedtime stories, but it's not the same as when your mom reads to you cuz they don't use the same voices." Her arms stilled before she folded them over her small chest. "That's what 'unknown' is."

I struggled to swallow the lump in my throat. *Is that how the girls felt when I was in the hospital?* I was so glad to be home. I clung to the hope that we could get through anything as a family. Hopes and dreams—that's what we build our future on. And lies. Lots of lies.

Chapter 9

I missed Pria's first home soccer game—at her request. "You sitting there might make things worse," she'd said before she left for school that morning. The knowledge that she was right tempted me to grind my teeth into little nubs. If only we could get the DNA results.

"I understand." I reached out to hug Pria, surprised when she hugged me back. "Grandma Rita and your dad will be there."

"Good. I'm sorry, Mom," she mumbled into my shirt.

"It's not your fault. Self-preservation is important, which is why I'll send Codi and Ali along with Grandma." I smiled and leaned back to look at Pria, the tiny, spunkier version of me. "Dad will take videos for me."

As much as I wanted to attend, it gave me an out. I wouldn't be subjected to staring, to wondering who was against me. I leaned in for a gentle hug, my shoulder and arm still healing from the knife wound. "I'm proud of you for sticking it out. And remember, we have people on our side."

Over the past few weeks, I'd questioned Luke on whether people said anything nasty to him or Pria.

His answer was always the same. "Don't worry about us. Focus on getting better."

Pria's slumped shoulders and shuffling feet made it impossible to pretend things were all rainbows in her world. Her emotional trauma concerned me more than my own. Unlike hers, I could ignore mine. Or medicate it. The wooden crutches I used were easily accepted. But my opioid crutch I kept hidden in the darkness of my conscience, along with an arsenal in the bathroom.

FIVE WEEKS AFTER DETECTIVE Boyle had requested a rush for the DNA results—eight weeks since the attack—the results were in. Detective Boyle called me early Friday afternoon, shortly before the girls were due to arrive home from school. Rita had left for Chicago after driving me to my occupational and physical therapy appointments earlier that day. I mentally gave myself a gold star for shunning my pain pills ever since Kara's visit on Monday. Boyle's news was my reward.

"You did good, Lily. Plenty of Dalton's DNA under your fingernails. His and nobody else's. Now the ball is in their court," Boyle said with a smile in his voice.

"What do we do now?" It was tempting to crack open my pills and celebrate into oblivion, but I didn't want to blur the good news.

"We wait, Lily. You sure you don't want to go to trial?"

"Yes, I'm sure. It will only make things worse for my family. I want it over and done with. And the monster behind bars for a long time." Even as I said the words, I knew. *We don't always get what we want.*

There was a slight pause on his end. "I'll call you once I hear from them. Have a good weekend, and let's hope the damn football team wins tonight."

"Hah! You sound like me, Detective, wishing for something that will probably never come true."

Two games and two losses against high school teams rated below them didn't look good for their game tonight against the team they'd played last year in the playoffs. I'd only known about those stats because Pria had ranted about it plenty over the past few days, hoping, like Boyle, that the team would turn things around. Hoping a win would wipe the angst from her life.

They lost 28-3.

BY THE END OF SEPTEMBER, the football team's record was zero wins and four losses. Pria's soccer team fared better with a two-two record so far. And with each passing week, Luke and I held our breaths, waiting to receive an update on a possible plea bargain.

It fueled my refills on pain meds, an errand Mom was more willing to drive me to than Luke was. After supper one night, Mom and I went to the grocery store, where I stopped at their small pharmacy while Mom picked up a few groceries. I turned to leave the counter, counting the days we'd waited to hear an update on the case, and ran right into an elderly person, almost knocking him over.

"Oomph. Sorry!" I reached out to steady his arm.

His fishing cap fell off-kilter, revealing black hair that looked like an Elvis Presley wig. He waved a gloved hand at me as if to say it wasn't a bother that I'd almost toppled him.

Gloves? It wasn't cold outside even though the sun was setting. Then I remembered how easily chilled I'd become after my injuries.

And I reminded myself to pay attention and stop worrying about what would happen next with the case. It was a topic of conversation in my fourth counseling session.

"I'm concerned that you feel everything will go back to normal if Dastard is convicted," Dr. Arlene said, using the nickname Dr. Arlene and I agreed to call the monster so I wouldn't have to validate him by speaking his name. I liked her, especially from the distance I kept her at. Unfortunately, she seemed determined to pull me in closer for inspection.

"It won't fix everything, but it's one step closer to getting back to our old life. People won't expect him to leave jail to play football, and they can turn their focus on the next local train wreck." It would come. It always did. And although I would like to have said that I never jumped on the gossip wagon when someone's personal life became fodder to chew on, it would have been one more lie coating my tongue.

"I think what we need to focus on here, Lily, is forgiving yourself. Don't worry about whether anyone else blames you. Concentrate on the reason *you* are blaming you." She rambled on about things we'd touched on in previous sessions—my upbringing, my family, my high expectation for myself. Nothing new there.

"Let's talk about your brother again. You've told me a bit about how Jacob turned to drinking, turned against your family, and built a wall between you after always being so close. Did you ever reach out to him to offer help and understanding?" She peered over her eyeglasses, her dark-brown eyes reaching into my soul. "You mentioned how difficult it was to watch him spiral, how it affected you and your parents."

I understood where she was going. I was in Jacob's shoes now, my actions affecting Pria, sending an electrical current through our previously smooth life. "That pretty much sums it up. I did ask Jacob what was wrong, why the change in his personality, but he never gave a reason if there was one. He'd become someone I didn't know, and then he left. That's it. I tried reaching out to him a few years ago and received no response."

"Do you feel an understanding toward Jacob now after everything you've gone through?" Dr. Arlene didn't add, "since your newfound penchant for pain meds," but it was implied. Oversharing Luke had met with her after my first appointment so she could get a feel about how things were from his point of view, and he'd managed to slip in that juicy tidbit about me. I wasn't sure how our counseling session had turned to talking about Jacob instead of Dastard.

Luke had thought he'd been helping me by telling her I turned to prescription relief too much—according to his unprofessional opinion. He'd attended my second session with Dr. Arlene, and when the meds were brought up, I shot back that the doctors and pharmacists wouldn't keep refilling my prescriptions if they didn't believe I needed it. He let it go.

But Dr. Arlene revisited it.

"Of course I miss Jacob. And yes, I think of him every time I reach for a pill." It was none of her business. "Why are we talking about him?"

She leaned forward and tipped her head to study me. "Because you carry a lot of guilt, and I think some of it goes back to when you and Jacob parted ways. You wanted to 'fix' him, and now you want an easy fix for what happened to you. And, as we've discussed, you feel a sense of guilt that Dastard's attack was somehow your fault."

I pinched the bridge of my nose to keep the tears where they belonged. I kept silent.

Dr. Arlene gave a small sigh. "I'm giving you an assignment for next week. I'd like you to reach out to Jacob, either by phone, snail mail, or email. Whatever option works best for you."

Give me PT or OT any day over this. I crossed my arms over my chest and took one of the deep, slow breaths that had become my daily routine ever since the attack. It was no longer to fend off pneumonia. It was so I wouldn't tell her to shove the idea. I had enough going on and didn't need to poke Jacob again so he could ignore me and add to my guilt. Yes, I reminded myself of a sulking student when I would ask them to quit talking out of turn or to stop picking their nose.

And like a small child antsy to bust out of school, I eyed the clock. *Five minutes left of this torture.* "I'll see what I can do."

After my session, I walked out to the waiting room, where Mom sat knitting a rainbow-colored cap. Maybe I would ask her later for

Jacob's phone number or email address, maybe not. Hell, maybe she didn't have either. They received a letter from him about once a year.

For the moment, I needed calm and comfort. "Can we stop by my school on the way home? I'd like to see my classroom, say hello to my coworkers, and take a peek at the new kindergarten students." Most people wouldn't consider visiting a grade school calming, but I wasn't most people. I craved the goals of teaching, the daily curiosity from my students, and the comradery with the team I'd worked with for nearly twenty years.

Mom packed away her knitting, opened the waiting room door, and quipped, "I can't believe you've waited three weeks since school began to ask me that favor."

IT WAS AFTER TWO O'CLOCK when Mom pulled into the school parking lot. Buses would line up within the hour. Ali and Codi attended the grade school two miles from home. My grade school was on the other side of town, a whopping ten-minute drive from home.

"I'll go to the grocery store while you visit," Mom said as she pulled up to the curb alongside the school front doors. "Milk, eggs, peanut butter... do you need more spinach for your smoothies?"

"I'm good. I've got plenty, blended and frozen." I opened the car door.

Mom eyed me as I stepped out, putting my weight on the door until I stabilized my footing.

"I'll be back out in half an hour so we can get out of here before school is dismissed." I shut the door.

"I'll watch for you. It won't take me long at the store." Mom smiled and fluttered her hand toward the school as if pushing me along. I appreciated her confidence in me, that I could make my way alone. If only she knew.

Mom pulled away, and I hobbled up the front walk to a school I'd scurried into a thousand times. Forced to a slower pace, I appreciated the brick building, the clean grounds, the playground off to the right, and the job it had given me over the years. One I enjoyed and missed.

I stopped in the front office and exchanged pleasantries with the staff before making my way to my friend Barb's kindergarten classroom, which was next door to mine. The door was closed, but I spotted Barb through the door window. As she stood in front of the class, her short silver hair shone in the sunlight reflecting through the windows across the room. I knocked.

The smile on her face as she spun around and our eyes connected through the glass welcomed me. She said something to her quiet class before opening the door and stepping into the hall to greet me.

"It's so good to see you again, Lily." She pulled me in for a hug. Barb, the friend I'd had the longest at school, had visited me in the hospital. She'd been teaching since she'd graduated from college thirty-plus years ago. She'd always been a cheerleader and supporter of new staff and was one of several teachers in our school who would retire in the next few years. I missed her already.

"Your class is so quiet. Did you threaten them or something?"

"Don't let it fool you. We've got a lively bunch of kindergartners again this year in all the classrooms. I just read them a book about friendly monsters, and they are working on their assignment now to draw a friendly monster. I wore them out good at recess earlier. We played tag, so I think they've lost their zip, thank goodness." Barb stood next to the door and cracked it enough so she could keep an ear out for them.

We caught up since our last visit in August.

"Do you have time to hang around so I can introduce you to the new staff?" she asked.

"Mom dropped me off and will be here soon to pick me up. I don't want to be here when class lets out. Once I can drive myself again—hopefully in the next couple of weeks—I'll come in and have lunch with all of you. Are there a lot of new staff?"

"We have a new first-grade teacher, Christina. She moved here last year from Colorado. She's in her early thirties and single. And they brought on a part-time teacher's aide who is assisting Maria. With a new substitute teacher covering for you, they hired Judith to rotate in the kindergarten classes with Maria. She's retired and widowed."

"How's the substitute teacher working out?" The villain in me hoped not well.

"She's good. Young and inexperienced but patient." Barb's face grew serious. "Do you still plan to return after the Christmas holiday? As much as I miss you, Lily, you tend to push yourself too hard. Everyone would understand if you needed to take more time. You need to put yourself first." Her hand reached for mine.

"I am. And to hold on to the bit of sanity I have left, I need to get back in the classroom. I'm bored to my toes at home."

"So you're up for an outing? We've been talking about having a party for you but weren't sure you were up for it."

"I am itching to get back out again—as long as I don't have to face Dalton supporters." As much as I hated saying his name, I couldn't call him Dastard in public. I'd already slipped once in front of Codi, who immediately broadcasted, "Mommy swore!" I hadn't bothered correcting her.

"Nobody allowed but staff, and certainly nobody who will throw spitballs at you." Barb winked. "I'll call you with some dates once I talk to the rest of the crew."

"Sounds good. Can we wait until my knee immobilizer is off so I can drive myself?" I wanted to feel like an adult again when I met up with my coworkers, not like some preteen who had to be dropped off at a party.

"You bet."

We parted ways as she went back into her classroom, where the noise level was rising. I hobbled down to the next classroom and peeked in the door window to see the kindergartners on the floor in a circle, the substitute teacher among them, as they sang a song.

Even when I went back to teaching, it would be months before I could sit cross-legged on the floor with the students again. Early January might be an optimistic goal for my return to the classroom, but I needed a goal, a reason to avoid the pain pills and continue with my therapy and counseling. A reason to hope.

Chapter 10

After last week's counseling session, I asked Mom for Jacob's mailing address. My parents didn't do email, and I was too chicken to ask for his phone number, not ready to hear his voice. Or hear the click of him hanging up on me.

Mom drove me to my next counseling session the first Thursday in October, and I put the letter in our mailbox before we left, hobbling down our driveway. I was scheduled to have my knee immobilizer removed the next day and couldn't wait to be able to drive and not feel like a child who needed babysitting. I'd been a real trooper over the past weeks with minimal pill popping and maximum determination.

Poor Mom had to be exhausted. Rita would have loved to move in with us for two months, but she had a husband who liked his home-cooked meals on the table when he walked in from a job he should have retired from by then. Mom wanted to be here for me, but she also wanted—and needed—to be back at the farm canning, cleaning up her garden, helping with chores, and monitoring Dad, who overworked himself even after a scary heart attack years ago.

"So, you wrote to your brother?" Dr. Arlene brought my thoughts back to our session.

"Yes, I wrote and apologized and asked if I could reconnect with him. I'll let you know how it goes." I wasn't holding my breath. I'd been a shitty older sister once he'd fallen apart.

Jacob must have felt alone in his pain while I was off at college, and he'd turned to drinking. Back then, I'd told him to "shape up and shake it off." Whatever "it" was. Those memories haunted me. I needed his comfort, support, and forgiveness. I wondered if it was twenty years too late to offer him mine.

THE DOCTOR REMOVED my knee immobilizer and gave me her stamp of approval for physical freedom, along with a word of caution to not overdo it. Mom and I celebrated after the appointment by stopping at the local coffee shop for pumpkin spice coffees, a treat neither of us would typically order.

"I'll drive home," I stated as we sat outside on the coffee shop's patio, the leaves on nearby maple trees beginning their progression into vibrant hues of reds and oranges.

Mom grimaced. "Uh, you haven't driven for over two months. Why don't you practice this weekend out on a country road?"

I chuckled. "It's like riding a bike, Mom. I doubt I forgot how to drive."

An hour later, I smiled like a teen with a new driver's license as I slid behind the wheel.

"Remember, hands at ten and two," Mom said.

"They don't say that anymore. Kids now only know digital time. Ten and two on a clock is as foreign to them as a rotary phone."

I sang "Freedom!" by George Michael all the way home. Mom braced herself, her right leg pressed hard on the floor in front of her where the brake pedal would be.

That afternoon, she prepared to leave for home, packing all the belongings she'd left behind over the past two-plus months. She whistled the same tune I'd sung earlier as she loaded her car, giving me a wink before leaning in for a kiss. Minutes later, she headed for our beloved farm in Wisconsin.

As Mom pulled out of the driveway, I gingerly walked up our sidewalk to the front door. Our neighbor Irene was in their yard, pruning shrubs. I'd seen her once since coming home from the hospital and had thanked her for stepping in to keep an eye on our girls while Luke drove to see me in the emergency room. By then, Dastard had been arrested, and her response had been icy. Irene didn't have it in her to be downright rude, but I felt the wall between us just the same.

Her youngest was a senior on the football team, following in his older brother's footsteps. Just one more family questioning the truth behind the attack. I thought she knew me better than that. We'd lived next to each other for fifteen years. But Irene and her husband were older, and we'd never hung out together.

And really, I was in too good a mood to worry about it. Irene looked up. I waved and smiled then received a solemn nod in return.

Every day, I held my breath, waiting for it all to be over but knowing that it could get worse before it got better.

That night, I lay in bed wondering how often I'd falsely accused someone based on rumors. People were wrongly convicted far more than we wanted to acknowledge. Eyewitnesses often misremembered facts, their brains distorting what had actually happened. Although I felt certain of the truth, I'd had no eyewitness. Yes, the DNA under my fingernails was incriminating. Black and white. What was gray was the "why" behind it all. Everyone wanted a reason for his attack—especially me. I wasn't sure I would ever get one.

"OUR FOOTBALL TEAM SUCKS! If they'd win, people wouldn't look at me in the halls at school as if I was the devil incarnate." Pria plunked down next to me on a patio chair overlooking our backyard.

Codi and Ali drew with chalk on the cement slab alongside our deck. The sun warmed our shoulders, the cool mid-October air offsetting its warmth. Fall was my favorite time of year. I breathed in the crisp air, which carried the earthy aroma of damp leaves.

"Wait, you aren't the devil incarnate?" I winked. Pria's volatility with me had leveled out since the attack, her patience outshining her few outbursts. "Imagine the team's frustration after their high hopes from the past two seasons."

"The score was zero to thirty-one last night." Pria had gone to the Friday night game with the two friends who'd stuck with her—a rare fun day for her. I'd taken her wanting to attend the game as a virtual slap until she'd explained, "It's better than sitting in my room alone."

Luke and I wanted her to enjoy high school, a challenge with everything that had happened. If it meant cheering on the football team alongside the ignoramuses in our community who had turned their back on our family, we would allow it. Anything to help offset the blame by association she suffered.

"Close game, huh?" I put my hand on hers across the patio table.

"I'm not kidding, Mom, it stinks."

I searched for a positive response. "Word is, the team has two good wide receivers, but without a spot-on quarterback to throw to them, it's tough." I switched the subject. "Are things going okay in your classes?" At least in her classes, teachers could moderate student behavior. I knew most of the teachers and sensed they were on my side.

"I swear, some kids stay up half the night to think of how they can piss me o—" Pria caught herself. "I mean, how they can make me angry."

Codi, several yards away, jerked her head up at Pria's slip. Her mouth formed a big *O*. "Mommy, Pria said a naughty word!" Little Miss Tattletale squealed over the chance to rat on her sister as if I hadn't heard Pria sitting next to me.

"How do you know it's a naughty word?" I pressed my lips together to stifle a laugh.

"Because you said it when Grandma Pat was here, and she scolded you." Codi's eyes sparkled as if reminding me would get her extra points.

"Hmm, should we have our mouths washed out with soap?" I asked Codi.

"Yes!" Codi's grin spread wide across her jubilant face as she leaned toward Ali. "Should we ask Daddy to wash their mouths out with soap?"

Ali shook her head at her younger sister. Codi tested both of her sisters' patience, especially Ali's.

While they were occupied, I turned to Pria. "Is it that bad?" *Please say no.*

Pria shrugged. "Well, only a few people have come right out and said anything to my face. The way they ignore me is even worse. Erin's got the same lunch hour I do, so we sit together. Sylvie's lunch hour is later, but I've got her in three of my classes, which helps."

"You have good friends in Erin and Sylvie—loyal friends. And I'm thankful for them." I had people I could turn to, so did Luke, but Pria's large circle of girlfriends—so crucial to teenagers—had dwindled since the attack. Our neighborhood friends we hung out with at the park for Thirsty Thursdays—the group we'd get together with to watch the Vikings football games—were still there for us.

Some of them had brought meals over in the first several weeks after the attack. Others, with young children, had invited Ali and Codi to their houses to play. Ali rarely went, but we appreciated the invitations. Not everyone was against us. It only felt that way.

I RELISHED MONDAY MORNING, the first day I'd had the house to myself. Luke had left for work, the girls were off to school, and I caught myself yawning several times by late morning. It had been a busy weekend, pushing myself to walk around our neighborhood with a cane. Between driving to run errands, getting some fresh air, and walking, it was more than I'd done in almost three months. Gone was the woman who could run ten miles without a single groan.

And I ached, something I would never admit to anyone. So I settled into the recliner, popped a pill from my stash, and soon, a cushiony cloud of calm wrapped itself around me.

I drifted off to a peaceful sleep.

The ringing telephone dragged me out of my happy slumber. By the time I was alert enough to reach for our landline phone, placed between the hospital bed and recliner, it quit ringing. A minute later, my cell phone, also on the same end table, rang.

"Hello?" My mouth felt like a desert, my voice hoarse.

"Hello, Mrs. Gallo. This is Shirley from Washington school. I'm following up with you to check if I misunderstood you earlier. Ali and Codi are still waiting for you to pick them up."

"Pick them up for what?" My brain pressed its way out of the fog.

"Their dentist appointments today. You called this morning stating you'd neglected to notify us beforehand that you'd need to pick them up at one-fifteen for dentist appointments. We pulled them from class. They've been sitting in the office with their things, waiting for you."

Shirley was around sixty, and—I had thought—efficient. I felt like a schoolgirl being reprimanded. The clock on the living room wall read 1:35 p.m. "I'm so sorry, Shirley! They've been sitting there for twenty minutes?"

I would remember if they had appointments. At least, I think I would've. And Luke wouldn't have made the appointments. That was my area. "I don't remember calling you. The girls don't have dentist appointments today. I apologize for the confusion. They can go back to class and take the bus home as usual."

Surely she'd confused me with another mother. But another mother would have shown up to pick up her child for a dentist appointment by then. *Poor Ali.* The unplanned glitch would test her. As if the upheaval of our lives hadn't tested us all enough already. There was no need to call Luke to find out if he'd made the appointment. He wouldn't have, and I'd only sound irresponsible. *No need to point that out to him.*

I might well have been losing my grip on reality. I'd already lost my coping mechanisms. I didn't want to lose Luke too.

WE MADE IT HALFWAY through supper before Luke busted me. Anyone who knew Ali would notice something was troubling her. She'd lined up the peas on her plate in three rows and was staring down the cheeseburger Luke had grilled, untouched on her plate.

I ignored her actions. Yes, I felt like a failure for my daughter's inability to eat. But I swore I hadn't called the school office. *Not. My. Fault.*

Luke had asked Ali what was bothering her. She didn't look at him and didn't answer.

Chatterbox Codi stepped in. "Mommy forgot us at school today, and we had to sit in the office and wait and wait for a super long time, Daddy."

"What's she talking about?" Luke squinted at me.

I glared back at him. "Shirley got her wires crossed in the office and accidentally pulled the girls out of their classrooms for a dentist appointment they didn't have. They ended up sitting in the office for a little while until she called me. Shirley's getting old." I gestured to my temple with my fork, insinuating Shirley's forgetfulness.

"Is that what's bothering you, Ali?" Luke's voice was soft.

Ali nodded.

"It all worked out though, didn't it? You went back to your classroom, and the best part?" Luke feigned enthusiasm. "You didn't have to go to the dentist." He slapped his knee as if he'd just delivered the best punchline.

I was not amused with his theatric attempt to smooth it over, as if I'd intentionally tossed Ali into a tailspin. I couldn't wait to get back to work. The less I was home alone, the less I could get blamed for.

Chapter 11

My parents arrived the following Thursday to attend Pria's last home soccer game of the season. Mom had been gone from our home for less than a week, and although she'd made it to several of Pria's earlier games, Dad had not. Their arrival was a welcome break from the guarded looks Luke gave me since Monday's nonexistent dentist appointment.

Mom was in the kitchen, making a soup to put in the crockpot for supper after Pria's game. They would stay overnight, and I'd have someone to talk to again. Three days alone in the house with nothing to do gave me too much time to focus on my pills. I hadn't taken a single one since Monday morning, but I thought of them every minute I was alone.

I was down to as-needed physical and occupational therapy appointments, my body healing on schedule. My sixth counseling appointment was supposed to be that morning, but I canceled it. I was fine. I'd had no pills the past few days, and unless she could cure my boredom, it was a waste of her time and mine.

Not that I had a lot on my schedule. There were daily walks with my cane and planning a supper for our family that took over fifteen minutes to prepare—a luxury I typically only had during my time off in the summer. I also went through the storage in our attic, which took up most of my day. After living in our house for fifteen years, there were a lot of boxes full of things we hadn't used. It was a time-consuming project, but it wasn't enough.

While Mom cooked, Dad and I visited in the living room. "Your hair's coming back in that straw-in-the-sunshine color I love." He'd always compared my hair color to a farm crop as if I'd forever be a farm girl. In my heart, I would.

"Thanks. I'm going to keep it short."

We talked about the farm, their decision to put it up for sale so they could travel while they still had their health.

"I'll miss the cows. Could you bring a few with you next time you visit us? And my flute too?" I smiled. Music and our cows had always calmed me growing up. They came to mind every time I thought of turning to pills. Every time I thought of Jacob, who had yet to respond to my letter.

Jacob's heavy drinking had begun the summer before his junior year of high school. I was back at the farm for the summer after my first year of college. Things were tense between him and our parents. After I helped Dad milk the cows, I would take solace in the nightly ritual of playing my flute in the barn. Both actions had brought me as much comfort as they had for the cows.

"Why don't you spend some time on the farm, kind of recharge?" Dad offered.

"I need to be here. We'll spend a few weeks there next summer if you haven't sold it." It had cut into my heart when Mom and Dad said they were putting the farm up for sale. With my precious memories of a perfect upbringing, I would miss the beloved farm like losing a limb.

"Farms aren't like houses. It will take time to find the right buyer. I'm sure we'll still be there. I think that's a great idea for next summer."

Dad and I sat side by side on the couch, my legs propped up on the ottoman, my head on his broad shoulder. "I need to toughen up and deal with things like you and Mom have always done." Colorful leaves swirled outside the living room window, reminding me that winter—and slippery ice—was just around the corner. "I thought I was tough. It's easy to be strong when nothing bad has ever happened. A lot harder when things go wrong." I swallowed hard after airing the lesson it had taken me decades to learn.

He kissed the top of my head. "You *are* tough. You're alive today because you didn't give up." He pulled away and studied me. "You'll get through this like you've done before, crossing the finish line with your head held high because you've given it your all." His face, lined from decades in the sun, calmed me. "Only the weak stumble, Lily. And you aren't weak."

I leaned my forehead into his and prayed that he was right.

LUKE MET US AT THE game. I'd only made it to one of Pria's games so far, cushioned between Rita and Luke, along with Ali and Codi. I'd pretended the rest of the crowd wasn't there. Today, I had a similar arsenal of family to protect me. Pria was more vulnerable out on the field but had her own protectors, which warmed me on the inside as much as the hot chocolate Luke brought me.

We all headed to the bottom row of the bleachers so I wouldn't have to maneuver steps and could avoid looking at anyone behind me. I wore a knit cap Mom made, even though the mid-October sunshine took the chill out of the air. Ever since the attack, I moved much slower and often felt chilled.

Pria scored one of the five goals her team made. I zeroed in on her interactions with teammates like a mother bear, ready to pounce if someone so much as flashed her a scowl. They appeared to treat her like everyone else. Same with her coach.

A few women stopped to chat with me, two from our neighborhood and one mother of one of Pria's teammates. And for those short periods, I could pretend nothing had changed those past few months. When each leaned down to hug me, I squeezed as hard as my body allowed, so thankful for the human connection and support. I would never take it for granted again.

After the game, I caught a few glares aimed at Luke and me as we walked from the bleachers to the car after Pria's team won. If that was the worst we would face, I'd take it any day over someone putting dead mice in Pria's locker. Luke and Pria assumed I didn't know.

Teachers stick together. If I found out who did that to Pria, they would be eating a dead mouse. Gone was the take-it-on-the-chin farm girl. I'd been through too much.

MY PARENTS STAYED OVERNIGHT and helped move me upstairs. I'd missed sleeping next to Luke, his familiar scent, and the comfort of him next to me. We'd worried about him kicking me during the night, but I was healing. And we had a king-size bed.

Over the past two weeks, I'd practice maneuvering the steps every night when Luke was home, something I wasn't allowed to attempt while alone. Between the railing and my cane, I'd managed okay.

After everyone left the next morning, I took my green smoothie and sat on our back porch, wrapped in a fleece blanket to ward off the cool October air. I focused on our farm and the things I'd learned over the years growing up there, things Ali and Codi would miss out on once it sold. When I'd been around nine, a girl I'd gone to school with had moved away. Her family had owned a nearby farm, and they couldn't keep up with it. I remembered helping Dad milk cows that night, talking about my classmate having to leave.

"Will that happen to us?" My tummy had ached that whole day in school, worrying we would have to move too.

Dad sat next to me on an overturned pail, hooking up a milking machine to one of the cows. He stopped, leaning his elbows on his knees, then turned to me. "No, it won't. We've worked hard, and our farm is doing well."

He reached for my hand then, which was damp from anxiety about our future. "Sometimes, people fail because they give up. Some don't try hard enough." He paused. "There was a song popular around the time you were born. The lyrics talked about how only the strong survive." He'd kissed my hand. "We're strong, Lily. Remember that."

I'd remembered it all right. And over the years, I'd heard various rumors about what had happened to their farm. Whatever the reason had been, I'd never forgotten Dad's message.

I used to train hard for my track events. I'd excelled in high school and college because I'd put everything I had into my running training and studying instead of giving it a half-assed attempt. We all got what we deserved—at least, that was what I used to believe. But I wasn't so sure anymore.

BARB CALLED WITH A date for the get together once I let her know I could drive again. The Monday night after Pria's last home game, I met several grade school teachers at Olive Garden. I'd had my hair styled into a pixie haircut, and I'd spent way too much time picking out an outfit, anxious about stepping back into "life" again.

As I hobbled into Olive Garden with the aid of a red cane, I held my head high, a soldier back from war. I wore a long red crepe skirt and a long-sleeved white sweater. When I walked into the meeting room in the back of the restaurant, cheering, balloons, Welcome Back banners, and about thirty smiling faces greeted me.

"I love your haircut. You look so chic," a young third-grade teacher said.

"Thank you," I said, relieved at the warm welcome. My happy marriage was common knowledge to my coworkers. The people I couldn't wait to join again after the holiday break. I sure as hell wouldn't throw myself at a teenage boy, and they knew it.

Barb introduced me to the new employees she'd mentioned when I'd visited the school recently. She led me to a shapely woman with long golden-brown hair that fell in perfect tendrils. "Lily, this is Christina, the new first-grade teacher."

I shook Christina's outstretched hand as we exchanged pleasantries for a few minutes. I asked her about Colorado and what sports she enjoyed, remembering the little information Barb had given me.

"I'm no runner, but if you ever want to go kayaking or hiking, I'm your girl." She smiled, revealing a dimple in her right cheek. Her skin was flawless, with no bags under her eyes.

That's what childless and early thirties look like. It would be fun having another younger woman in the lower grades. Barb, in her early fifties, was a great friend but was also over a decade older than me.

Next, Barb led me to a woman I guessed to be in her sixties. "This is Judith, our efficient newbie and part-time assistant." Barb gestured to the woman with a faded-red pageboy and blue eyes accentuated by wrinkles. She looked like everyone's grandma.

"It's so nice to meet you, Lily. I'm looking forward to assisting you in the classroom," Judith said.

When I went back to teaching, I would have Maria—reliable, calm, and close to retirement—until I regained my balance in the classroom. She had been a full-time educational assistant, or EA, for over two decades, dividing her time between Barb's classroom and mine. Once I was comfortable with things again, Judith and Maria would rotate as my EA. I couldn't wait.

On the drive home, I passed through our neighborhood, the houses decorated for Halloween. I thought of the school festivities I'd missed and the daily connection to the coworkers and students

I loved. It was what kept me pushing toward physical recovery and what kept me pushing the tempting pills away.

AFTER THE DNA RESULTS had come in, Prosecutor Katz and Dastard's attorney had played volleyball with a plea bargain agreement. Katz pressed for first-degree assault. They bartered with third-degree, which could still land him in prison for up to five years.

And during that time, I, with the help of Brook, wrote up a victim impact statement covering how the crime had affected me and my family, what I felt his punishment should be, and why. In the end, they agreed to leave it up to a judge. One I hoped had a heart.

Three months after the attack and over a month since the DNA results had arrived, I received a call from Detective Boyle. Both he and Brook had taught me that nothing happened fast in the judicial system. "Can you and Luke meet us at Katz's office after lunch?"

"I can. I'll call Luke at work to make sure he's free. One o'clock?" Fridays were busy at Luke's office, but October was the wind-down period after summer's seasonal customers left.

After we hung up, I called Luke.

"Hell yes, I'll be there. Did he hint if it was good news?"

"You know Boyle, always a poker face, no giveaway in his voice." And really, I wasn't ready to know the outcome. Living in la-la land had its perks.

Two hours later, we sat across from Prosecutor Katz at his desk. Brook and Detective Boyle waited in chairs against the wall. I was literally on the edge of my seat.

"The judge settled on third-degree assault." The prosecutor leaned back, letting the words settle in around us. He was around my age, more broad-necked than Luke. For a man who'd devoted his life to the judicial system, it surprised me Katz had one of those faces that looked perpetually happy.

"And...?" Sentencing could be so broad, so forgiving.

"Remember the juvenile record where Dalton attacked his mother's 'friend' with a knife?" Katz asked. "At that time, he'd been living with his grandparents, doing okay after being in and out of foster care. Their health declined, and he ended up back with his mom, who was supposedly clean." Katz took a sip of water. "But she'd gone back to her old ways. A drug dealer attacked Dalton's mother with a knife, so Dalton stepped in and turned the knife on the dealer, claiming self-defense."

Brook added to the details. "He went beyond self-defense. The man suffered eleven knife wounds. Dalton spent time in juvenile detention. He attended anger management classes and was released back into the foster care system." She tapped a pen against her knee as she continued. "Dalton's been in a great foster home since—the same one he was living in before his arrest. That's when he moved to our area, took up running and football thanks to encouragement from his active foster family, and buckled down in school."

"What made him derail?" I rubbed the scar on my head, an action I found soothing.

"We think his mother is what happened." Detective Boyle studied his handwritten notes. "She had been showing up at his foster care home, causing trouble. We assume she was trying to take him away again for a final boost of financial gain from Social Services, which she would have received if he lived with her his senior year of high school."

"We know how that worked out," Luke said. "She sounds like a nightmare of a mom."

"Yes, which brings us back to the judge's decision." Katz addressed the reason we were gathered.

Luke clutched my hand, and we braced as if riding a roller coaster that had gone off the track.

Five years, please. He would only serve two-thirds of the sentence behind bars, the other third on probation, but that would mean Dastard would spend at least three years in a correctional facility.

"His sentence is five hundred fifty days." Prosecutor Katz's eyes resembled a puppy dog's, begging forgiveness even though he'd done nothing wrong.

I flinched. So did Luke.

"Are you freakin' kidding?" Luke's voice rose an octave.

"I wish I was." Katz rubbed a beefy hand over his face, his smile gone. "I was afraid they'd go light on Dalton, but I didn't think they'd go this easy on him. The sentence is roughly a year and a day or so behind bars and then six months of probation. The upside is it means he'll be in a correctional facility instead of the local jail."

"One measly year?" I clutched my chest as if I was having a heart attack. Maybe I was. Only instead of it stopping, it zoomed full throttle into overdrive. I'd tried to brace for the news of a lighter sentence, but hearing it out loud made me want to throw something. "I should have pushed for a trial!" I balled my fists, sending shooting pain through my healing fingers, but it kept me from hitting something.

Luke put his arm around me, and Boyle and Brook came to stand next to me.

Brook took my hand. "You did what you could. There's no guarantee a trial would have brought a better outcome."

She was right, and I needed to remind myself why I'd bailed on a trial, had to visualize sitting in there, listening to the monster and his lies, dragging my family—and me—through a lengthy public display of torture.

"One year is better than nothing. Let's focus on that." Luke's words cut into my thoughts. He hugged me to his chest as if he could shield me from the injustice of the decision.

I felt anything but gracious toward the judicial system at the moment, but I stood and thanked Katz for his help. He'd done what he could with no trial. Luke and I shook his hand before walking out the door, Brook and Boyle behind us.

In the parking lot, Brook turned to us. "We'll keep in touch. Even though Dalton is behind bars, please feel free to contact us with questions or concerns. Right, Doyle?"

The detective whistled a Star Trek tune. "Sure, I'll be around. Like a bad rash." He forced a half smile. "You've got my number." He nodded a goodbye to us then walked to his vehicle.

"Same goes for me. I'm here for you, and I'll be checking to make sure you stick with your counseling, okay?" Brook lifted my chin so she could read my expression.

I grimaced. "This is nuts. I'm happy it's over and sad at the same time. I feel like Christmas when you still get presents but find out there's no Santa Claus."

"What? There's no Santa Claus?" Brook deadpanned. With her keys in hand, she waved goodbye.

For three months, we'd relied on those people for guidance. Now, along with closure came an aching emptiness. The victory didn't taste as sweet as we'd hoped.

Chapter 12

I holed up in our house for three days after the verdict, licking my wounds like an animal that had chosen to walk into a steel trap instead of waiting to see if there was a better route. I'd taken the quick, less painful route by avoiding a trial, and I had nobody to blame but myself for the pathetic outcome.

So, he'll spend a year in a correctional facility? Big freakin' deal. With credit for time served, he would be out next August. He'd miss one year of his youth. I, on the other hand, would forever live with the emotional—and possibly some of the physical—trauma. The scar on my head was easy to cover up, and the one on my shoulder would fade. It would still be several months before I could run again, and now my immediate concern was slipping on the ice this winter as I hobbled with a cane.

By the following Tuesday, I was forced out of my self-imposed captivity. Pria had a band concert that night, one which I refused to miss. I'd caved the past few days, taking a pain pill every day by midafternoon, hoping to numb my mind enough so I could sleep at night.

Luke had dropped Pria off at the high school early to get set up with the rest of her band class. An hour later, the four of us arrived, the cool late-October night putting a thin sheen of ice over the puddles in the parking lot from yesterday's rain. Codi had insisted on wearing a sundress, and I hadn't had it in me to battle with her. To offset the forty-degree temps, she wore leggings and a jacket over the dress.

Ali, ever obedient, wore jeans, tennis shoes, and her favorite purple sweater. I went the sensible route, wearing flat-heeled ankle boots with good tread on the bottom. I'd dressed for the cool weather, aiming toward stylish with my new stretchy dark jeans and black turtleneck sweater that Luke had helped me into.

When Pria had joined the band in sixth grade, I'd coaxed her to choose the flute like I had. Instead, she'd selected the drums. As we sat through several songs, one being "In the Air Tonight," where each drummer played a part of the drum solo, I understood her choice. It was a perfect way to release some of that pent-up energy and frustration. It made me want to buy a drum set for myself. Or play my flute again.

Pride enveloped Luke and me as we slid out of our seats a few minutes early. Luke took Codi and Ali's hands and let me set the pace with my cane. Pria had kept her chin up through her first difficult months of high school. I was glad that everything was over so she—and the rest of our family—could put it all behind and move forward.

That joy left my heart when we walked out to our SUV. The streetlight above our vehicle illuminated raw eggs splattered all over it.

"Dammit!" Luke kicked a tire as if it was to blame instead of whoever in our community couldn't let things go.

I stood beside him, leaning on my cane, my mouth and eyes wide, feeling as if I'd been slapped. He opened one of the back doors then hustled Ali and Codi inside, shutting the door on a list of several questions shooting from Codi. We'd told Pria we would meet her at the side door by the band room. I cringed at having to pick Pria up in our egg-encrusted vehicle and embarrass her further.

"I'll clean this up." Luke's chin jutted out in defiance. He opened the passenger door for me and assisted me into the seat.

"I can help, Luke. There should be towels in the far back." I kept a tote with random things in the back of our SUV. Hats and mittens, toilet paper, towels, snacks, and other things we might need on any road trip with the girls. Too bad I'd taken out the water bottles recently since they would soon freeze if left in the car.

"That's okay. I've got this." Luke, usually calm and cool, was anything but. I sensed he felt the same way I did. We thought it would be over once Dastard was sentenced. Instead, the sentence had poured gasoline on an unlit match.

He turned on the vehicle and cranked up the heat before collecting towels from the back of the SUV. He found a nearby puddle, chipped the ice skimming the top with his shoe, then dunked the towel in.

We'd left early so I could walk at my own pace and avoid the crowd. Now, families made their way out the doors and into the parking lot.

Our neighbor friend Shawn walked toward Luke, his gaze taking in our messy vehicle. I rolled down our window a crack to hear their conversation.

"Hey, Luke. I've got some rags in the back of my truck and some water bottles rolling around in back. I'll get those." Shawn, the epitome of tall, dark, and handsome, owned a contractor business. He and his family lived a few blocks away in our development.

Shawn was back a moment later with a few rags and two plastic bottles of water.

"Thanks, man." Luke slapped him on the back.

Shawn's gesture choked me up, swinging my emotion from pissed off one minute to grateful the next.

They dumped water on the rags and wiped off the windows. As Luke worked on the front window and Shawn went to the driver's side, Luke jumped when someone appeared next to him with their own wet towel. It was a man whose wife taught fifth grade at my school.

"This shit's got to stop," his deep voice boomed as he helped Luke clean the window. He turned his damp towel over to continue wiping.

After the windows were presentable, the three did a lot of patting each other's backs. When my husband climbed behind the wheel, he reached for my hand and drove with the other to the school's side door to pick up Pria, with a sense of hope between us. We weren't alone.

I hoped Pria wasn't either.

I CANCELED MY NEXT counseling session two days later. I'd gone last week and answered the none-of-her-business questions about me and my family. But unless she could fix the mindset of those who blamed me for the demise of Dastard's football career, there was no point.

Instead, I dove into more boxes in the basement, re-boxing things we no longer used as if that would somehow organize my emotional clutter. And yes, I coated that pain with pills.

Friday night was the last football game of the season, and Pria stayed overnight at Sylvie's after they'd attended the football game. Saturday morning, Luke took Codi out for a bike ride to burn off some of her energy while I helped Ali get ready for a classmate's birthday party later. She was a ball of nerves and excitement, wrapped up with a bow of uncertainty.

"It will be fun. Remember, these are your classmates, and if you don't feel like playing a game, just say, 'No, thank you.'" It was the first party invitation she'd accepted and was from a friend who'd been in her class since kindergarten. "Daddy will be at work today, catching up on some things. You can call him if you need to leave early, but I bet you'll want to stay the whole time." I hugged her, feeling the softness of her long hair on my hands, the warmth of her cheek through my T-shirt. Luke's office was only a few minutes away from where Ali's friend lived, so it would be easier for him to pick her up than for me to since it was fifteen minutes from our house.

Her friend's mother was aware of Ali's quirks and need for consistency and calm. She'd been kind enough to call me last week with the food menu of pizza and ice cream cake, confirming Ali's pizza would need to be cut into squares, not triangles.

Luke dropped Ali off at the party on his way to the office. He reminded her that she could call his work phone, and he would pick her up early. Otherwise, he planned to arrive at three o'clock, the scheduled time on the party invitation.

I looked forward to a quiet Saturday with Codi before the frenzy of Halloween tomorrow. My shoulder ached from overuse thanks to my incessant unpacking and packing of our stored items. The recent dip in temperature only added to my aches and pains. While Codi colored at the table, I took inventory of my pill stash in our master bathroom.

Luke was aware of the pills in the medicine cabinet, the ones I "rarely" relied on now. Achiness traveled down my arm, pulsated in my right leg, which was still healing, and filtered through my thoughts like a lightning bolt that refused to move on.

I tried to ignore the pain and failed. Again. I was down to six pills. I put them back. I had a bottle hidden behind the wine glasses on the top shelf in our kitchen cabinet. While Codi concentrated on coloring a picture of Belle from *Beauty and the Beast*, I reached behind the stemware and let out a sigh when my fingers located the pill container.

Nine pills left in that one. I would need to call the pharmacy on Monday. *Or get this damn monkey off my back.* I'd been doing better until the verdict. Until the egging of our SUV. Until the aches and pains overtook my body, along with lack of exercise.

I popped a Vicodin in my mouth and chased it with a drink of water before replacing the pill container. Codi was still at work at the table.

"Want to play a game?" I ruffled her curls.

"Sure!" She slapped the color book shut. "Chutes and Ladders?"

"Fine with me."

She ran into the living room then came back with the board game. We played on the kitchen table as the Vicodin slowly worked its magic. I made it through one game before the fatigue hit me.

"I need to rest, okay? I'll make your lunch, and then we can cuddle on the couch while you watch cartoons." It was early for lunch, but I would never be able to keep my eyes open until noon. "PB and J?"

Codi nodded.

We sat at the kitchen table while I wished Codi would pick up the pace with her sandwich. After she finished, I flipped on the TV. I settled in with a blanket on the couch, waiting for Vicodin to wipe out the worry playing like a never-ending movie in my head.

I drifted off, waking periodically to make sure Codi was in the room with me. A Minnie Mouse cartoon was on TV. Codi had a bowl of animal crackers and the water bottle I'd filled earlier and was playing on the floor with her paper dolls.

The pain in my shoulder poked at me, begging for another Vicodin. I would take the next from the stash in the master bathroom. I made myself another cup of tea and downed it. Before I settled back in, I cut up apple slices and cheese for Codi then crawled back under my blanket on the recliner. The level of relaxation was a fantastic fluffy burrito, wrapping itself around my body and mind.

I didn't hear the phone ring. It wasn't until Codi pressed the receiver of our cordless phone to my cheek that I fought to get out of the cotton ball haze.

"What?" I blinked at Codi, a cracker crumb stuck in her hair.

"It's Pria, Mommy." She studied me like I was one of her dolls coming alive.

"Hullo?" *Where is Pria? At school? What day is it?*

"Mom, you said you'd pick me up at one. It's almost two! What's taking so long?" Accusation edged her words. As I struggled to remember where she was, I looked at the clock above our fireplace. 1:50 p.m. My right leg tingled with sleep as I attempted to stand.

"I'll be right there. I'm sorry. I must have dozed off." My tongue was as thick as a hockey puck as I tried to form words.

Think, Lily. Where is Pria? I didn't dare ask her.

When I hung up, I turned to Codi. "Where is Pria again?"

She'd gone back to putting a puzzle together, one I didn't remember her getting out. *How long had I been asleep?*

Codi focused on her puzzle. "'Member? She's at Sylvie's."

Ah yes, her friend Sylvie's. Pria had slept at her house. Today was Saturday. I went to the bathroom, splashed water on my face, then fluffed my matted hair with my fingers. I guzzled a glass of water and located my keys, moving like a pixilated image.

"Come on, Codi. We've got to go!" I called over my shoulder as I headed for our attached garage. I hit the garage door opener button, and Codi ran up behind me.

Dang, it's cold out! I started the vehicle, opened the back door for Codi, then backed down our driveway, not allowing the car to warm up.

I hadn't been to Sylvie's home for a few months, but after driving there enough times over the years, our SUV could have probably driven itself. *Why is Pria's underwear in a twist?* She'd never complained about spending extra time at her friend's house.

I made it there in ten minutes. Pria stood outside their front door with her backpack on her shoulder. She ran down their walkway to the vehicle before I'd even put it in park. Every movement of hers seemed so fast compared to the speed of my thoughts and actions.

"What's the hurry?"

Pria leveled me with a stink-eye she'd shelved since the attack.

I backed down the long driveway then caught the curb as I turned the wheel. I giggled, finding humor in the sudden bump.

"Mommmm!" Pria's tone felt like a virtual slap.

"What? What?" Her yelling flustered me as I attempted to pull out from their side street into the busy oncoming traffic. I clenched the steering wheel while merging into traffic.

"You have your slippers on, and your shirt is buttoned up wrong." Her face contorted as she looked me up and down. She might as well have said, "You flew to Sylvie's house on your broomstick."

I snuck a peek at my plaid shirt. So my buttons were off by a couple. At least I had a shirt on. I'd have commented on her nastiness, but I needed every ounce of concentration for driving. *Why isn't everyone home on this dreary day?*

Pria turned her focus to Codi in the back seat. "Hey, Codi. Whatcha been doing all day?"

"Playing." Codi, a girl who could win a chatter contest, summarized her day with one word. Guilt pushed itself inside my heart as I realized I had no idea what Codi *had* been doing. She was six going on sixteen at times. I didn't trust her. Maybe I hadn't been sleeping for long.

Pria reached back to tickle Codi, seated behind her. "Hey, you aren't strapped in!" She screamed, and I jumped, swerving out of my lane.

"Jesus, Pria!"

A man laid on his horn in the car next to me.

"Pull over, Mom!" Pria yelled as if our vehicle was on fire.

I glanced at the back window to make sure no flames were coming out of the car.

I huffed, veering over to the side of the road. *What is the big deal?*

Pria undid her seat belt, hopped out, then opened Codi's door to belt her in. "Oh, sweetie. Aren't your feet cold?"

I turned around to see Pria rubbing Codi's bare feet. *Where are her socks and shoes?* Pria reached around her neck and took off the winter scarf she'd been wearing, wrapping Codi's feet together in it like a turban. I busted out laughing, imagining Codi turned upside down, the scarf being her head and her walking on her arms.

"Not. Funny," Pria said between gritted teeth.

Codi giggled with me, reinforcing my funny bone.

Pria mumbled under her breath before stomping back into the front seat.

"What's that?" I leaned toward her, unsure if she was talking to me or crabbing about me. *Please shut up, Pria! I can't focus on driving, let alone worry about your random teenage rant.*

"Go." Pria fumed. "I wish I was sixteen so I could drive. *You* shouldn't be driving. You should get help, that's what you need. *Help.*" Sarcasm dripped from each word.

I flinched at the sting of her accusation. Moisture distorted my vision while I drove in silence. As I neared our driveway, a jolt to the front of the vehicle combined with a loud thud.

"What was that?" I stopped the SUV in our driveway, put it in park, then looked at Pria, her mouth hanging open wide enough for my fist.

"Holy shit, Mom. You knocked over our mailbox!" She reached over and turned off the ignition, got out, then helped Codi from her car seat. She hustled up the rest of our driveway, balancing Codi in one arm and her backpack in the other.

I was going to have to talk to that girl about her attitude.

Chapter 13

P*ria must think I've gone deaf.* Yes, things were a little fuzzy around the edges, and yes, I may have made a mess of our mailbox, but I'd picked her up, and we were all fine. Okay, Codi's feet may have been a little cold, but the girl was a hotbox all the time. It wasn't my fault she ran around barefoot in the house. She was in kindergarten, for heaven's sake. She could put her own damn socks and shoes on. And fasten the seatbelt over herself in the car.

I'd shuffled to the living room. Codi had gone off to play. Pria, on the other hand, was ripping me a new one to Luke on the phone. I picked up the landline phone next to me and listened in.

"Slow down, Pria." Even I could hear Luke's patience waning in his voice. "I can't understand what you're saying."

I heard her loud and clear, in stereo, her voice carrying from the kitchen and also from the phone clutched to my ear. Two words stuck out. "Mom" and "bonkers."

"Take a deep breath." Luke slowed his words. "Now, is everyone safe?"

"Yeah." Pria drew the word out as if she wasn't sure.

"Who else is there? Do I need to come home?"

"Codi. Mom's in the driveway right now." A little squeak followed her words. "Dad?"

"Yes?" Luke sounded like he didn't want to hear what she would say next.

"I think Mom is on drugs. Or drunk." Pria's words were muffled as if she'd covered her mouth. "She knocked over our mailbox.

And"—her words rushed out like a powerful wind—"Codi wasn't buckled in when they picked me up. And she was barefoot!"

I covered the receiver so Pria wouldn't hear my gasp. *How dare she point fingers at me?* She hadn't been paying attention herself. She hadn't heard me open the front door and shuffle in. Shame on her for throwing me under the bus.

"I was going to leave in an hour anyway to pick up Ali from the birthday party. I'll leave now. The car is shut off, right?" Luke said.

"Yes. I turned it off before Codi and I got out."

"Smart girl. Leave your mother be. Would you please get Codi a snack and play a game with her? I'll be there in twenty minutes."

After they hung up, I did too. Pria was banging cupboard doors in the kitchen, likely getting a snack for her and Codi. I snuck from the living room up to our bedroom to put myself together before landing under Luke's scrutiny. My leg ached by the time I reached the top of the steps, leaning on my cane. If only I could take another pill. I didn't dare.

I stood in front of our bathroom mirror. *Dang, Pria was right. How did my blouse get buttoned up wrong?* I'd started the day with a T-shirt. I didn't know when I'd changed. I fluffed up my matted-down hair, brushed my teeth, then downed two glasses of water.

Back in our bedroom, I looked out the window to our driveway below. *Ooh, so the mailbox is a total mess.* I cringed, certain I'd put a few scratches on our vehicle. My head ached, pulsating like it did when I ran too fast in the heat. I flopped back on our bed and closed my eyes, wishing for the day to be over so I could start fresh.

A few minutes later, I heard Luke downstairs. I pushed myself off the bed and walked down the hall. Pria's bedroom door was shut. Whispers and giggles filtered into the hall from under her door. I knocked before turning the doorknob.

"Hi, Mommy! Are you all better now?" Codi jumped off Pria's bed and came barreling at me, her arms open wide. I pulled her in for a hug and eyed Pria, reclining against her pillows on the bed with paper dolls strewn all over the covers. They'd been laughing a second ago. But then, as our eyes met, I read fear in Pria's.

"Thanks for keeping her occupied," I mouthed over Codi's head as she rested it on my waist.

Pria's lips pressed together, and her chin quivered. I turned away, unable to handle what I was doing to my family.

Codi ran to the bed and brought back a paper doll. "So, the dude here is wearing a bikini. Hmmm, I wonder who dressed him."

I attempted a smile at Codi. I sensed Luke's presence behind me in the doorway.

"Are you girls hungry?"

Codi's eyes lit up. She jumped off the bed then headed downstairs.

"I'll take that as a yes. There's pepperoni pizza and breadsticks downstairs. Early supper, I guess," Luke said.

I turned and watched Codi hurry down the steps.

"I'm hungry too. We didn't eat much at Sylvie's," Pria said to Luke, ignoring me as she walked past me.

"What? No big breakfast? Sylvie's dad usually cooks up a storm for you two. Pancakes, eggs, bacon..."

She avoided his eyes. Something hiccupped in my mind.

"Not today." Without another word, she went downstairs.

Luke turned to me, his eyes hooded. "We'll talk later." It wasn't a question.

Although I wasn't hungry, I needed food to offset the pills I'd taken earlier. Mastering going down the steps had been more difficult than going up. I took my time. It wasn't as if my family was eager to have me in the kitchen with them.

"I'll whip up a salad." Luke's voice carried from the kitchen.

Salads had typically been my area. I'd been the one making sure the girls ate somewhat healthy. Not anymore. It wasn't that I didn't care. There was only so much energy and willpower left. It was like my body had a slow, continuous leak of my former self.

I rounded the corner to the kitchen, where Luke dished up a plate for Codi. Two pizza boxes and a bag of cheesy bread from our favorite pizza place sat on the counter.

"I'll set aside enough for Ali and your mom," he told Codi. Luke turned to Pria. "I need to leave to pick up Ali. You going to be okay until I get back?"

I hid behind the wall, fuming. *Jeez, he's acting like he's leaving them alone with a monster.* I was fine. Well, still tired and achy, and the day felt out of focus like someone had blurred the lines.

"We'll be okay," Pria answered.

Fine, they don't need me. I turned and hobbled back upstairs, wishing my body would allow me to stomp. All I wanted to do was nap.

BY THE TIME I WOKE up, the sky was darkening. From our bedroom window, I could see that Luke had pulled out our damaged mailbox and post. He'd also moved my vehicle out of the driveway and into the garage. It was time to go downstairs and face the music.

The house was quiet as I made my way down the steps. Although it was almost six o'clock, I spotted the four of them in the backyard, playing catch with a football. In the kitchen, Luke had left a note on the counter. *Pizza and salad in the fridge.*

I took out the pizza and salad bowl. Six squares of pizza remained, and I forced myself to eat one. What I wanted was a green smoothie—something to make me feel better about what I'd been doing to my body. Instead, I ate the last of the lettuce, tomato, and pepper salad Luke had put together.

My family soon joined me. Codi rebounded from the day as if nothing odd had happened. Ali—sheltered from my actions thanks to the birthday party—was her usual quiet self, and Pria was back to acting like I'd murdered everyone on our block.

Luke stepped in, probably forgiving me an inch since I was eating and looked like a somewhat sane version of myself. "Ali, do you want to tell your mom about the party?"

I smiled up at him for throwing me a lifeline. "Yes, Ali. I want to hear about your day." I patted the chair next to me, then Ali sat with a proud smile on her face.

"It was fun. And I stayed the whole time! I only didn't play one game. They were blindfolded and had to pin a hat on the drawing of the Halloween witch. I didn't want to be blindfolded, but I cheered for my friends."

I touched her cheek with my palm. "I'm so proud of you. And so glad you had fun."

"Okay, let's get you girls cleaned up." Luke rubbed his hands together. "Ali, you shower first, and then I'll bathe Codi. Pria, your mom and I would like to talk with you later."

My eyebrows shot up. *We would? About what?*

"Okay." Pria averted her eyes. "I'll be in my room."

"Go get your pajamas, Codi. I'll be upstairs in a few minutes," Luke said.

After our girls left, Luke came to stand by my chair. "I called your mom while you were sleeping. We can talk about this later, but I've asked her to come to stay here again for a while. You need help, Lily, and I can't leave you here alone again. Or alone with our children." His words sounded like an apology. As if he was sorry he had to say them.

Not as sorry as I felt hearing them. "Okay. Um, what are we talking to Pria about later?"

"Her stay at Sylvie's. I think they were there alone without Sylvie's parents."

I nodded, vaguely remembering feeling something was off with Pria. It was her insistence I pick her up on time instead of relishing extra time with her friend.

"By the way, your mom suggested we look for your flute. She remembers how it calmed you as a teen. It might help now."

I nodded before he turned and left me alone in the kitchen with a bucket full of remorse.

Not being able to run anytime soon added to my agitation. No release of endorphins as I pounded the pavement. *But music? Hell yes.* Although it might be difficult navigating my fingers to play the flute or our piano. Another stress reliever was teaching. I was scheduled to go back to the classroom after the first of the year, which was a little over two months away. Physically, I was on the road to recovery. It was the emotional healing that shredded me.

Luke waited until Ali and Codi were in bed with Pria still holed up in her bedroom before he suggested we talk. We chose the corner of the living room where my hospital bed had been, a quiet corner of our home.

He took my hand as we sat next to each other on the couch. "Your mom will be here Monday afternoon and will stay through the week again until things improve." Luke cleared his throat and turned his body to look me in the eye. "This is what I see, Lily. The strong farm girl in you has been replaced with an emotionally battered woman who has tried to be too damn strong. You're too stubborn to think you need help. But you do."

I blinked back tears, and he thumbed one off my cheek. "While you were sleeping, I checked every cabinet and drawer in our house. I found OxyContin, Tizanidine, Vicodin, and other pills I don't recognize that weren't in containers."

I squeezed my eyes shut, wishing it all away. The pills. The pain. The guilt.

"Do you remember what happened today when you picked up Pria at Sylvie's?"

"Sort of." I opened my eyes to look at the man I'd loved for almost twenty years. Handsome, kind, smart, and the best father and husband anyone could ask for. *Will he leave me?* No, Luke—like me—wasn't a quitter. Yet maybe he thought I'd quit on my family by turning to the pills.

His hand caressed the top of mine. "As much as we wish that asshole hadn't attacked you, we can't change that it happened. But we can keep it from wrecking our family, which is why we need to talk about the opioids." He paused, waiting for affirmation from me.

I nodded, feeling like a bobblehead with my incessant agreeing.

"I'll tell you what I know happened, and then Pria will join us to fill in the blanks. You took something and fell asleep. Codi answered the phone when Pria called because you were late in picking her up from Sylvie's. You and Codi drove to pick Pria up."

Yes, that all sounded somewhat familiar. A scene tucked behind clouds.

Luke let go of my hands and cracked his knuckles. "Pria got in the car and noticed Codi didn't have her seatbelt fastened and that she was barefoot. She belted Codi in—even though we know Codi can, and should have, done it herself. Then she wrapped her winter scarf around Codi's freezing feet."

He stood and paced. "Not only did you neglect to buckle Codi in, but you mowed over our mailbox. I'll buy a new one on Monday. It put a nice scratch on the side of our vehicle."

I winced as he continued. "I don't give a rat's ass about the car or mailbox. I only care that you get help, that you and the girls are safe. They weren't today, and the mailbox could have been a person out for a walk."

I leaned forward and buried my face in my hands. "I want to see our car." I forced myself to stand and face reality.

Luke handed me my cane, then we headed to the garage. I flipped on the light and fingered the long scratches along the driver's door.

"I'm so sorry!" I leaned my head on the side window as if apologizing to the SUV.

Luke hugged me from behind. My tears dampened his hands. "We'll get you better, but you need to be one hundred percent in the game, Lily. No more pretending everything is okay."

I turned and clung to Luke as if he was a lifeguard who could dive into the ocean to save me. Although he couldn't swim well, we were on dry land, and his determination helped ground me. "I'm trying, Luke. I am. But it's like everything is stacked against us. It's not fair!"

He pulled his face away to look at me. "Nobody said life was fair. You know that."

I did, but I'd never lived it before now.

"We can only control so much, and everyone needs help at times. Even you."

I gave up the fight of holding back emotion and sobbed in his arms, the first thing that had felt good all day. He didn't release me until my hiccups of tears subsided.

"Ready to talk to Pria now? I've got questions for her."

"Yes." I mopped my face with my sleeve and followed Luke into the kitchen.

I took a seat, and he went up upstairs to get Pria. My stomach curled as if I'd drunk sour milk, imagining if our mailbox had been a child. I could have hurt someone today. *I* did *hurt someone today.* More than one person. My entire family. And only I could make sure that it never happened again.

Chapter 14

Pria followed Luke into the kitchen, looking anywhere except at me. I didn't blame her. I wasn't happy with myself either.

"I'm so sorry, Pria." I reached across the table, but she kept her hands folded in her lap. The realization that I could have harmed my children, and possibly others, jolted me like the time I'd tripped on the electric fence at the farm.

My lower lip trembled. "I took a pill or two. I can't remember. My shoulder has been bothering me, and I needed to rest a bit while Codi played. I must have dozed off." The mug of tea warmed my hands as the rest of me shivered. "I shouldn't have been driving. When you called, I should have contacted your dad and asked him to pick you up."

Pria picked at her cuticles.

"Why did it matter that I was late?" I asked. "I'm surprised Sylvie's parents didn't offer to bring you home. They usually do."

Especially since the attack.

"That's what I wondered," Luke said. "And I found it odd that Sylvie's dad didn't whip up his famous breakfast."

Pria squirmed in her chair.

He folded his arms over his chest. "Is there something you want to tell us? Were her parents gone and on their way home, and that's why you needed to leave?"

Pria shrugged. "So what? Her older sister was there. We didn't do anything wrong."

My parental antenna shot up a day too late. "Then why lie to us?"

"I didn't lie. You never asked if Sylvie's parents would be there."

That was true. Pria was a teenager, one who hadn't pushed her boundaries before and suddenly had plenty of chances with an absentminded mother. I remembered what those years had been like and what I'd gotten away with, or at least tried to. "No boys over? No drinking?"

She wasn't as good a liar as I had been at her age. When Jacob's drinking had escalated, I'd become a pro at lying to myself and my parents, pretending all was fine. On the rare occasion I'd caught Pria in a lie, I'd noticed her blink several times, just as she was doing at that moment. Luke picked up on it as well.

"So, I guess the answer is yes to at least one of those questions. Alcohol stays in your body for hours. Should I go buy a Breathalyzer kit at Walmart?" He leaned forward.

Pria shoved back from the table. "At least I didn't get behind the wheel." Her eyes turned a deep green, her glare slicing my body like a laser.

"Don't you talk to your mother like that!"

Poor Luke. I'd made it a trying day for him. It was time I took the reins.

"You're right, Pria. I need help." I swallowed a painful lump of admission, and Luke placed his hand over mine. "I promise to do better, to be a better example for you. We remember what it's like to be your age. You're not a child anymore. You want to be an adult, yet you aren't. Still, we rely on you a lot to act like an adult... especially these past few months." Shame coated my words. "I've leaned on you too much, expecting you to step in and cover for me."

Pria's rigid body softened.

"Your dad and I talked about me getting help. Today has been the incentive I needed. Thank you for stepping in to make sure Codi was okay."

Pria's jaw dropped. A thank-you was probably not what she'd expected.

"No sleepovers for a month though. And I promise, next time, I'll be clearheaded enough to make sure parents are home and that I'm okay to pick you up." I got up, stood behind my daughter, then wrapped my arms around her shoulders. "Deal?"

After a few seconds, she reached back and placed a hand over mine. She hadn't given up on me.

After she went back to her room, Luke and I talked. "Didn't you say the counselor suggested aqua therapy for you? I think you need some sort of physical workout to replace running, something to help you like running did." He knew what relaxed me.

"My physical therapist suggested it." My body craved a daily serotonin boost.

"Okay, well, I think it's a good idea. Also, you need to keep your counseling appointments. I'm afraid if you don't do these things, you'll need to go in for treatment." Luke's eyes watered as he leaned his face on his hand, his elbow on the table. Weariness pulled at his features. Keeping our family together and cleaning up my crap had likely subtracted years from his life.

"I can't leave the girls, or you, for a month." It was the standard treatment time.

Did Jacob ever seek help? Does he still drink? The fall after I'd met Luke, Jacob had stumbled down the dorm steps at college in a drunken stupor. Jacob's injuries were the excuse he'd needed to ramp up his drinking. He'd missed our wedding the following summer. I'd labeled him as weak. He was human. So was I.

And he'd yet to write back to me. It had taken me years to forgive Jacob, and if I was honest, it'd only happened because I could relate to him all those years later. I didn't know how long it would be before I could forgive myself. First, I needed to conquer the pills. I had the support system to do that. But Jacob hadn't. We'd bailed on him.

"Let's consider the treatment center as our last option." Luke leaned in and kissed me. "I just want you to be okay," he uttered against my lips before pulling back. "You need help to get rid of the guilt you're carrying around. I suspect it's what pushes you to reach for a pill or a drink." I wasn't much of a drinker, but as I'd weaned myself off the pills in September, I'd replaced them with a drink. Or two. Or three.

"I'm so lucky to have you. And maybe that's part of my problem—thinking I don't deserve you. That you'd be better off with a woman who doesn't cry in her sleep, who isn't so needy, who hasn't turned people against you." Insecurity cut like razor blades inside my throat.

He put both hands on my cheeks, his face so close to mine I could count his dark eyelashes. "Don't think that. It's not true. We need to tackle this together and remember all the people who *are* behind us. Sometimes, we forget to listen to those who aren't shouting."

THAT NIGHT, BEFORE we went to bed, Luke stood next to me in our bathroom with the opioids I had stashed in various hiding places. I flushed each one down the toilet. It was painful, cleansing, and frightening. Those pills had become my security blanket.

"I'm amazed at how easy it's been to allow something so small to wreck my life."

Luke put his hand on my shoulder. "I'm concerned you'll have withdrawals."

"I did okay before the judge's verdict. I think between that and someone egging our vehicle, I felt like someone stomped me back down a black hole. I understand it's a roller-coaster ride to recovery. One day at a time, right? Aquatic therapy and counseling will help. And music. I need to find my flute." I needed a lot of things.

MONDAY WELCOMED NOVEMBER and my poor mom back to our house. She arrived early afternoon, armed with a new craft project.

"I've got some things I need to finish before Christmas."

I helped her set up shop in a corner of our living room. "Must be quite a project to start two months ahead of time." Mom could never sit still, always had ten things on her to-do list. I'd been that way. I could be again.

"Thank goodness it's sewing instead of knitting, or I'd worry you were making us all ugly Christmas sweaters again." We laughed at the memory of the god-awful one she'd knitted for me a few years earlier for our school's Ugly Sweater Contest. I'd won. Nobody could compete with a woman who'd crafted a double-sided cow sweater complete with silver glitter yarn in his teeth for braces, tiny cowbells, a puffy nose that squeaked, and a knit cow tail sticking out of the back. Sometimes, she made me damn proud.

I'd struggled through Halloween yesterday, tucking myself into bed after handing out candy until Luke came home from trick-or-treating with Ali and Codi. That morning, I hadn't made our bed, skipped showering, and scarfed down two pieces of toast with butter and cinnamon sugar. My bed and hygiene hardly mattered. I'd used my brainpower to focus on not punching the walls, which would've hurt my fingers.

But before Mom arrived, I'd been proactive. I'd called the aquatic therapy number my PT had given me and set up sessions every Monday and Wednesday. And I'd located my flute in one of the boxes in our basement.

After a few minutes of rusty playing, I set it aside. Practicing would be minimal for a while. I'd recently finished OT for my fingers and would concentrate on playing the piano—another instrument I'd cast aside years ago—until my fingers could handle the flute.

As dinner baked in the oven—roasted chicken, potatoes, and squash—Mom and I sat at the kitchen table, a notebook between us.

"I want to make a schedule with goals for each day—something for me to focus on, something to give me purpose." I twirled a pencil.

Mom pushed back her faded blond hair and smiled. "That's my girl."

I drew a chart. "Okay, water therapy is every Monday and Wednesday, counseling every Thursday. I thought of even scheduling a walk twice a day until the roads get too slippery. And music. I'll keep trying my flute, and my fingers are okay to play the piano. What do you think?" I drummed the pencil on the paper.

"I think scheduling as much as you can is a good idea. You're a goal-oriented person, and I believe the busier you can make your day, the better. Even when the weather turns and the sidewalks are slushy, we could drive to the mall and walk around in there."

"Aw, Mom. Only old people walk around in the mall." But I grinned and agreed I might have to resort to it for a while.

An hour later, the girls were home from school, followed soon by Luke. It wasn't until everyone was in bed that I felt the pressure cooker ready to erupt inside me. Luke slept next to me, his breathing quiet and even. I slipped out of bed then made my way downstairs.

I walked around our main floor, sipping warm milk, and stared out the windows into the darkness that reflected the demons haunting me. The structured mornings of sending the girls off to school, counseling, and water therapy would help get me up and dressed. But in between busy moments, the edge of need crept in, filling the cracks. My heart raced, an agitation I'd never experienced before the attack. There'd been times of stress in my teens, but I'd been able to run it off. *Dammit. I need to run!*

At my first session on Wednesday, the aquatic therapist and I discussed that craving.

"I bet you'll find water therapy a good replacement for now," she said. "It isn't an aerobic exercise to the extent running is, but it will give you a workout that will strengthen your body, boost your mood, and hopefully, calm your mind." The therapist looked to be a decade younger than me. "Once you feel strong enough, we can get you into swim lessons if you'd like."

"I'd like that. My entire family needs lessons."

"It's the one sport that can save your life."

I liked the option of swim lessons until I could run again. I napped that afternoon after the first session, but that kept me awake again late into the night. The restlessness that overtook me each night made me want to unzip my skin and crawl right out of it. *If only it were that easy.* The aches that had been subdued the past few months came back like an unwanted guest who refused to leave. They may have been "phantom" pains from weaning off the pills, but they sure as hell were real to me.

Warm milk hadn't helped at night. Neither had pacing. So it was that I found myself in our basement at 3:30 a.m., screaming at the top of my lungs a stream of words like "unfair," "justice," and "assholes." My anger took in every person, even though 99.9 percent of them had done nothing wrong.

On our way to the counselor on Thursday, Mom said, "I heard you screaming in the basement last night. It's a good idea, especially if it helps you blow off steam. Feel free to do it in the comfort of your main floor during the day." She cast a look at me as she drove.

"How did you hear me?" She should have been sleeping upstairs like the rest of my family. *Oh, no. Did they hear?*

"I got up to use the bathroom, came downstairs for a drink of water, and heard you."

"Busted." I hoped to make light of it as if I wouldn't be back in the basement tonight doing the same thing. "Maybe it's the gloomy November weather."

Mom just nodded, keeping her thoughts to herself. Neither of us believed it was the weather or I wouldn't be on my way to purge to Dr. Arlene.

By Saturday, I wanted to gnaw my arm off. Six days with no opioids, and agitation still pulsated through me. I wasn't the most pleasant person to be around. Poor Ali. Luke did his best to keep her away from the tension I radiated. Pria kept her distance, and Codi had a high tolerance level on just about everything, including me.

Mom arrived the following Monday morning to drive me to swim therapy. Apparently, they didn't trust me yet to attend alone. That afternoon, when my nerves pushed me toward a scream fest, she said, "Let's watch a movie instead. I picked one up for us yesterday."

A movie was the last thing I wanted—sitting still instead of walking and screaming my anxiety out. Mom inserted the DVD, and *Steel Magnolias* popped up on the screen. I hadn't watched the movie since it'd come out in the late 1980s.

"Really, Mom? A movie about a daughter dying is going to cheer me up and calm me?" I eyed her as I settled in next to her on the couch, my legs propped up on the ottoman.

"I think it will be therapeutic." Mom reached for my hand.

"I don't even remember most of the story, but I remember Julia Roberts's character dies. Should be a real mood booster." Nonetheless, I relaxed from my mother's calming touch.

As usual, Mom was right. I lost myself in the story, forgetting my pain. And in the scene where Sally Field's character fell apart on the day she had to bury her daughter and she screamed she wanted to know *why* she'd lost something so precious, I understood.

There were too many "whys" in the world that would never get answered, and I had to accept that. I might never understand why he attacked me, and all my screaming—just as Sally Field had—might relieve my internal pain, but it wouldn't bring me answers.

When it was suggested Sally Field's character punch Shirley MacLaine's character, "Ouiser", Mom and I busted out laughing.

In the next instant, Mom stood and pulled me up. "Punch me."

I pulled my face back and studied her. "Are you kidding? I'm not going to hit you!"

"Quick, who do you want to hit? If you could punch someone, who would it be?"

"Dastard. Duh." She was familiar with my name for the monster.

"Yes, but he's behind bars. If you had your choice of punching him or him sitting behind bars for a year, which would you choose?"

As badly as I wanted to hurt him, the answer was obvious. Losing a year of his life while sitting in the correctional facility did more damage than any punch I could throw.

"You can't undo what happened, and you can't change what some townspeople think. You can only move forward with your head held high and realize that sometimes, we don't get an answer to 'why.'"

I fell into Mom's arms, and as she wrapped them around me, her warmth and comfort working like a healing balm, I thought of the characters in the movie. Yes, it was fiction, but reality had just as many painful stories. At least I was alive.

Two days later, my primary physician put me on a low-dose anxiety pill. "This is temporary. Things will improve. The medication, along with continued counseling and your music and exercise therapy, will get you past this rough spot."

IT TOOK A LITTLE OVER a week before my anxiety subsided. Water therapy wore me out physically, and counseling wore me out emotionally. And, because I understood she couldn't help me if I didn't allow her in, I let my guard down with Dr. Arlene.

"Tell me about the guilt weighing on you." She addressed what I'd avoided in previous sessions—the incessant storm clashing over my head.

I closed my eyes, unable to look at her as I confessed something I hadn't admitted to anyone. "I feel guilty for not fighting hard enough against Dastard. For the trauma I've brought to my family—especially Pria—and for not running with pepper spray or a cell phone." I pinched the bridge of my nose to dam the emotion threatening to burst. "And I hadn't been paying attention like I should have been. Hadn't been aware of my surroundings. I've drilled that into my children yet hadn't done it myself that morning."

She nodded along with each admission, looking as if she'd already known about them. And with each passing session, the guilt peeled away like an unfurling peony, releasing a fragrant scent of hope and rebirth.

Along with rebuilding my emotional fortitude, my body strengthened. After several water therapy sessions, my therapist agreed it was time to add in swim lessons. I would start them the week after Thanksgiving, another physical routine that would get me through each day. Slowly, endorphins replaced the pills and booze. And I kept my eye on the prize—my family.

If I hadn't flushed my medications down the toilet—I found out later that I should have turned them in at the clinic—there were several times I would have reached for pills. The verdict was out on whether I would need to refrain from drinking. Until I had a firm grip on things, I'd cut out booze even though I'd never had a problem until the last few months. Luke did his best to help me curb my cravings. His charitable personality led him to help the homeless or any child selling something, and it flowed into his urge to help me. I hadn't made it easy for him.

Though raised in different worlds, we respected our unique strengths. Farm life forced flexibility. Chores changed depending on any emergency. A heifer with a breech calf needing manipulation. A crop in need of harvesting before an impending storm. A malfunctioning piece of equipment. All challenges I'd embraced. Yet I'd struggled to adjust after the attack.

Luke could fart on command thanks to his father's rigid years in the service. After our children came along, he relaxed his need to have a schedule for everything. That forced flexibility had no doubt saved his sanity in dealing with my erratic behavior.

Chapter 15

After three weeks—with time off for good behavior on my part—Mom was relieved of Lily-watch duty. She left Thursday when Luke arrived home from work, both of them certain that I'd made great strides on my road to recovery.

In a little over six weeks, I planned to be back teaching. I hadn't had a scream fest in over a week, the anxiety pills had kicked in, and after three soul-baring sessions with Dr. Arlene, she agreed that I was healing emotionally. Life was back on even ground until Friday night.

Pria had gone right from school to her friend Erin's house to hang out until they attended a girls' basketball game at seven. Ali and Codi were home from school, and I was frying ground beef for the chili simmering on the stove when the doorbell rang.

"Can you get that, Ali?" She sat at the kitchen table doing homework, Codi beside her, coloring. Luke would be home soon from work.

"Mom, he needs money," Ali said as she entered the kitchen.

"Who does?"

"The pizza man at the door. You ordered a lot of pizzas!" Ali's eyes lit up, and Codi jumped down from the chair, hopping around as if it was her birthday.

"Pizza?" I turned down the temperature on the stove, washed my hands, then followed Ali to the front door. Surely it was a mistake.

"Mrs. Gallo?" the gangly teen asked. Four large pizza boxes rested on his forearm, a receipt taped to the box.

"Yes, but I didn't order any pizzas. Are you sure you're at the right place?"

Codi clapped next to me, bouncing on the soles of her feet. If these had been meant for a neighbor, Codi would've invited herself there for dinner.

He handed me the receipt. "That's your address and phone number, right? She said you ordered eight large pizzas—four pepperonis, four sausages. You got a teenager who is having a party? That's what you told her when you placed the order."

"*Eight* pizzas?" I checked the information on the slip of paper. It was correct.

He handed me the four pizza boxes, turned, then headed back to his car to get the rest. I didn't have time to dissect whether I'd placed the order.

"Ali, can you get my purse, please?" I headed to the kitchen with the boxes.

Ali ran to the living room, where my purse hung by our coats. Five minutes later, I was over a hundred dollars poorer, and we had enough pizza to feed the kids in our neighborhood, even if some of those families no longer spoke to us.

I lifted the lid off a box, surprised to find the pizza cut into triangular pieces. We always requested to have ours cut into squares or Ali wouldn't eat, further proof I hadn't ordered them. I finished frying the hamburger then added it to the other chili ingredients before cutting a triangle piece into squares for Ali.

The girls were eating pepperoni slices when Luke arrived home. Six of the pizzas were in the fridge. I wasn't a big pizza fan. No matter how hungry the girls and Luke were, they couldn't polish off eight large pizzas in the next few days. Not without upset stomachs.

"Pizza for supper?" He peered over my shoulder after we kissed, no doubt wondering why I had chili on the stove while Ali and Codi crammed pizza in their mouths.

"It was a mistake. Honestly, I didn't order them. I think this is someone else's pizza order. I bet there's a party somewhere with a bunch of starving kids." That was the only explanation I could come up with, even though the delivery driver called The Pizza Pad, our favorite pizza place, and double-checked the delivery information before I paid him.

Luke shrugged. "Oh, well. It's only two pizzas." He walked over to the kitchen table, kissed the girls' sauce-covered faces, then opened the box marked "sausage."

"Um, no. It's eight pizzas." I opened the refrigerator for him to see. I'd moved food around to fit the boxes inside.

"Jesus, Lily!" Luke cracked his knuckles.

"I swear, I didn't order them. See? These are cut into triangles, not squares. And besides, I was making chili for supper."

We refrained from discussing it in front of the girls, but I read distrust in Luke's eyes. It hurt me more than if we'd had a knock-down, drag-out shouting match.

TENSION BUILT A WALL between us in bed. I lay there, eyes closed, my mind in a hamster wheel of silent self-defense. I tried to put myself in Luke's position, tried to look at tonight as he did—a fiasco on the heels of my other opioid decision-making.

Next week was Thanksgiving, a time for us to give thanks for all we had. And as I thought of the holiday, I remembered a special Thanksgiving eighteen years ago. The weekend Luke had asked me to marry him. It was also the first time our parents had met.

Unbeknownst to me, he'd driven from his Minneapolis apartment to the farm the week before Thanksgiving, five months after we'd met, to ask their permission to marry me.

My favorite spot was the barn. I would hop up on the milk cooler and play the flute while Dad corralled the cows into their stanchions.

Thanksgiving night, after our meal with our parents, he'd offered to replace Dad so we could milk the cows together. When we'd finished, Luke asked me to play the flute. We sat shoulder to shoulder on the milk cooler as I took my flute case off the shelf nearby and opened it.

"What the...?" I lifted the toy train engine he'd tucked in the case, a Christmas ornament symbolizing our first meeting.

"The doors open." He pointed to the engine's side door.

"Oh!" I turned to Luke, stunned. Inside was an engagement ring.

He picked up the ring and held my left hand. "I was already falling in love with you before the first time I came to visit you here. Your mom told me I'd find you in the barn. As I walked over, the night carried notes of a slow rendition of 'Old MacDonald Had a Farm' from your flute. I'd thought of you as this tough farm girl. Then I found you serenading the cows. It showed me your softer side. It was another reason for me to want to spend the rest of my life with you."

I dabbed my damp cheeks with the bottom of my sleeve, speechless.

"I realize this is a simple and, okay, tiny solitaire, but its size in no way reflects the depth of my love for you. It only reflects my small bank account right now and—"

I stopped his rambling with my fingers before replacing them with my lips. "Yes," I'd whispered between kisses. "My answer to the question you meant to ask? It's yes."

I never regretted marrying Luke, and I sensed, underneath his frustration, he still felt the same about me.

THE FOLLOWING MORNING, Luke woke me up with a kiss, his sign he'd put yesterday's pizza fiasco behind us. We had a fun weekend ahead of us. I was scheduled to attend a potluck with coworkers at Maria's house on Saturday evening. I called Maria that morning.

"I know you've got me down for bringing a salad, but can we change that to pizza from The Pizza Pad? Like, four large pizzas?" I explained the ordering error to Maria.

"That would be great. I'll make a salad instead of barbeque meatballs. See you at six."

Luke and I spent Saturday afternoon with the girls at the bowling alley. I couldn't bowl with my fingers, so I was the scorekeeper and cheerleader. They ate leftover pizza for supper as I dressed for Maria's, and I spent the next few hours with old and new friends as if nothing had changed besides Judith and Christina getting hired at the school.

Sunday was Luke's turn for fun. He attended the Minnesota Vikings game against their rival, the Green Bay Packers, with some of his friends from our neighborhood. And although the Vikings lost, by Sunday night, we'd both forgotten about Friday's pizza delivery.

AS THE GIRLS GOT READY for school Tuesday morning, I asked if they would like to grocery shop with me after school. "We can pick you up at school, Pria, if you'd like to come with. I'll let you three decide what desserts we should make for Thanksgiving."

Pria enjoyed working in the kitchen more than I did, and since the bus dropped her off an hour later than Ali and Codi, I didn't want to wait.

"Sure. I pick chocolate pumpkin pie." She shrugged into her winter jacket.

It had snowed overnight, yet the temperatures hovered around freezing. I'd managed without my cane for the past two weeks, but I would take it with me today for the trip to the store.

After Ali and Codi arrived home that afternoon, I drove us to the high school. I pulled into the school parking lot, where several older kids pulverized each other with snowballs. We faced the front doors of the school, waiting for Pria to walk out.

Suddenly, the vehicle jolted. Something had hit the side window. I looked up to see the teens, twenty feet away, pummeling our vehicle with snowballs. I might have convinced myself it was all in fun if not for their scowls and the *tings* against the car door. The small rocks packed inside the snowball would surely damage our SUV. Ali sniffled. Codi was silent.

"Why are they doing that?" Ali's voice quivered.

I didn't want to worry them. "Snowball fights can be fun. Kids do it all the time when the snow is right, like when we make snowmen." Something I would struggle to do that winter. Bending down to roll the snow would be painful for me. "They're just playing."

If I rolled down the window and yelled at them, I might get blasted in the face with snowballs. I could get out and stomp over there, but worried I might slip and fall or be assaulted with snowballs myself. When Pria walked out of the front doors, she became their vulnerable target.

Pick on me? Fine. Pick on my kids? Hell no.

"I'll be back in a minute," I told Ali and Codi. "Stay inside." My cane rested between the front seats. It would take away from the badass vibe I needed, so I left it behind. I wore sturdy, flat boots. They would work.

I opened the vehicle door, holding steady until I had both feet planted, and then shut the door before they whipped a snowball inside our vehicle. Their attention turned from Pria to me. I held their attention as I walked toward them, feeling as if fire sparked from my body.

"Hey, it's Dalton's cougar!" One of the four teen boys sneered.

I flinched at the sting of the nasty rumor. They actually believed I'd gone after him for sex. I ignored that battle for now.

"Hey, bullies. Real men don't pick on women."

They paused in their throwing. A car door slammed behind me. Pria was safe.

"You have a beef with me? Fine, but stop bothering Pria. If you're angry about Dalton's arrest, focus it on him, not us. Pay him a visit, and ask why he beat the hell out of me and cut me with a knife."

The boys' mouths hung open at my words. I'd left my coat in the car. I yanked the neck on my hoodie aside and stepped closer, giving them a decent view of my shoulder scar.

"Get your facts straight before you take sides." I kept my voice calm. "What happened to me could have happened to your mother. How would you want people to treat her?"

I didn't get a response. I hadn't expected one. I carefully made my way back to our SUV, and we left the parking lot without another snowball thrown.

Was that all it took? If I needed to call a school-wide conference in the gymnasium and educate the students and parents, I would.

In the seven miles to the grocery store, I received several side glances from Pria. Codi and Ali were quiet. I didn't have the energy to pretend it had been all fun and games for their sakes. I wouldn't expect Pria to either.

I pulled into the grocery parking lot. Pria helped Codi out of the back seat. I waited for Ali to unbuckle herself, thankful the girls were old enough to do their seat belts since my fingers struggled with the buckles now. Ali typically secured Codi since, if given a choice, she would rather bounce around like a pinball inside the car.

"Off we go to the baking aisle!" I forced cheeriness into my voice as if it would erase the handful of dings I noticed on the driver's side of our vehicle. Luke would be furious—an emotion I'd never witnessed in him until those last few months. In the past, it had been easy for us to be levelheaded. Nobody had mistreated our family before.

Pria pushed the cart while I led Ali and Codi to aisle twelve.

"Hey, Codi. We don't need a dozen bags of chocolate chips."

She continued to fling them into the cart as if pitching hay in a barn.

After I removed several of the bags, we stocked up on flour, sugar, and spices before heading to the dairy section. Pria placed packs of butter in the cart while I studied our list.

A deep voice from behind surprised me. "Must be nice to get out and enjoy time with your family while others sit behind bars for Thanksgiving."

The man's words stopped my daughters. Ali stepped behind me, clinging to my jacket, and Codi slipped her hand in mine, her eyes wide.

I straightened my back and turned around, taking a breath large enough to inflate a Thanksgiving Day parade balloon. "Excuse me?"

I didn't recognize him, but the woman standing next to him looked familiar. They appeared to be my age or older. I'd seen her at school events before. *The blowfish must be her husband.* Her cheeks flushed, and she looked away.

His top lip curled. "You heard me."

"I just got rid of walking with a cane, and now with the snow, I've got to be careful with every step I take so I don't get hurt *again*, Mr..."

Pria led Ali and Codi away to the chips aisle.

"Name's Ed. My son's a senior, a football player with Dalton. He said Dalton's a great guy, wouldn't hurt a flea. Yet you're out in public as if you didn't wreck his life or the football team's chances at state." He stepped closer to me. "You should be ashamed."

I stood my ground, his attempts to intimidate me whipping up my mood like a sudden storm. "There are around two hundred fifty boys in each grade, which means over seven hundred boys in high school. Dalton isn't the team, nor is he the only solution." My voice held grit. "And I'm not the problem. He is. If he hadn't attacked me, he could've played football." I would have kept going, but I worried that my children might be within earshot.

"Quit twisting the truth. Nobody believes Dalton would go after *you*. Why you?"

It was a question I'd asked myself a thousand times. I was a good person. I didn't deserve to be attacked. I fed him the reasoning Detective Boyle had given me. "People attack others all the time for no reason. Sounds like Dalton's had some anger issues in the past. Maybe you should pay him a visit at the correctional facility and ask him yourself." My hands curled into painful fists at my side. I'd never hit a person before in my life. There was a first for everything.

Lucky for Ed, his wife stepped in, pulling at his arm, muttering about how they should leave me alone and pick up the steaks they'd come in for.

"You've wrecked Dalton's chance at college football!" Ed harrumphed as if it was the worst thing that could happen to someone.

"He wrecked my family's life and could have killed me. Did you think about that?" I pointed at him. "You want to see the scars he left?" I pulled my shirt to the side to show my shoulder wound before sweeping back my short hair to uncover the scar on my skull, displaying my wounds for the second time in less than an hour. "I can give you the gory details. They're forever etched in my mind, *Ed!*" I tried to keep my voice down but failed.

Ed's wife's tear-filled eyes met mine. "I'm sorry," she mouthed.

I turned away to avoid her sympathy. All I wanted was to do some damn grocery shopping with my girls and pretend our life was normal.

Ed opened his mouth as if he might defend himself then clamped it shut when Pria stepped around the corner with Ali and Codi holding her hands. He turned and walked away without another word, pulled along behind his wife.

"Oh my God, Mom!" Pria let go of her sister's hands and covered her face with her hands.

Did I embarrass her again?

But when she peeled her hands away, instead of teenage angst, she radiated pride. "You rock, Mom!" She stepped forward and gave me a fist bump.

The anger and dread I'd been holding inside dissipated, and I smiled. "I'm done being a doormat. He can scrape his crap on someone else. Not me."

I'm done with these accusations and the shit slinging.

Pride and accomplishment filled me until I noticed Ali's pale face, her body shaking. "I'm so sorry that you heard all of that, Ali. But it's going to be okay. I'm okay." I crouched, wincing at the pain in my knee, and hugged her hard.

When I stood, I spotted the contents of our grocery cart. It contained two boxes of Chicken In a Biskit crackers—Ali and Codi's favorite. One box was open, Pria's way of keeping them occupied. They wouldn't be hungry for supper. I didn't care.

Ali picked up one of the open boxes then handed it to me. "Here, Mommy. You need some Biskits. They'll make you feel better."

Her tenderness melted the rest of my anger. Pure love was standing right in front of me. To hell with the Eds of our town. What mattered was my family. I guided my children and our grocery cart to the cracker aisle then picked up four more boxes of their beloved crackers. I also tossed in four boxes of Pria's favorite, Cheez-It crackers. She deserved a whole cart full.

BY THE TIME WE ARRIVED home, Luke was back from work. I showed him the little dings on the driver's side of our vehicle. I would save our grocery store confrontation for later. No need to overload him. He leaned in to inspect the damage.

"Seniors, you think?" He fingered the small dents.

"I'm guessing. They looked older than Pria. I haven't asked her who they were. I wasn't sure if I should put her on the spot. It may make things worse for her."

He leaned against the SUV and took me in his arms. "Don't worry about it. I can fix them with a hairdryer and canned air." He kissed the top of my head. "I'm not worried about the car. I'm worried about the ignorance that continues to flow from people around here. If they treated you that way, what are they doing to Pria at school? She won't tell me. I've asked."

I pushed back from his chest and looked at him. "You mean besides the dead mouse in her locker last fall?"

His eyebrows rose.

"Yes, I found out. I've asked Pria how things are going, too, and she always says she's fine. We know she's not. I'm not sure if I should drag her to the counselor with me or meet with the high school principal."

Luke walked with me to the kitchen. "Did Pria act as if she knew them?"

I shook my head. "I'm sure she knows *who* they are. If she reports them, she'll pay the price." Pria had paid enough already. Neither of us wanted to make things worse for her.

It wasn't until the girls were in bed that I told Luke what had happened at the store.

"Ed Southers?" Luke paced our bedroom, cracking his knuckles.

I'd described Ed—muscular, trim, midforties, with short graying hair—and his wife. "Yes, I think that's their last name."

Luke frowned and stopped pacing. "He always seemed like a decent guy to me. Guess you don't know what people are really like until someone pushes their buttons."

I'd always been a glass-half-full person, but I thought of how I'd acted once "life" had pushed my buttons. It wasn't something I was proud of, but it was something I could control. And I'd taken that first step today.

Chapter 16

Swim lessons started the last Monday in November, the hour following my water therapy. I had regained muscle strength, and the sessions gave me renewed energy and confidence. On the day of my fourth session, I fired up the car to let it warm up then ambled down our driveway to check the mail. On the way back, I spotted a package on our doorstep.

The package wrapped in white freezer paper had Early Christmas Gift written in large letters. I brought it inside, curious since there was no postage or name. Someone must've hand-delivered it. I ripped into the paper, revealing what looked like a bakery box. I lifted the lid.

Inside were three freakish-looking dolls with wild hair, enormous eyes, and a mouth resembling a frozen scream. I recognized them from shopping at Target—they were the latest fad for kids to collect. They were supposed to look like they were singing. To me, they looked creepy. Their removable limbs and heads made it worse. In the box, the dolls' limbs had been pulled off, their heads popped off and lined up.

A chill ran down my spine as I counted the dolls again. *Is this a threat?* They might represent our daughters. Two of them were the exact ones I'd bought for Codi and Ali.

Sudden nausea twisted my stomach. *Are these their dolls?* I itched to dash upstairs to check. Instead of taking the stairs three at a time, I gripped the handrail and carefully walked up to their rooms. I thought I'd left their dolls on the dresser. I let out a breath. There they sat. Whoever had sent the package hadn't entered our house. One small comfort.

I would deal with this later. I tossed the box on the front seat of the vehicle, not wanting to leave it as if it might put a hex on our home.

On my way to my therapy session, I called Kara. I'd come clean to her about my pain pill crutch the day after I ran over our mailbox. Kara's calm reaction hadn't been what I'd expected. I hadn't done as good a job at hiding my addiction as I'd thought.

"I'm not judging you, Lily, but I *am* here for you, twenty-four seven. Next time you want to reach for a pill, reach out to me. I promise, I'll be there." Her words had enveloped me like a soft hug.

Kara picked up, and I relayed the contents of the "gift."

"Are you freaking kidding me? Someone's threatening you. We know Dastard can't be ordering them, right?" Kara liked the nickname Dr. Arlene and I used, though I didn't share it with my children. "Whoever it is, that's low to insinuate harm to your daughters!"

"I'm beyond pissed." There were too many possible suspects to dwell on right now.

"Are you going to show them to Luke?"

"Yes, but I don't want the girls to see them. No need to freak them out."

Will Luke believe me? Before the attack, neither of us questioned each other. But my craving for meds hadn't painted me as trustworthy. I didn't blame him for the caution in his eyes.

After a pause, I made up my mind. "I'm going to call Detective Boyle when I get home."

"That's a good idea." She sighed into the phone. "I can't figure out if someone is threatening you or trying to frame you to make you appear unbalanced."

"I'll let you know what Boyle thinks. Just so you know, this isn't me back on drugs."

"Hey, I believe you. And news flash, Lily—you're human. Something had to give. Everybody needs something when their life spirals. People find something they can control. Whatever twisted soul sent those dolls, they obviously turned to shopping. Although I don't think this is therapy for them. More like revenge. Some people turn to food, some gamble, or some turn to sex. You turned to your meds. I get it, Lily, I do."

"Some turn to their leaf blower."

Kara snorted. "Luke at it again? What's he using it for now? Snow?"

"Yep. The constant droning noise can push me over the edge. I assumed he'd pack it up once he rid our lawn of the last leaf. Not this year. Now he's using it on the driveway and sidewalk if we get even a dusting of snow."

Luke had relied on a leaf blower ever since we'd bought our house with the spacious yard years ago. But his usage had amped up once I'd come home from the hospital. He could control the leaves if nothing else.

"See what I mean? We all need something we can control when life spirals," Kara said.

We hung up with a promise from me to let her know about Luke and Boyle's take on the dolls. And as I walked through the parking lot to water therapy and swim lessons, I thought of why Jacob had felt the need to turn to booze. *What had he hoped to control in his life?*

Mom and Dad raised us in a buck-up, suck-it-up world. Wounded, cut, or sick, the farm did not wait for us. Snow, hail, sweltering heat—the animals and crops had their own schedules. They didn't care about our struggles. Farming was needy and demanding. Jacob had buckled. So had I. I would write to him again. Next time, I would include my phone numbers. I couldn't give up on us again.

I PLACED A CALL TO Detective Boyle after I arrived home from swimming, filling him in on the dolls. “It may sound juvenile, but I want it on record.”

“I’ll make note of it. I’d say we could dust the package and dolls for fingerprints, but they could have multiple fingerprints on them. And it’s not an actual threat to your safety, although it probably feels like one,” Boyle said.

I thanked him, and after we hung up, I decided to wait to speak with Luke until he got home from work. No need to bother him. He had enough interruptions in his job thanks to me.

As we got ready for bed that night, I said, “I have something to show you.”

He stopped unbuttoning his work shirt and wiggled his eyebrows. A grin spread across his face. I had a good idea of what he *wanted* me to show him. We hadn’t had sex since the night before Dalton’s attack. I couldn’t muster up the nerve to approach him with my damaged self, and Luke was too much a gentleman to ask.

I pulled out the box I’d hidden under our bed. “I found this package on our doorstep today.” I unfolded the paper with Early Christmas Present printed on it.

Luke studied the creepy dismembered dolls before looking back at me. “I don’t get it. Are these the dolls you recently bought Ali and Codi?”

“Nope. That’s what I figured at first too. Theirs are still on their dressers.”

He touched one of the doll heads as if it would burst into flames at any second.

I closed the lid. “I feel like these are a threat. I called Boyle earlier today to let him know. He made a note of it.”

Luke pulled me to his chest and rested his chin on the top of my head. Neither of us understood what was going on, but I added it to the phone calls I'd been certain I hadn't made. If someone was out to make me appear unstable—again—I would have to be on high alert.

MY LAST APPOINTMENT with Dr. Arlene was mid-December. Somewhere along the line, she'd gone from a nosy counselor to one who wanted me emotionally healed. She hadn't changed. I had.

"Remember, I'm here for you if you feel yourself struggling at all," she said as I stood to leave at the end of my session.

"Thank you for all your help—help I didn't think I needed. Guess I was wrong."

We smiled at each other as she walked me to the door. She'd connected the dots for me on my feelings of helplessness with Jacob years ago—the impact and guilt—and the similar feelings I'd had after my attack and the aftereffects on Pria.

In just a few weeks, I would be back teaching, back to having a purpose. The children would be out of school in a week for the holiday season break. After Ali and Codi arrived home for the day, we made a trip to our local candy shop for holiday gifts for their teachers.

Sweets N Such was busy with an onslaught of holiday buyers. While we waited in line, Ali and Codi studied their gift options behind the glass cases.

"Look at those, Mommy. Can I buy those for my teacher?" Codi pointed to large pecan caramel clusters.

"They look yummy, don't they?" I peered into the case beside Codi. "But they have nuts in them, and some people are allergic to nuts. Let's pick something else, okay?"

After a lengthy explanation of what an allergy was, using Morgan, the office manager at Luke's work, as an example of someone severely allergic to nuts, Codi agreed she didn't want to bring something that could make her teacher—or anyone in her family since

I knew she was married with three children—sick. In the end, they both settled on gourmet chocolate-covered potato chips.

THE FIVE OF US SPENT the weekend decorating the inside of our home for Christmas. Afterward, Luke wrapped the girls' gifts, a job too difficult for my fingers yet. Our daughters helped me bake Christmas cookies, and the following Monday, four days before my parents would arrive on Christmas Eve, I worked on finishing up the baking. Luke's parents were going to his sister's house for Christmas, and although our holiday gathering would be small, I wanted to drop off cookies for my coworkers and Luke's.

It was after lunch when Luke pulled into the driveway. *What's he doing home so early?* He didn't open the garage door, instead coming through our front door.

"Hey, Lily. I'm home," he called from the entryway.

I rounded the corner from the kitchen, a spatula in one hand, a cookie sheet full of nutmeg logs in the other. I smiled at him, wearing my Kiss This Crazy Cook apron, and he leaned down and accepted the invitation.

"Did you smell the cookies all the way from your office? Are you here to be my taste-tester?" I led the way back to the kitchen.

"Well, I thought I should make sure they're okay before Codi eats them all." He chose a wreath-shaped sugar cookie from the cooling rack and ate it in one bite. "Very acceptable." Luke studied me with a guarded look that told me he hadn't come home to eat cookies.

"What's up?"

"I need to talk to you about the gift you had delivered to Morgan at work today."

I furrowed my brow. "You mean the baby gift? I dropped it off at her house a couple of weeks ago." Morgan lived near a classmate of

Codi's, so I'd dropped it off that Saturday when I'd picked Codi up at her friend's house. Realization hit me. "Oh, didn't she like it?"

"You brought a baby gift to Morgan's home and then sent her something at work?"

"No. Just the baby bathtub and sleepers. She opened them when I was at her house. Did she think I sent another gift to work? Should I have? Did they have a shower for her there?" My face flushed with concern that I'd embarrassed Luke by not sending a gift.

He folded his arms across his chest and cleared his throat. "Sweets N Such delivered a glass canister of mixed nuts to her at work."

"What? But Morgan's allergic to nuts, right?" I turned my back to the cookie dough.

"Yep. Guess who sent them?" He didn't give me time to answer. "You." The one word dripped with accusation.

I gasped, as surprised at the nuts sent to Morgan as I was at my husband's tone.

"The card had your name on it."

"I didn't send anything to her at the office. I know Morgan's allergic to nuts. It must have been an error on their end." Even as I said the words, they sounded too familiar. I'd accused The Pizza Pad of a similar error.

Yes, I sounded defensive. I understood why Luke would look at me with an untrusting squint. But dammit, I hadn't placed either of those orders. Without another word, I turned around and rolled out dough to form more nutmeg logs. When he stepped up beside me and tried kissing my cheek, I turned my head in dismissal.

"I'm sorry," he said to my back.

I kept silent while Luke walked back out the front door, leaving a trail of mistrust behind him. My life had changed from some of the community not believing me to my husband feeling the same way. After he was gone, I sat at the kitchen table, unable to stop the tears.

Either I'd lost my memory, or Kara had been right. Someone was framing me. I wasn't sure if I wanted to know the answer.

LUKE'S LIPS WERE PRESSED together when he walked in hours later after work. I had a roast in the oven and had asked Pria to watch her sisters. I was going for a short drive with her dad.

"We need to talk." I met him in the entryway between our garage and kitchen and put on my winter jacket. "Let's go for a drive." I pointed to the garage door he'd just shut.

Luke nodded, turned on his heels, then led the way back to his vehicle. "Where to?"

"Park at the end of our road if you want. I don't care. I just didn't want the girls to hear us, and this conversation can't wait." I made it through the sentences without breaking down.

Luke parked on a dead-end road a few blocks from our neighborhood so that none of our friends would see us. He leaned his forearms on the steering wheel and took a deep breath. "If this is about the canister of nuts sent to Morgan, I said I'm sorry."

He turned to me. "But you know what? I'm not sure what in the hell I'm sorry for. Your name was on the card! I was working in the central office when I heard a loud ruckus in the front office. The service technicians were out of the office on work calls, and my concern was that something happened to someone, so I jogged down the hall to the front near Morgan's office. The women had gathered around Morgan's desk. I worried she'd fallen, fainted, or, worse yet, was in early labor." He rubbed a hand over his eyes.

"A few women stepped away from Morgan's desk, revealing a large glass canister full of mixed nuts, with a small gift card open on the desk. The one signed with your name on it." He shook his head. "I apologized every which way but sideways to Morgan, whisked the canister from her desk, and said I'd get to the bottom of it. That's when I drove home."

"But I didn't send it." My voice sounded as weak as my defense. "In fact, I just used Morgan's nut allergy as an example to Codi when we were there last week to pick up gifts for her and Ali's teachers." I recited our conversation to Luke.

"I'm trying to be honest with you. Sometimes I feel you don't believe anything I say anymore." I was generalizing to make my point. "We used to trust each other."

Luke pushed back from the steering wheel and looked out his window at the dusk surrounding us. It was a full minute before he spoke, before he could look at me.

"Okay, what I'm going to tell you isn't me making excuses about how I've acted. I'm only trying to get you to understand what I've seen and heard... things I don't believe you remember. Reasons why I sometimes question what you've done or haven't done. Promise you'll listen and wait to ask questions?" He reached for my hand. "Because I only want to say these things once, and then I want to put them in the past."

I braced myself for what was to come. *What the hell? Did I kill someone?*

He blew out a long breath. "Remember how I told you Mom taught me how to dance the merengue when I was a teen? Every day since July has felt like I've been doing that. Our lives move forward, and our lives move backward, stepping in both directions. And things keep happening. I feel like we will never step out of the endless circling of the dance, that I'll never feel like I'm not spinning in a what's-the-truth cyclone."

His chin quivered, and I longed to stop him from saying anything more, but I'd promised to wait. He swallowed several times. "Back in October, Erin called for Pria, and you answered the phone. You went off on a rant about demons chasing you at night, the procedure to castrate a bull on the farm, and the size of a horse's penis before hanging up on a traumatized Erin. And I don't think you remembered a single thing about that conversation."

How did I not remember? My cheeks burned, and I braced for more embarrassment. "Poor Erin. Poor Pria!"

"There have been little things, like finding our dirty laundry in the trash outside. Or the day you insisted the girls try a green smoothie, and I think you accidentally added chili pepper instead of cinnamon."

Our daughters had never wanted to try my green tea or smoothies. That I'd somehow convinced them, and then messed up the ingredients, only solidified the girls' decision to never try them again. I didn't have time to think about when it might have happened.

"Kara came to visit you one day, and you must have forgotten she was coming. You answered the door with green smoothie spilled down your shirt. Your words were slurred, your eyes glazed over." Luke leaned his head back against the headrest and rubbed his eyes. "Kara called me at work, and I drove home. We cleaned you up, put you to bed, and you slept it off."

That explained why Kara hadn't been surprised when I confessed my taste for pain meds.

As Luke recited each situation, a vague remembering danced in my mind. I couldn't deny any of it. And it explained why he was hesitant to trust me. I braced myself for another guilt trip.

"I'm not trying to make you feel bad. I just want you to see why I'm a little hesitant to believe you didn't order those pizzas or the nuts." He started up the vehicle. "Remember last month, when I found a baggie with six pills in the back of our bathroom cupboard?" He'd been looking for a new tube of toothpaste and found a stash I'd forgotten about.

"Yes." I nodded. "I get it. All I can tell you is that I haven't taken a pill since the day I hit our mailbox. I don't know what's going on."

To blame an invisible person would only make me appear unhinged, but I was certain those last two incidents—and the dismembered dolls—hadn't been me.

My attacker was behind bars. I didn't know how in the world I was going to convince anyone that another person was after me. I still didn't understand why Dastard had assaulted me, which made it all the more difficult to prove anyone else was out to frame me.

Chapter 17

The following morning, I drove to Sweets N Such after it opened at ten a.m. As with several of the small businesses in our town, we had a charge account there. They would have a record of my orders.

"Good morning, Lily. Back for more chocolate-covered potato chips?" Bald and stocky, Joe had been a fixture in the town for years. He'd taken our order last Thursday.

"Not today, thanks. I am wondering about another order I placed though. Can you pull up our account please?"

"Sure. What are you looking for?"

"Does it show that I ordered a delivery of a canister of mixed nuts to Luke's office?" I aimed at sounding unconcerned, hiding the tidal wave of angst surging inside me.

He peered at the screen over his glasses. "Yes. Looks like you called in the order last Friday morning." Joe looked up at me. "Says it was a gift delivered to a Morgan who works there?" He tipped his head to the side, studying me. "Did we mess up your order?"

Hell if I know. "No. Any chance it shows who took the call?"

"Tony. He's in the back. Did you have a question for him?" I didn't know who Tony was, but before I could answer, Joe stuck his head in the back and called Tony's name.

A young man rounded the corner, one I recognized from last summer. He worked there when he was home from college. "Hi, Mrs. Gallo. Do you have a question about your order?"

"Yes. Do you remember me calling this order in?" I sounded strange asking him about an order that wasn't anything special.

He shrugged. "Only that you said you'd been in here the day before and forgot to place this order for delivery Monday."

I nodded, taking his words in. There'd been a long line of people there last Thursday. And people sitting at the few nearby tables, eating sweets. Anyone could have heard me explain to Codi how Morgan at Luke's office had a severe nut allergy.

"Okay. Thank you, Tony. Thanks, Joe." I smiled at them before turning to leave, understanding that any explanation of why I'd questioned my order would only make me sound more confused.

MY PARENTS ARRIVED the day before Christmas, loaded with enough food and presents for our entire neighborhood.

No worries about that happening. If we invited our old neighborhood friends, probably a quarter of them wouldn't show up now. I referred to it as the "Dalton Divide." Like the Berlin Wall, it tore a chunk of our community apart even after football season ended.

"I'm excited for you and the girls to open your special presents." Mom and I worked in the kitchen, slicing and dicing vegetables to go with the spinach-artichoke dip she'd made.

"Special presents? What, you didn't bring enough already?"

"Actually, it's a present for you." She smiled. "You'll see."

"Should we open them tonight?" Our family tradition had always been to allow the girls to choose two presents to open on Christmas Eve, and on Christmas morning, they got one gift from Santa and a few more from family. We'd never showered our kids with presents. No matter how tough those last few months had been, we didn't believe in compensating with gifts.

"Yes, if you don't mind," Mom said.

Luke, Dad, and the girls played Chutes and Ladders at the kitchen table. Mom whipped up homemade rolls, and I added last-minute ingredients to our taco soup. Ali would pick out the beans, Codi, the tomato chunks, and they would both fill up on the light and flaky rolls.

Cheerful conversation reverberated off the dining room walls during our meal. Afterward, we left the dishes in the sink. Pria took Ali and Codi upstairs to her room so they could wrap the homemade Christmas ornaments they'd made for Mom and Dad.

Luke, my parents, and I sat at the table, a plate of Christmas cookies in the center, along with a pot of decaf coffee. Mom fiddled with her cup.

"We received a letter from Jacob." Dad rarely spoke of Jacob. It was Mom who usually brought my brother into a conversation.

I choked on a sip of hot green tea. "Really?" Optimism coated me. Mom was aware of my letter to Jacob in early October and that I hadn't heard from him.

"His letter is in response to one your mom wrote to him about the attack. Your mother wanted to let him know about your injuries and also that we had the farm up for sale on the odd chance he'd stop to visit again." Dad leaned back, his legs crossed in front of him as if my parents received letters from Jacob every week. They occurred as often as a seven-year itch.

Mom had written her letter months before I'd mailed mine, and it had taken Jacob months to respond. "What did he say?" I asked.

"I'll get it, and you can read it for yourself." Mom stood, dug in her purse on the bench by our living room, then handed me the letter.

Jacob lived on the Iron Range, the northeastern part of Minnesota a few hours from our house. He wished the "bastard who attacked Lily would get hung by his nuts." He gave Mom and Dad his blessing on selling the farm. And he claimed to be content with his life.

I read the letter twice. "Jacob sounds like he's doing okay, right?"

"I think so," Mom agreed. "He's been living there for so long. It's home to him now."

"I miss him," I whispered. I'd spoken more of him to Luke in those past months than I had in the last seventeen years. Luke barely knew Jacob, never knew my younger brother the way I remembered him. I needed to see him. Soon. I'd planned to write to Jacob again and had found a hundred reasons not to. Not anymore. Once the holidays were over, I would write and include my phone numbers.

Codi ran into the kitchen to tell us they were ready. She led the way into the living room, where the Christmas tree illuminated everything. Four gifts sat off to the side with goofy-looking Christmas wrapping. Upon closer inspection, I spotted farm animals in pajamas.

"Hmmm, that's interesting. Where did you get this wrapping paper?" I asked Mom.

"At your local farm supply store. Duh." She jostled me with her elbow before turning to Luke. "You should talk to the school about selling it so you can have some in your enormous stash."

We all laughed. Everyone knew Luke was a sucker for buying things from school fundraisers. The only birthday and Christmas wrapping paper we owned came from them.

I turned to our daughters, now sitting on the living room floor. "These are special presents from Grandma and Grandpa. They want you to open them tonight." I set their matching gifts in front of them and one in front of Luke.

Pria looked up from her spot on the floor where she leaned up against the couch. "Where's yours?"

"She's sort of getting her present vicariously through all of you," Mom said.

"Huh? Curiously through us?" Codi's brow furrowed at her grandma.

Dad scooped Codi up onto his knee. "Grandma means that in a way, your presents are also a gift for your mommy." He looked over at me settled in the couch recliner, Pria by my feet.

"Come on, open those presents for me!" I rubbed my hands together in anticipation.

They agreed to all open them at once. Ali was the quickest, pulling out folded black-and-white spotted material. Luke stopped unwrapping to check out her gift. She laid it on the carpet, unfolding two arms, two legs, and a mask. *A cow costume?*

Pria had hers open and laid out a larger version of Ali's.

Mom beamed, and I clapped, understanding the gift. Luke raised his eyebrows, giving Mom a curious look while I helped Codi unwrap her little cow costume.

"Get it, Luke?" Mom asked.

"Um, no. I don't. I'm a cow. And the girls?"

"Yes, yes!" Mom applauded as if he'd won a spot on a game show. "Lily misses our cows. I hoped these would help. I made you all cow pajamas so she can play her flute for you."

He came to kneel next to me. "Are you going to play 'Brian's Song,' 'The Dance,' and that slow version of 'Old MacDonald' for us like you did for the cows?"

Memories took me back to the scents and sounds of the barn—the low moos, the earthy hay scent, the whooshing noise of the milk machines. And me, sitting on top of the metal chest cooler, leaning against the wall, and playing music to soothe the cows for milking.

"You played music for cows?" Codi piped up, maneuvering her small body next to my legs. She bounced on her knees at the idea of her mom playing songs for animals.

"I forgot about that," Pria said, smiling. "I remember you telling me about how the cows liked music." Her smile faded when she looked at the cow pajamas in her lap. I could only ask so much of the girl at this point.

Obedient Ali tried on her cow pajamas and mask and let out a soft "Moo."

Overcome with emotion, I stood, walked over to Mom, then hugged her.

"Should I go get your flute?" Luke asked.

I nodded.

"When I get back, I expect to see three cows sitting in our living room." He winked.

Pria's mouth twitched. "Only if you put yours on when you get back." She stood and helped Codi with her cow pajamas.

When Luke returned with my flute, all three girls had their costumes on and sat on the floor by me. My parents sat to the side of us, wearing cow ears on a headband and a cow nose held by an elastic band. Dad grimaced, but his eyes smiled. I stifled the urge to get our camera.

Instead, while Luke stepped into his cow pajamas, I stretched my fingers. I'd played a few songs over the past month or so. Every week, my fingers gained flexibility. With everyone settled, I played "Silent Night." Codi and Ali sat with their mouths hanging open. I followed it with "White Christmas."

When I finished, Ali and Codi let out enthusiastic "Moos." My fingers might ache tomorrow, but my heart was full tonight.

WE WERE ON OUR WAY to a normal life again, and overdue to resurrect our sex life that had been kicked to the curb after the attack. New Year's Eve offered us the perfect opportunity.

I'd given myself enough pep talks about sex, body image, and self-confidence that I could head up a women's rally on the topic. I'd been with Luke for almost half of my life, a man who'd had a front-row seat of my vagina when our daughters were born. But I wasn't that person anymore. I didn't look the same. I didn't feel the same.

Pria was spending the night at a friend's house. After playing several board games with Ali and Codi, Luke and I tucked them into bed. Luke showered before I did, and after I showered, I blow-dried my short hair, something I rarely did before bed. I pumped out the almond-scented lotion I'd bought for our anniversary trip to Chicago last July, slathered it on my body, and slipped into a shimmery silver nightie that Kara gifted me after the birth of Codi.

The slinky-soft material massaged my erogenous zones yet did nothing for my nerves. I shoved an oblong box of Kleenex under the negligee where my less-than-bountiful-breasts left plenty of room. I took a deep breath before sashaying into our bedroom. Luke had never rejected me before, but our marriage had been challenged.

He sat propped up against pillows, reading a magazine. When he looked up, a loud guffaw erupted as he eyed my box breasts before working their way down the rest of me. His eyes darkened with a desire I'd missed, one I hoped like hell to reciprocate.

When he reached for me, Luke's gentle touch dissolved those fears. Time hadn't changed his body, his bare chest still firm above a flat stomach. He had always been active, playing basketball, baseball, and soccer as he'd done in high school.

His dark hair was still damp. "Lily." It was a question, a whisper, and a promise all rolled into one as he moved from the bed, his hands guiding me to him. "I've missed you so much. Everything about you. Not only *this*." His finger wagged at the small space between our bodies.

I studied those full lips, his dimples, and every inch of that face that'd hit me like an electrical zap the day I spotted it in his rearview mirror while waiting for the train. Never once had I regretted marrying him. I hoped he could still say the same thing about me.

He tucked a stray hair behind my ear, leaned in, and kissed my neck as if I was a dessert he'd been deprived of for years. My heart picked up its pace.

His arms wrapped around my lower back, pulling me flush against him. He leaned his forehead against mine. "Please tell me if I hurt you or it doesn't feel right, and we'll stop, okay?"

I nodded, emotion expanding in my throat. I *needed* him to show that he desired me, loved me.

Luke scooped me up and carried me to our bed, gently laying me on the turned-down sheets with ease. He kneeled over me and took my open hands in his, bringing them to his lips and kissing each fingertip. He let out a slow breath then busted out laughing.

"What's so funny?"

"I'm turned on just from kissing your fingers. My teenage sex drive's reappeared." His hands moved softly down my back, sending shivers to my core.

"You don't know this about me, dead-sexy man, but I battle dragons for a living. The last one clawed my neck before I did him in." I nodded to my scar, wiggling my shoulder to reflect my battle wounds before flexing my new muscles, thanks to swimming. "I'm a total badass."

"I'm turned on just thinking of you wielding a sword." He bent down and kissed my scar before his lips traveled to mine.

I snuggled into his warm body, turning my feet up so that the bottoms connected with his warm legs.

Luke pulled back, letting out a shriek. "You know what hasn't changed with you? Your cold feet. Your toes are still tiny ice cubes." He reached under the covers and took one of my feet between his hands to rub some warmth into it. "I missed them when you were in the hospital."

"I hated not having you next to me every night," I whispered, understanding it was time to live in the present, this moment, this reconnection with Luke. It had nothing to do with sex. It had everything to do with acceptance.

Chapter 18

The following week, I was back in my classroom. Maria, Judith, Barb, and several others applauded as I walked—cane-free—down the polished hall toward the classroom I'd missed and the students I'd only peeked at through a window.

"Welcome back!" Kindergarten and first-grade teachers and EAs cheered me on, lightening my load of concern that I was back too soon, that I was no longer needed.

"Thank you." I stopped in the hall to visit with them. "I've missed this so much." I couldn't put into words how much I'd needed those coworkers, my students, the structure of work, and purpose in my life.

My first week back, Maria was my guiding light. After introductions, I asked each child what their favorite animal was, what they wanted to be when they grew up, and what their favorite food was. It gave me a glimpse of their personalities, and I answered with my own. Penguin, teacher—of course—and green smoothies and tea. When I explained why the yogurt-based smoothie was green, thanks to spinach, the twenty-two students wrinkled their noses in disgust just as I'd predicted. Maria's answer of nachos as her favorite food was much more acceptable.

Each day became more comfortable, like trying on an old sweater that at first felt stiff until it had been worn in. And each night, I fell into bed with a happy exhaustion. It reminded me of running a race I hadn't trained enough for. I would get through it, but not without a lot of huffing, puffing, and sheer exhaustion by the time you finish.

I'D BEEN BACK TEACHING two weeks before I had the energy and brainpower to sit down and write another heartfelt letter to Jacob. It was early Saturday morning. Though the house was quiet, my thoughts were not. With no landline number for him, no email address, I had no way to contact him other than snail mail.

I all but pleaded in the letter for him to call me, listing both my cell number and our landline number. We had voice mail on both. *If I don't answer, please, please, please leave me your call-back number.*

It was then that I realized that I hadn't checked the voice mail on our landline since I'd gone back to work. I picked up the receiver from the end table next to the recliner and heard the fast *beep-beep-beep* that meant we had messages.

The first was from last Monday. Our local mechanic had called, reminding Luke of an appointment to have the tires rotated on our SUV, something he'd taken care of three days ago.

The next voice mail was from our pharmacy. Medication was ready for pick up. I replayed the message to see if it was for me or Luke. He wasn't on any regular medication, and neither was I, other than my low-dose anxiety medication that I'd recently had filled. The message hadn't dictated who the prescription was for.

But the third message, also from the pharmacy yesterday, did. The medication was for me, and the message stated they would hold it until Tuesday.

When the pharmacy opened at nine, I called. It was a refill for Vicodin, a prescription I hadn't taken in over two months. *Shit.* I had to deal with it. And tell Luke. He was outside shoveling our sidewalk, the snow too heavy for his leaf blower.

I waited until he came inside, meeting him in the entryway as he took off his winter boots and coat. "There's a voice mail message from the pharmacy saying my prescription for Vicodin is ready." I met his eyes. "Please believe me. I didn't call in the refill."

Luke's arm stopped midway from hanging up his coat on the coat rack. "Are you serious?" He shook his head.

"Yes, and I'm driving there this morning to put a password on any prescription orders." I had time to think about what had happened over the past couple of months since I'd stopped taking the opioids. I had to believe in myself, or nobody else would.

If I wasn't making those calls, someone else was. Someone who knew where we shopped and enough about me to order things like my pills, who may have been nearby when I'd placed similar orders in the past. I'd never worried about protecting my personal information before.

"I'll go with you. Pria can stay with Ali and Codi until we get back." She was going ice skating with some friends that afternoon, her life almost back to normal. Mine, not so much.

We drove to the pharmacy, canceled the Vicodin refill, and set up a safe password for any future call-ins. I didn't bother asking who took the call for a refill. I couldn't keep interrogating others as if they could point me toward someone out to sabotage my life.

And while Luke and I drove home in silence, each deep in our thoughts, worry swirled with my certainty. I wanted to be positive I'd not placed those calls. The doctors had assured me over the past several months that I'd had no brain damage from the attack. So I was either diving off the deep end, or someone was messing with me. I'd tried that route with Luke and read skepticism in his eyes. Kara was on board with me, but I'd told nobody else besides Boyle. And I hadn't kept him up-to-date on calls that, by themselves, seemed innocent.

But not to me. I had started a list of where the call was made to and when. If I ever needed it, I didn't want to have to rely on my memory.

I didn't need my coworkers thinking I'd become paranoid. I wasn't worried I'd be out of a job, thanks to the Minnesota Teachers

Union, but the higher-ups would toss me back into counseling and who knows what else. They sure wouldn't want me teaching young minds if they thought I was unstable.

A STORM HIT OVERNIGHT, turning the roads into an ice rink. We were out of milk, bread, and cheese, and after the plow trucks sanded the roads, Luke drove to the grocery store. He arrived home an hour later.

"That was a nail-biter." Luke set the groceries on the counter and cracked his knuckles, a habit I'd seen him do in record amounts in the past six months.

"I'm glad you made it home safe." I leaned in and kissed his cold cheek.

"I almost hit a dog on the corner down our road. It ran in front, and I hit the brakes." He shook his head. "Barely missed it. But it gave me an idea."

I raised an eyebrow. "What? Remember to pump your brakes next time?"

"Nope. I'll tell you and the girls over lunch." He chucked me under the chin, seeming in an unusually good mood after driving in an ice storm.

Tomorrow was Martin Luther King Day, which meant the schools were closed. Luke could do some of his central office work from home if needed. I hoped the storm would pass soon. Even though we could hole up at home tomorrow, many others could not.

The girls had requested tacos for lunch, hence the need for cheese, and Luke brought up his idea while we ate. Ali's structured meal requirements had improved over the past couple of years. Her new willingness to try foods where the ingredients touched made meal choices an easier decision for our family.

Luke leaned over his plate and rubbed his hands together. His beautiful green eyes lit up. "So, what do you all think about us getting a dog?"

I clapped and bounced in my seat, reminding myself of Codi. "That's a great idea!"

We'd had a golden retriever when Pria was young. He had died from cancer by the time she was five. After a couple of years, we'd talked of getting another pet, but I'd been pregnant with Ali, and Codi followed two years later. Planning to look for another dog was like the trips overseas Luke and I always talked of taking, something for the distant future.

"We could check out the animal shelter," I suggested.

Codi hopped out of her chair and did a cartwheel right in our kitchen.

Ali, more subdued but smiling, said, "Can we help name it?"

"For sure," Luke said. "It will have to be a dog we all agree on and a name we all can live with." If we left it up to Codi, she would name the dog something like "Spaghetti" or "Trash Can." I thought everyone was on board until I looked at Pria.

Pria, for whatever reason—it could have been something as simple as me breathing the same air as her—spoke up. "I'll be going off to college in a few years. I don't care if we get a dog or not."

It was wishful thinking on her part that once she left for college, she would no longer be a part of the family. Her full-out sympathy after the attack had boomeranged back to her volatile teenage-roller-coaster of emotions. And I got the brunt of it.

BY THREE O'CLOCK, THE storm had passed. "Should I call the animal shelter?" Luke asked.

It seemed so spur of the moment, yet the timing was good. We had tomorrow off, and we'd decided we wouldn't get a puppy. "I guess. I could run home at lunch and let it out."

Luke shook his head. "You barely have time to eat at school. I'll come home for lunch every day. It wouldn't be alone for more than a few hours at a time." His days were longer than mine and also more flexible. Luke called the shelter, surprised when someone answered on a Sunday, especially after a storm.

"I'll be here until five if you can make it in by then," the woman said.

Luke thanked her and promised we would be there within half an hour. He ran up the stairs where the girls were in their rooms.

We drove on well-sanded roads. Codi and Ali raced for the front door when Luke shut off the vehicle. Pria dragged her heels behind us. We hadn't let her stay overnight at Erin's house last night, and she would not let us forget it.

As I stepped inside, the damp, visceral scent of animals tugged at my heart. *How did we go so long without a pet?*

"Thank you for thinking of this," I said to Luke as Ali and Codi ran in front of us. Even Pria went off on her own to browse the kennels.

Codi wanted the first dog she spotted. Ali was pickier, but not by much. We were so busy refereeing their choices that we didn't hear Pria at first, calling to us from the back of the shelter.

"Mom. Dad. Come back here. Oh, he's so ugly, he's cute!"

We followed her to an open kennel near the back where a worker held a small fluffy dog that looked like a pug-Pekingese mutt. It was no beauty. Before I could ask what the attraction was, Pria pulled me toward the woman holding the dog.

"Look." She took the dog and held its face close to mine. "See? He lost an eye in a dog fight, Mom. And he's got a limp. Someone put him in a *dog fight*. And he survived." Pria's chin wobbled. She didn't need to say anything else. She'd picked that dog for me. An abused dog with permanent scars, yet he'd persevered. And needed us. Almost as much as I needed him.

I embraced Pria, who, for the moment, forgot not to care. "He's perfect."

Our family agreed on the name Percy, short for persevere. His battle wounds tugged at my heartstrings. A dog who would accompany us on walks, and who would heal along with us.

I'D BEEN BACK TEACHING for three weeks and felt almost up to speed again in the classroom. They'd changed our computer system last September, but it was nothing I couldn't handle. January twenty-first was National Hugging Day. Each year, kindergarten through third-grade classes put on a skit. Each grade would sing songs about hugging. I was as excited as our students for their parents and grandparents to watch the performance.

That morning, our five kindergarten classes lined up in the hallway, and I shushed my students as their excitement magnified. Avery, a boy in my class who expelled excessive energy, stood in front of the line.

"Okay, class. One, two, three, eyes on me." I cupped my ears then zipped my lips, knowing that, mostly, my students would follow my actions.

The other four classrooms lowered their volume, too, and we all made our way, as quietly as over one hundred kindergartners could, to the gymnasium.

Our students performed a skit before each grade sang two songs about hugging. The kindergartner's excitement stretched as wide as their little arms when they sang about "Four hugs a day. That's the minimum, not the maximum."

As our grade completed their last song, I labeled their performance a success, although I noticed several of the children from my class looking sad as they searched the crowd. It wasn't until the kindergartners lined up at our spot in the hallway then made their way to the cookies and milk line that some burst into tears, Avery among them.

"What's wrong? You all did great!" I wondered if I'd seemed disappointed in them.

"My mom and dad aren't here!" Avery busted out a full-body wail as if he'd been holding it in until I asked the question.

"Neither is my grandma!" Another student sobbed from the back of the line. Several children hopped on the where-is-my-family bandwagon. Many parents had to work, although families often tried to at least send grandparents to attend. Based on the whining, my classroom seemed to be the only one with minimal family in the auditorium.

I pulled Barb aside. "Do most of your students have family here in the audience?"

"Yes, why? Don't your students?" Barb looked around the crowd.

"I don't think so." I swallowed the concern that I'd somehow messed up. But it was too soon to point a finger at myself. "I'll talk to you after the students leave." That would give me time to check with the other teachers.

At lunch, I casually asked the others if they'd heard complaints from their students, and found that no other class was as underrepresented as mine.

My first week back, I'd had Maria as my full-time EA, and Judith helped a few hours each day, alternating between Barb's classroom and mine. After that, they'd gone back to alternating in my classroom so that I had help full-time for the first month.

As Maria occupied the students with story time, I scrolled back in my emails. With our new software, I could create graphics and information and use them as an attachment to send to parents. I searched in my email, looking for "hugging," and found nothing. Maybe I hadn't used it in the subject line, but I remembered emailing the parents two weeks ago, my first Friday back at teaching.

My heart dropped when I found an email to the parents that day. The subject line read "Reminder," but the attachment wasn't the National Hugging Day program information. It was a reminder that school would be closed on January 17 for Martin Luther King Day.

Without notifying Maria, I walked as calmly as I could down the hall to the empty teacher's lounge, shut the door, then bawled.

What is wrong with me? I'd been back three weeks and already failed my students. I couldn't even blame the new software. The attachment had worked. It was just the wrong one.

Pulling myself together, I dried my tears and made it through the last two hours of the school day. After everyone left, Barb stayed and met with me in my classroom.

I showed her my mistake. "The thing is, I swore I put a hard copy of the program flyer in their backpacks."

Kindergartners weren't too reliable about handing over paperwork to their parents, but most parents were responsible enough to check their children's backpacks.

"Who knows? Some of your students had family here, so you must have notified them. Don't worry about it." Barb patted my back. "People will understand."

I hoped so, or it might be one more chapter in the Lily's-gone-off-the-deep-end story. I refrained from pointing out to Barb that my students who had family in attendance were children who had older siblings—siblings who would have notified their parents of the program. I gave myself a big F in teaching and vowed to do better. I *had* to do better.

Chapter 19

Over the years, several of us at school had become involved with a program for needy families, a cause close to our hearts that affected children within a one-hour radius from our town. We met every other Wednesday night during the school year, working on fundraisers, gathering supplies, and doing what we could to help.

I'd missed those gatherings in the months I'd been off, and I'd skipped the first one in January, still getting back in the groove of teaching and regaining my energy. I'd attended the second one at Maria's house, and tonight, the first Wednesday in February, I would host. We rotated homes, often just a handful of us attending.

Christina had been one of the hosts last fall. I took her spot now since her apartment was so small. We all ate supper ahead of time so the host didn't have to mess with food. Luke stayed at work to catch up on central office work, and the girls watched a Disney movie in our living room. Barb, Maria, Judith, Christina, and I worked at our kitchen table on the latest project, collecting knitted hats, mittens, scarves.

It was one of my favorites. With leftover yarn dropped off in the boxes we'd placed in churches and businesses throughout our community, people took that yarn and knitted or crocheted items for area children in need.

Outside our classrooms, volunteering together gave me a chance to get to know Judith and Christina better, even to know other coworkers I'd worked with for years. Everyone acted differently away from our job, more relaxed and fun. Barb brought up an upcoming weekend getaway with her husband for Valentine's Day, less than two weeks away.

"Where are you going?" I asked.

"Skiing in Lutsen. I've got Friday the eleventh off of work." Lutsen, a beautiful town on the shores of Lake Superior, was a four-hour drive north.

"Luke has talked of us getting away, but our moms have been here so much over the months that we don't want to bother them again." He'd brought up an overnight trip to downtown Minneapolis for us—a chance for us to be alone together—but I couldn't bring myself to ask either of our parents.

"I'll watch your girls," Maria said. "Are you thinking the weekend before or after Valentine's Day since it falls on a Monday?"

"Not the weekend after," Barb said, wagging a finger. "Remember, that's our post-holiday party at my house." Barb's annual potluck was a good break in the winter doldrums. She turned to Judith and Christina. "You've got it on your calendars, right?"

Christina, her thick hair piled high on her head, nodded. "Yep. Cleared any potential date from that Saturday night." She winked.

"You can bring a date," Barb said then turned to Judith. "You too."

Judith was in her sixties and widowed. "I'm smart enough to not go down that road again at my age." She chuckled. "Any man I'd date now would be one I'd have to care for later on." There was wistfulness in her smile, and I guessed she'd been more than happy to care for her late husband, who she spoke of often.

"Is your offer serious, Maria? We'd just stay overnight Saturday night. Luke had wanted to get a hotel room in downtown Minneapolis. If you aren't busy with your own grandkids, we'd love for you to watch the girls." Our children knew Maria and would be comfortable with her. And I trusted her 100 percent.

"I sure am." Maria nodded, her silky dark hair brushing her shoulders.

After Luke arrived home later that night, I told him about Maria's offer. By the time we crawled into bed, he'd made reservations at a downtown Minneapolis hotel for the Saturday night before Valentine's Day.

He leaned on his elbow, his head above mine. "I checked into horse-drawn carriage rides along the Mississippi River near downtown. They decorate the streets with those little twinkle lights. What do you think?"

I pulled him toward me, his body flush with mine. "I think it sounds perfect."

THE FOLLOWING MONDAY morning, on my drive to school through several inches of fresh snow, I thought of Jacob. For around half of his life, we'd been apart. Jacob had been my best friend until I met Kara in grade school. In our youth, Jacob and I had milked the cows together, baled hay together, fed the chickens and pigs together, and shared stories late at night by the barn. We'd played hide-and-seek behind the hay bales in the barn loft, chased each other through the muck in the pigpen, and chucked dried cow dung in the open fields.

When he got stepped on by one of our cows, I cried with him all the way to the hospital as Dad drove like a maniac. Jacob and I had commiserated over our favorite pig, Babylon, a runt that hadn't made it to her first year. We had fishing contests in the creek down the road, using grub worms we'd dug up in the cow piles as bait.

Every childhood memory involved Jacob. But few adult ones did. We'd had a bond I'd thought was unbreakable. Now, I understood every bond could break, which was why I couldn't wait until the weekend when Luke and I would get a night away together to reconnect.

That afternoon, I left school and trudged through freshly fallen snow in the parking lot. I couldn't find my vehicle. Again. It had happened one of my first days back when I'd been preoccupied. Although I'd thought I'd parked in the employee rows, my SUV hadn't been there. I'd found it several rows away, where parents and visitors typically parked.

Today, the lot wasn't that full. Several teachers had already left, and parents who'd picked up their children were long gone. After walking the rows of employee vehicles, I stopped and took a calming breath as I scanned the rest of the parking lot.

Unless it had grown wings and flown away, our SUV was there somewhere. The wind howled like a dog in heat, blowing snow in my face. I sheltered my eyes from the snow and squinted, zeroing in on a vehicle that looked similar to ours. It was so hard to tell with snow covering most of it.

I never would've parked there. Or did I? Maybe I'd been so focused on it being Jacob's birthday that morning that I'd spaced out, but I didn't think so. Still, no other explanation made sense. The driver's side faced a side street. When I rounded the vehicle, I saw SLUT written in large letters across the snow-encrusted side doors.

I looked around as if the culprit would stand there waiting for me to nab them. I yanked open the door, pulled out some napkins from the glove compartment, then wiped the word off. Inside the vehicle, I let it warm up while I hung my head over the steering wheel. I needed to tell Luke, but there was only so much he could take. The past several months had been a hell not mentioned in our wedding vows. Being young and in love, we'd promised to love each other for better and for worse but had never, for one second, thought about the "for worse" part.

Our wedding day had been the first time I'd met his older sister, Rachel, and older brother, Isaac. Jacob, MIA at our wedding, just as with most of the past twenty years, wouldn't meet Luke until he came home to the farm after Dad's heart attack eleven years ago. When Dad had back surgery a few years later and Jacob went home to help out, Luke and I'd missed that visit since I'd been due any day to deliver Ali. The weekend of our wedding, Luke's family, who all lived around the Chicago area, had made it to Wisconsin to stay at his aunt and uncle's farm.

We set our simple wedding up in the spacious yard at my parents' farm. His family had come over ahead of time to help with the preparations. I'd been nervous about meeting Rachel and Isaac. They were city. I was country.

"Don't worry," Luke said two days before the event. "They'll love you and vice versa."

He'd been right. A few hours before our wedding, Isaac had been helping me put white plastic tablecloths on the picnic tables. Everyone had given up lecturing me that I should get ready. The busier I was, the less I'd stress.

"Ask Luke about the time he played outside with his friends in his underwear," Isaac said as we unfolded tablecloths.

I laughed at the image of a young Luke playing outside in his undies. "How old was he?"

"Twelve." Isaac smirked. "Okay, maybe five. I was twelve. I'd convinced him that the Superman underwear I'd bought him for his birthday converted to a Superman cape and tights that others could see when he stepped outside. Poor kid believed me and went out to play with the neighborhood kids, thinking they could see his Superman outfit."

"That's why nobody likes their brothers," I joked. I loved mine. And wished like hell Jacob had shown up for our special day. Clean and sober.

Later, as Rachel and I sat in the shade on our wrap-around deck, frosting cupcakes, she added her own Luke story. "Mom's parents died in a house fire when we were teenagers. I was a senior in high school, so Luke would've been in eighth grade. Isaac was off at college, I was self-absorbed like a typical teenager, and Luke was his usual thoughtful self—even at thirteen." She continued spreading the cream cheese frosting on cupcakes as I stopped to listen.

"He took money he got from mowing lawns and walked two miles to the nearest florist shop to buy Mom a dozen white roses. Then he walked back, glass vase and all." She looked over at me, my butter knife hovering between me and the cupcakes. "I don't remember what he wrote on the card, but I remember crying when I read it. Luke was way more thoughtful than the rest of us put together."

Hearing stories from Luke's siblings about his youth had only magnified my love for him. We were married a few hours later in a ten-minute ceremony under a large white tent awning two hundred feet from the home I'd grown up in. Kara had been my maid of honor, and Isaac, Luke's best man.

Ever since that day, I'd witnessed a thousand examples of Luke's big-hearted nature, his goal of making people happy. It was one of my favorite things about him.

I smiled at the memory as I drove home, willing it to erase the nagging idea that someone was harassing me. If nothing else, someone at school believed I'd gone after Dastard for sex. Or someone in the community had taken the time to drive to our school to vandalize my vehicle.

I'd struggled to locate my vehicle in a sea of SUVs. Yet whoever had written the word had found it. Never for one second did I think they meant it for anyone else but me.

WHILE LUKE AND I CLEANED up the kitchen, shooing our daughters out to put their folded laundry away in their rooms, I relayed the word on the SUV to Luke in a monotone voice, neither of us surprised at the action, which in itself made me sad.

"And you said you couldn't find your car... again? This has happened more than once?"

"The first time was my first week back at school. I think I was just preoccupied when I'd parked that morning. And today's Jacob's birthday. Maybe I was distracted again." I shrugged as I wiped off the counter.

Luke, a dish towel tossed over his shoulder, stopped loading the dishwasher and turned to me. "I think we need to tell Detective Boyle."

I pressed my lips together and nodded. "I will." And I would give Boyle my updated list of phone calls that I was positive—almost positive—I hadn't made.

I made the call on my lunch break the following day. "Can I stop by your office about four-thirty today? I've got a couple of things I'd like to talk to you about." I hadn't spoken with him or Brook since before Christmas, and although I didn't miss the need for their services, I missed them and their expertise.

I imagined Brook and Boyle had heard plenty of crazier things than what I sensed was happening to me. Luke knew some of it, Boyle should know it all.

"I'll be in my office all afternoon. See you then," he said.

After Pria got off the bus that afternoon, I left her to keep an eye on her younger sisters and said I would be back in an hour. I had an errand to run. I drove the few miles to Boyle's office. He met me down the hall and led me to his messy-yet-organized office, where Brook sat.

"Hi, Lily. Doyle told me you were stopping by." Brook stood and shook my hand and then patted the empty seat next to hers. "What's up?"

I felt comfortable with Brook hearing my limp list of reasoning that someone wanted to make me look as if I should be locked up. The office smelled of peppermint and black licorice.

"I just missed this big iron marshmallow's wit." I winked.

Boyle slapped his leg and gave a hearty laugh.

Brook chimed in. "You mean this old dude that refuses to be kicked to the curb?"

"Oh, stifle it, both of you." Detective Boyle grinned as he turned to me. "You doing okay? How's it going back in the classroom?"

"I'm glad to be back teaching. I had too much alone time at home last fall. And yes, I'm doing much better. We adopted a dog. Percy has been an incentive to go for walks, no matter what the weather is like."

We caught up on how things were going better for Pria at school—as far as I knew—and whether Boyle was seriously considering retirement.

Brook rolled her eyes. "He's been promising to retire since I became a victim advocate."

He stage-whispered to me, "I'd retire, but who would antagonize Brook?"

"Well, I'm glad it won't be soon." I leaned down and took a slip of paper from my purse on the floor. "Because I need your help again." I slid my documented list of phone calls to the school, to the pizza place, to the sweet shop, and the pharmacy—calls I hadn't made.

"There are other things too. Some I told you about already." I looked at Boyle. "And although none of these on their own seem like much, the phone calls, the orders, the dismembered dolls. Overall, it feels like *something* to me. A threat."

Brook reached for my hand when I mentioned dismembered dolls.

Boyle took a notebook from his desk and jotted down the details. "Can I take a photocopy of your list?" He nodded to the paper.

"Sure." I slid it toward him. "You don't think I'm crazy, do you?" I aimed for carefree in my voice. I doubted either of them bought it.

"No, I don't. It could be a disgruntled football fan. Who knows? Not an obvious, dangerous threat, but as I said before, it feels like a threat to you, which is what they want, especially when they stack one on top of the other." Boyle stood and made a copy on the machine in his office.

I thought of Ed, the jerk in the grocery store. I wondered if someone like that would go through all the work to follow me around and figure out places to call to set me up.

"Doyle is right. If it was one or two things, we might blame your memory. You've been through a lot. But this sounds excessive." She took a drink of her Diet Coke. "What does Luke say about it?"

"I haven't told him all of it. He knows a few things, but I've leaned on him so much already." I clasped my hands. "And you two don't act like I'm three fries short of a happy meal. I'm afraid Luke will. I get a lot of sideways glances from him." I could feel a lump forming in my throat and swallowed it back down.

Boyle reached in his shirt pocket and pulled out a business card. He wrote on it then handed it to me. "My home and cell numbers are on there. Don't hesitate to call me. I mean it."

"Yes. Same with me," Brook said.

We all stood, and Boyle patted me on the shoulder before I left his office, followed by Brook. She walked down the hall with me, giving me a solid hug before I headed out into the cold. I'd neglected to mention my penchant for pills last fall. That was probably why they'd had an easier time swallowing my theory than my husband had.

Chapter 20

We left late Saturday morning after I covered a hundred instructions with Maria.

"We'll be okay, won't we, girls?" Maria turned to Ali and Codi, who bounced on the balls of her feet.

"Yes! Are you going now so we can play Go Fish?" Codi directed her enthusiastic question at Luke and me. She might as well have said, "Leave us alone."

"Okay, okay. Try not to miss us too much. I'll start the car." Luke ruffled Codi's hair and gave me a "let's go" look.

"Pria and Sylvie will be here by six," I told Maria. They worked the same shift today at the grocery store, then Sylvie would drive them to our house.

After several sloppy kisses and quick hugs from the girls, we left for our first overnight date since before the attack.

Luke had planned our brief trip, but I had a bonus for him packed in my suitcase. I saved it until later. We checked into the hotel, unpacked, and it was dusk by the time we walked the few blocks to where the horse-drawn carriage would pick us up.

As if in a Hallmark movie, light snow blanketed us, and red and white lights decorated trees along the river and cobblestone roads. We snuggled under a blanket as the clip-clop of the horses' hooves beat in time with our hearts.

"This was such a great idea." I wrapped my arms around Luke's waist.

He kissed me. "I figure, an overnight date isn't too much to do for the woman I kind of, sort of, love." Our weekend anniversary trip to Chicago last July seemed like eons ago. So much had happened since then.

Afterward, we walked to a downtown restaurant where we had reservations, found a nightclub where we danced more than we had since the first year we'd met, then went back to our hotel, reveling in the glow of reconnecting.

Luke suggested a joint shower, but I had other plans first. I pulled out the deck of cards from my overnight bag.

"First, strip poker." I grinned, thinking of all the extra jewelry I'd scrounged up for the game. I rarely wore any, other than my wedding ring and earrings. I'd dug out an old toe ring, ankle bracelet, several bangle bracelets, and a necklace. And under my jeans, I wore biker shorts, and I had on two tank tops under my sweater. But Luke was a better poker player. I needed the advantage.

"I like how you think." His grin reminded me of a teenager guaranteed his first kiss from a girl he'd crushed on for months.

We sat on the bed with our backs against the headboard and placed my hard-sided overnight suitcase between us as the game table. Within a few hands, Luke realized I wasn't making it easy for him.

"Are you kidding me? A toe ring? Do you have one on every toe?" He feigned sexual frustration, although I wasn't sure it was all pretense.

"Maybe. Guess you'll find out." I smiled coyly.

Luke chuckled. "I've got all night. And I'm a patient man."

He was right on both accounts. It was after midnight when we called a truce. Luke was down to one sock, and I had on a pair of lacy underwear and one earring.

It was worth the wait.

WHILE I SLEPT IN—UNUSUAL for me—Luke walked down the street from the hotel to pick up breakfast for us. The aroma of fresh coffee and baked goods enticed me out of bed. Bakery items were a treat since I was attempting to regain my healthy eating habits. He handed me a coffee and set our juices on the hotel table.

"Thanks." I dug into the bag and pulled out a bacon-and-egg bagel for Luke, a tomato-herb bagel for me. The receipt was in with the napkins. I pulled it out and grinned. Four coffees, four orange juices, and six bagels.

I reached for Luke's hand. "Let me guess. The two homeless guys outside our hotel last night?" The two men with long gray hair and beards had looked thin and scruffy. They could have been forty or seventy. It was hard to tell. They'd huddled in sleeping bags in the alley. Last night, Luke had given them wrapped-up dinner rolls from our meal at an Italian restaurant and a twenty-dollar bill.

It didn't surprise me. I'd have been more shocked if he'd ignored them. He downplayed the question with a shrug. He'd inherited his mother's soft heart. Rita had been volunteering for decades at one of the food bank outlets in Chicago and also at the Humane Society.

We made it home before noon, gone a mere twenty-four hours. But those hours together had been just the break we'd needed from the frenzy and fear over the past several months. Ali and Codi greeted us at the door, bouncing off the walls to tell us all about their activities with Maria. I gave myself a gold star for only calling her twice during our absence.

Maria's weathered hands dealt Old Maid cards at our kitchen table. "Sylvie picked up Pria an hour ago for their shift at work." Maria's smile illuminated her round face.

Ali and Codi hurried back to their chairs and picked up their hands.

"Have you been playing cards since we left?" I asked. Codi had rambled on about so many things that I'd missed most of it. "And what was that I heard about 'dog' and 'sliding'?"

Maria shook her head. "Nope. This is only our third game of cards this morning. Yesterday afternoon, we walked to the sledding hill by the park. Percy slid down the hill with them, and Judith and her two dogs met us there." Judith lived on the other side of our development. Close in age and both widows, they'd become friends.

"We had fun with the dogs!" Ali's eyes sparkled. In the past several months, the upheaval, chaos, and uncertainty of our lives had had an upside—it had pushed Ali to adjust—somewhat—to an unscheduled life. We were also seeing the results of the special one-on-one classes at school and her after-school program.

"I hope that's okay," Maria said. "Judith's two collies got along well with Percy."

I sat in the kitchen chair next to Maria. "Of course it is. The girls have wanted to go sledding. I'm glad the weather cooperated."

We visited as the girls filled me in on every detail of their sliding, the snow angels they'd made, Judith and her dogs coming over to our house for hot chocolate, Maria whipping up spaghetti—their favorite meal—for supper, their two games of Trouble, and several card games of Go Fish. *Poor Maria.*

"You must be exhausted," I said.

"I won't deny a nap might be in my plans this afternoon, but it's been fun. I miss my grandkids being young and their energy and zest for everything."

"Don't you get your fill of that at school?"

"I do, but it's not the same as the one-on-one time."

After their card game, we gave Maria a thank-you card containing gift cards to restaurants in our town. I walked her to her car in our driveway. "Thanks again for everything. It was reassuring to know the girls were in excellent hands."

"Anytime, Lily. I mean it." She fired up her car. We hugged, and I reminded myself how lucky I was to have coworkers whom I considered friends. As I walked up our sidewalk, I thought of how even the football diehards had weakened in their "Lily War." Time healed most wounds.

After making Ali and Codi grilled cheese sandwiches for lunch, I settled for a small glass of green smoothie from the container I kept in our fridge, hoping to offset the heavy food I'd eaten for dinner and breakfast. I was back in my healthy eating habits. Swimming had replaced my daily running for the moment. Soon, the roads would be dry enough for me to work back up to running again. I couldn't wait.

By Sunday afternoon, I struggled to function, and my concentration waned. Luke had left to go grocery shop before picking up Pria when her shift was over. After they arrived home, Pria went upstairs to shower, and I helped Luke unpack the groceries.

"The assistant manager said they're pleased with Pria's work," he said as he put away the refrigerated items.

I restocked the canned goods in our pantry, my body moving in slow motion.

"They didn't say she was moody or that she complained?" Pria was a typical teenager who saved those emotions for her home life.

"What?" Luke shut the fridge door. I caught his forehead furrowing.

I repeated myself. My tongue felt as if someone had inflated it with a bike pump.

Luke came and stood in front of me. "You okay?" He put his hand against my forehead.

"I think so, just super tired." I sounded like I'd submerged my face in a fishbowl.

His cool hand soothed my perspiring face. "I'll finish this. Why don't you go lie down? I promised Codi and Ali that I'd play cards with them after I'm done here."

Pria was in her bedroom with the door closed when I walked upstairs. Sometimes, I itched to fling the door open, lie on her bed, and hang out with the daughter who had become a stranger. Judith had mentioned she'd lost her only child, a daughter, to drugs. It hit home to me for two reasons—that could have been me if I hadn't gotten help, and also, it could happen to any of our girls. I needed to open that door and keep us connected. But it was not the time.

I woke up hours later, woozy as if I was hungover. I'd never been good at napping and attributed it to that. Luke studied me off and on as I roasted chicken and baked potatoes for supper. Other than asking if I was okay, we dropped any discussion of my odd behavior. I had no explanation, and he was past questioning every single strange thing that happened.

He would leave for North Carolina two weeks from tomorrow for the Central Office Upgrade Training, and I dreaded it. He had enrolled in online training last month, which would at least lessen the duration of the trip. I wasn't sure I could have handled him being gone a full month.

BARB'S POST-HOLIDAY potluck was the following Saturday. Other than our solo night out last weekend, Luke and I had been homebodies since last summer. I needed a night out with friends and an excuse to dress up.

Pria stayed home to watch Ali and Codi, and we'd agreed Sylvie and Erin could spend the night. I dressed in black leggings, a long red tunic top, added a few curls in my short hair, and applied makeup with more care than the two-minute toss I did before work every morning. Luke wore a pair of new khakis and a crisp kelly-green shirt that brought out his beautiful eyes and contrasted his darker skin.

When we entered the kitchen, they offered us a choice of beer or wine despite it being a BYOB and side-dish party. Luke and I had discussed booze consumption ahead of time. I'd had one glass of wine at our Christmas dinner, and that was it. No craving for seconds—or the entire bottle. I would have one drink at the party. I wanted to show I was in control again, although nothing seemed to be a sure thing for me anymore.

I accepted a glass of white wine from Barb's husband then added the bottle I'd brought to the other beverages sitting on the drink cart. Luke set our crockpot containing taco dip down on the counter and plugged it in next to an array of appetizers.

After eating healthy again those past few months, I was concerned about the food choices tonight. But if I didn't eat something, even one drink would go to my head. Luke held my hand as we walked into the living room, where Barb and other teachers visited with fellow school employees and significant others.

I introduced Luke to the few people he didn't know. Christina and a new fifth-grade teacher hadn't yet arrived. Not everyone brought a guest. Christina arrived about an hour after us in a bronze-colored top that hugged her curves. Her long brown hair curled around her face. Christina exuded a vitality that I hadn't possessed since, well, since before Pria was born.

I barely remembered the single life, and mine hadn't been half as exciting as Christina's. During our lunch breaks at school, she talked of trips to New Zealand, Paris, and China, her summer job as a white water rafting guide when she lived in Colorado, and the training she'd begun for climbing Yosemite's Half Dome next summer. It all reminded me of the trips I hadn't taken. Yet.

Her colorful life made for interesting conversation. Christina might not have been the most beautiful woman in the room, but she was sexy and fun, a heady combination that attracted men. She sat at the portable bar in Barb's living room, surrounded by men—including Luke—as she shared photos of wildlife from her weekend rafting trip last summer.

Rafting in Colorado was on our wish list for trips. I assured myself Luke was only interested in her pictures. However, I noticed how Christina seemed to lean into him more than any other guy, her hand on his shoulder, her head close to his as they studied the photos. Maybe I was imagining it, but her low-cut top seemed strategically placed below Luke's line of vision.

"Don't worry." Barb's voice startled me as she came up from behind.

"So you see it too?" Her eyes followed mine to Christina, who looked like an appendage of Luke. I realized I hadn't introduced them to each other since Christina had arrived late. She wouldn't know Luke and I were married, but the shiny silver band on his ring finger should've alerted her he was *someone's* husband.

"Is she always this friendly with men?" My fingers clenched the wine glass stem, itching to break it like a turkey wishbone. *Easy, girl. Next, you'll be foaming at the mouth!*

Barb tilted her head. "Friendly? I guess. No rumors of her cheating with a married man though. But I don't know her that well yet. She's had her share of boyfriends from the stories I've heard these past five months. But Christina isn't blind, and Luke is darn handsome." Barb turned to me. "Sorry, I'm just stating the obvious. Come on. Let's get more wine." She led me by the arm.

I could have drowned my worries in another glass, but I wanted to prove I had self-control. And Christina wasn't his "type." After we'd dated a few months, he told me of a girl he'd dated his senior year of college who looked similar to me—petite with long blond hair like I used to have. I'd worried he'd go back to her after our first summer together. He assured me that wouldn't happen.

He'd found out she was already pregnant before they'd begun dating. "We met at a New Year's Eve party and only dated around a month. After I found out about her pregnancy, I told her I didn't want to date her anymore. That's when I realized appearances were deceiving. Outside, she had this wholesome image, but inside? She was unhinged." Luke shook his head. "She'd come unglued when I said I didn't want to date someone pregnant with another guy's baby, whether or not she kept the child. She flew into a rant about how we could be a family. In her twisted mind, she didn't seem to understand I'd never been serious about her."

My jealousy had evaporated then, and I hadn't experienced it since. Until tonight. When the necklace Christina wore somehow got caught on Luke's watch, placing his hand close to the neckline of her top, I kept my cool. I took a long drink of water to wet my frozen smile before heading over to assist with their entanglement.

That was when Christina realized who Luke belonged to. Yes, I didn't "own" him, but he was my husband. The father of my children. Christina's well-arched eyebrows rose. A blush crawled across her face, and she dropped her gaze. My less-than-nimble fingers freed his watch from her delicate necklace chain. Party over—at least for Christina.

I trusted him. But even angels' wings got broken. Luke was wonderful. He was also human. He never left my side for the rest of the night.

CHRISTINA APOLOGIZED at school on Tuesday, our first day back after having President's Day off from school. We sat at a table in the teacher's lounge, picking at our lunches.

"I bet you think I have no moral compass." She pushed her salad around in the bowl.

I remained silent.

"Yes, I noticed his wedding ring, but he didn't have a woman hanging around him. Also, Gabe told me he might bring a recently widowed friend along. I hoped your husband was that widower." She shrugged as if to say, "Hey, a girl can dream."

"So, did Gabe bring his friend?" I tried to remember if I'd seen Gabe, a sixth-grade teacher, at the party.

"Yes, they showed up later. I guess it took a lot of prodding on Gabe's part. His friend didn't feel right having fun so soon after his wife's death."

"I get that," I said.

"So, back to Luke. I'm sorry for flirting with your holy-hell-he's-gorgeous husband." She held up her hand like a police officer instructing me to stop. "I mean, I'm not surprised that he's your husband. You're adorable, and you certainly deserve him." She palmed her forehead. "Shut up, Christina. You sound creepier by the second!"

I laughed. "You're forgiven. I understand. You think Luke is cute and hoped he was the widower." I finished my last bite of tuna salad, struggling to swallow. If that police dog hadn't found me in time, Luke would be a widower. I took a drink of green smoothie, washing that ugly image down. It festered in the pit of my stomach.

Chapter 21

My cell phone rang in the kitchen while I was upstairs, tucking Ali and Codi into bed on Wednesday night. I received very few calls on my cell, and when I checked it later, I didn't recognize the number. But they'd left a voice mail message. Specifically, *Jacob* had left a message.

Over five weeks had passed since I'd mailed the second letter to him. I'd almost given up on getting a response and figured if he did, it would be by letter, not a phone call. My hand shook as I listened to his voice mail, plopping my butt in a chair so I wouldn't faint.

"Hey, sis." He cleared his throat. "You're right. We're way overdue to talk. Um, I get the feeling Mom and Dad have kept you in the dark about things. I'm not pointing the finger at them. I asked them to keep you out of it years ago. Anyway, sorry it's taken me a while to get back to you. I travel once in a while for work, and although I'd like to say that's the reason it's taken me so long, it's a lie, and you'd bust me on it." He chuckled. "With the shit you've gone through these past months, maybe it's time we talk. You've got my number now. Tag, you're it."

I pressed my lips together, blinking enough to fill a novel of Morse code as if I could stop the tears. I listened to his message three times before I searched Luke out, working on our water heater in the basement.

I shoved my phone to his ear. "Listen." My voice may have sounded carefree, but my thoughts and heart were doing backflips.

Luke's face didn't reflect whatever thoughts he had while listening to Jacob's message. He handed me the phone. "He sounds good." His voice held no emotion, and I understood Luke worried I'd only get hurt again by Jacob if we didn't have the perfect, all-is-forgiven reunion I hoped for.

I'd never imagined when I'd seen Jacob after Dad's heart attack that it would be eleven years before we saw each other again. My only sibling had become a stranger to me. And it was probably more my fault than his.

Luke would leave for training in North Carolina next Monday. I needed to see Jacob before then, while Luke was here to stay with our daughters.

In the privacy of our basement, I called Jacob back. When he answered, emotion overtook my throat, and I sounded like an elderly woman with a quivering voice. "It's so, so good to hear your voice again!" I thumbed tears away.

"Good to hear yours too, sis." Jacob's voice held a hitch too, warming my heart. "So, you want to meet somewhere?"

I'd asked Jacob in my letters if I could see him. Anything we needed to talk about deserved to be said face-to-face. "Are you busy this Saturday? We could meet somewhere, or I'd gladly drive to your house. Whatever you want." Hell, I would meet him on the moon if that was what it took to see my brother again.

"You're a few hours away, right? You want to come see where I live? I'll make us lunch."

My heart burst with excitement. "I'd love that!" I wanted a glimpse into Jacob's adult life, hoping it would reassure me he was happy, healthy, and sober. That he was okay. Some part of me felt that if Jacob was fine, I could be fine.

I promised to leave early Saturday, the weather forecast looking to cooperate for the last weekend in February. And as I fell asleep Friday night, anticipation bouncing around inside of me, I couldn't help but wonder what Jacob had meant in his message that Mom and Dad had kept me in the dark about something. Whatever it was, I would find out soon.

BEFORE THE SUN PEEKED above the horizon Saturday morning, I pulled out of our driveway with detailed directions to Jacob's house for the three-hour drive. On the way there, I thought of everything I wanted to say—how I realized my focus years ago had been on myself. How his drinking and absence still affected me. Never once had I put myself in his place—something I'd expected Luke to do with my situation. All I'd thought about was my extra workload, the stress on our parents, and how Jacob had "wronged" us. When he'd missed our wedding, our daughters' births, everything important in my adult life, I'd labeled Jacob as selfish.

Instead, I'd been self-centered. I hoped our visit today would give our relationship a new beginning. If he forgave me, I would be better equipped to forgive myself.

Jacob's driveway had no mailbox, no sign with his name. There was nothing but the green sign with his address number to tell me I had the right place. He owned forty acres with his home and promised he would plow his long gravel driveway. I slowed the vehicle down to a crawl as I drove down the single lane surrounded by dense woods and fresh snow. It was like driving into a Christmas card, with snow blanketing tall pine trees along the driveway.

When his one-level, log-sided home appeared, smoke curling from the rock chimney above the roof, my pulse quickened. I turned off the car, grabbed my purse, then took a long drink from a water bottle.

The front door opened. Jacob jogged across the deck and down the stairs toward my vehicle, his hands shoved in his jeans pockets. I stepped out then couldn't move. The apprehension in my chest grounded me. As Jacob neared, I caught his grin, surrounded by his beard and mustache, and I reached for him with my heart in my throat.

I breathed in the woody scent on Jacob's clothing, felt the whiskers from his beard catching in my short hair, and closed my eyes at the strength of his embrace.

Jacob, half a foot taller than me, pulled away, holding my arms in his. I took in his blond hair, several shades darker than I remembered, the fine lines forming around his eyes, and the few gray hairs in his beard. I leaned in for another Jacob hug. I'd missed the hell out of them.

"I'm so sorry, Jacob, so, so sorry that I wasn't there for you." My eyes and nose ran, and I fished a tissue from my coat pocket. My chest convulsed against his sturdy one.

"I know." His voice muffled against my head. He squeezed me hard before letting go and stepping back to study me. "So, it's a butch haircut for you now, eh?"

"I'm going for the Tinkerbell look. Still working on the wings." I dried my eyes.

"The mother clucker should've been hung by his nuts." His jaw clenched.

I grinned at Jacob's euphemism, a term we'd often said growing up on the farm, but I cringed at the image of Dastard hanging. "I don't understand why he picked me."

He folded his arms across his chest and tipped his head, studying me. "Why not you, Lily? You think bad things don't happen to good people?"

I tensed my shoulders. I deserved his scrutiny. And yes, my answer to his question, until recently, would have been "yes."

"I just meant I don't get his reason and why that day. I'd seen him many other times while running on that trail, so this attack came out of nowhere." I backpedaled, not wanting to start off on the wrong foot with Jacob.

He rocked on his heels, arms still shielding his chest, his heart. He looked out on the snowy yard, and we stood in silence, listening to the light breeze through the trees.

He blew out a long sigh as his shoulders slumped, and he broke the silence. "Let's go inside."

I followed him up the walkway and deck as he opened the front door for me. The temperature hovered at freezing, and I hadn't dressed for it. The warmth from the living room fireplace welcomed me. He toed off his winter boots on the entryway rug, and I hung up my button-up sweater.

"Your place is nice." The living room opened to a dining nook and kitchen.

"Thanks. I built it about ten years ago." He nodded toward the hallway. "Follow me." Jacob gave me a thirty-second tour of his bedroom, an extra bedroom, and a bathroom. "It's the perfect size for me. I spend half of my time at home either outside or working in the garage." His detached garage was as large as the house.

"No farm animals here?" I looked out the kitchen window at a snow-covered yard that spread into surrounding woods. There looked to be several trails worn down by deer, other critters, and probably Jacob.

He came to stand next to me. "About the only animals I miss are the cows."

I turned to him. "They're what I miss the most too. With all of this land, I'm surprised you don't have a cow." Maybe it wasn't zoned for farm animals.

"Living alone, it's not worth the work."

"No woman in your life?" Jacob had rugged good looks and, thankfully, appeared healthy. No bloodshot eyes, no broken capillaries on his nose and cheeks. I'd worried he spent his free time swimming in booze. I'd judged him before and realized I was still doing it, even after going down a challenging path myself.

He busied himself making coffee, not answering me. Jacob's shoulders were much broader now. He'd been a late-blooming teen.

"I'm sorry. I shouldn't have asked. It's just that I have so many questions, so much I want to understand."

Jacob braced both hands against the butcher-block counter and took a deep breath. "I'm not sure you want to hear everything I've got to say."

I sat on a kitchen chair, sensing his confession might buckle me at the knees.

Jacob turned around and met my eyes. "I decided that after the hell you've gone through, you can handle the shit I'm going to spread at your feet."

His words brought back one of the many happy memories of our youth together—we used to play a game in the cow pasture, seeing who could Frisbee a dried "cow pie" the farthest.

I'd won every time. By the time Jacob had passed me in height and made it more of a competition, his cheery disposition had changed. Our parents blamed it on hormones. I blamed myself for deserting him for college while he struggled with something. That summer before college was the first time he'd won at the shit-flinging game, yet he quit wanting to play. I'd never understood why.

He set two mugs of coffee on the wood table. "Half and half okay for you?" Jacob opened the fridge and waved a red-and-white carton at me. We'd grown up on fresh cream for our coffee.

"Yes. Thanks." I poured coffee into mugs decorated with timber wolves while he pulled out a loaf of wild rice bread from a cupboard.

"I made this yesterday. It's Mom's recipe."

We settled in at the kitchen table with the bread, butter, and coffee.

Jacob folded his hands in a fist under his chin and studied me. "I take it Mom and Dad never said a word about what happened on the farm?"

"You mean when we were growing up?"

"Yes, before you left for college."

"No, nothing." My nose tingled, a precursor to crying. I hadn't even heard his story yet.

He took a drink of coffee. "Okay, hold off on your endless questions until I'm finished." He shot me an "I mean it" look.

"Okay." My stomach roiled as if someone had strapped me into a chair to witness a friend's slaying. I wanted to cover my ears. But I'd come for the truth. And because I missed my brother like an appendage.

"You remember Earl."

It wasn't a question. Earl, our parents' farmhand, had been around since I'd been old enough to walk. It was a surprise when he'd quit and moved out of state to work on a ranch in Colorado several years ago. I nodded.

"The May before my junior year in high school, when Earl arrived back at the farm for the season, he suggested to Dad I help him with the more physical work since Dad's back had been bothering him." Dad and Earl had worked hard from spring through fall in the fields and with the livestock. Mom took care of the massive garden, canning, and caring for some of the farm animals. We thought of Earl as an older uncle, roughly twenty years older than me.

I reined in my walk down memory lane to focus on Jacob's words, ones that tumbled out. He clenched his hands on the table, studying them. "Remember the small mechanic's shed down the road where Dad kept the older farm equipment in need of repair? In that shed, the summer before my junior year, that's when it first happened. It was a rainy day, and Mom and Dad had gone into town to sign papers for some acreage they bought."

I leaned so far over the table toward Jacob, hanging on his every word, I almost fell forward. "What happened?" He'd said hold the questions, but I had to ask. My instincts screamed in warning.

His Adam's apple bobbed up and down. "Rape. It was the day Earl first raped me." The words gritted between his teeth as he pinched the bridge of his nose.

I choked on my spit, trying to swallow a horror I didn't want to visualize.

"How? I mean, I know 'how,' but how did he keep you from telling Mom and Dad?"

"Earl was clever. He pointed out that he'd helped Dad for years on the farm, how Dad relied on him, how he called Earl his brother, and how there was no way in hell Dad would believe me." Jacob folded his arms across his chest.

Earl was only a few years younger than Dad and had been his right-hand man for years. Still, I couldn't imagine that Dad would ever think Jacob had made something like that up. "Did you ever try telling Dad? Or Mom?" I couldn't stifle my questions.

"I told Dad the following summer. Foolishly, I'd hoped when Earl came back the next spring that it would stop. When it didn't, I mustered up the courage to tell Dad. And got the same response Earl said I'd get." Jacob pushed his chair back, stood, then paced the small kitchen. "Dad got pissed at me. Said it was outrageous. He figured I was trying to get out of work, even though I pointed out that if he fired Earl, it would make more work for me. As if I'd rather get raped than work more hours in the field."

Jacob stopped pacing, his body tense with pent-up emotion. "At the time, I figured Dad was more worried about extra work for *him*. Remember that song he said was popular when he was a teen, the one he always sang?"

My head was ready to explode from the toxic news Jacob had spilled. I couldn't think of any particular song Dad had sung back then. Music was everywhere on the farm. The radio played twenty-four seven in the barn. We had transistor radios cranked up on every tractor, Mom's oldie station played nonstop in the kitchen, and Dad listened to oldies in his truck and work shed.

"The one about walking a mile in his shoes before you criticize or accuse... or something like that." Jacob folded his arms close to his chest. "I took it as Dad hinting that I shouldn't accuse Earl of something so hideous."

My tongue itched with more questions.

"I started drinking, easy to do since Earl always had a flask of whiskey with him. I used alcohol to get through Earl's abuse. It helped me ignore the guilt—as if it was my fault—and helped me deal with anger toward Dad for not believing me. For not protecting me."

"I'm so sorry, Jacob. I wish I had known." My words were of no comfort now, gifted too many years later. It had taken my life unraveling before I understood the shift in his behavior. Shame on me.

"The only thing I was thankful for was that Earl came after me instead of you. That I'd protected you in some way."

"When did it stop? How did it stop?" Jacob had quit living at the farm as soon as he graduated from high school, causing an enormous rift between him and Dad. Back then, I'd blamed Jacob for deserting Dad, who'd needed his help. Now I saw it in a different light. Earl was at the farm. Jacob was an adult. He didn't have to live there anymore.

"The spring before I graduated, I beat the ever-living shit out of the mother clucker the first night he was back. He'd abused me for two summers, and I wanted to make damn sure it never happened again. I was finally big enough to take him on, and I had the element of surprise on my side. I snuck into his cabin and waited for him that night with a two-by-four."

I remembered when I'd come home from college that summer, Earl's face had had several marks from a "bar fight" he'd been in the month before.

Jacob sat back down, and for the next hour, told of his battle with alcohol. He might have left his abuser behind, but his booze crutch had followed him to college, escalating until the night he'd fallen down the dorm stairs. Those injuries fueled his dependency. The rape—and Dad's disbelief—kept him away from the farm. After that, Jacob had made his way to the Iron Range in northeastern Minnesota, where there was more land than people.

It was why he hadn't come back to the farm for my wedding, why he'd broken contact with our parents, and why he'd started life over somewhere else.

"Did you go through treatment?"

Jacob shook his head. "My old boss pushed me to meet with a counselor. I was working at an area mine in the machinery department, showing up drunk half the time. He said I could either purge my demons to a counselor or get sent away for a month to dry out. I chose the counselor, and it changed my life."

He'd quit drinking years ago, put his life back together, and I'd never known it. *We're together now. That's all that matters.*

"Did you know Earl left the farm about a decade ago?" I assumed our parents had told him. It had happened the year before Dad's heart attack. We hadn't discussed Earl's departure on the one day Jacob and I spent together when we'd gone to help at the farm that winter.

"Yep. He was caught raping a teenage boy in town and was arrested. I got a call from Dad the next day, apologizing for not believing me. Ten years after I'd told him about Earl." Jacob ran a hand through his short beard. "Mom called that night, crying and apologizing for not knowing. She told me that Dad torched the old mechanic's shed that morning."

Shock riveted me to the chair. Yes, the shed had burned down, and Earl had moved away, but I'd never known the truth behind those events. Jacob had opened up to me, paving the way for me to dig up the sludge of my secrets. I told him of my opioid reliance, my struggle with moving on after the attack, and the sureness that someone was still out to ruin my life.

"I'm at the point where I don't trust anyone," I confessed.

"Hey, I understand, Lily. All too well."

Of course he did. I couldn't imagine how alone Jacob must have felt as an abused teen, and his father not believing him. It reminded me of the sexual abuse in the Catholic Church, aired after decades of secrets.

Our visit flew by too fast, and I wished I'd packed an overnight bag, but Luke was leaving Monday for North Carolina. I wanted to spend Sunday with Luke, and I also wanted to spend another day, week, or lifetime with Jacob. I couldn't let a rift form between us ever again.

As Jacob walked me to the car, I asked about the one thing I still didn't understand. "Why didn't Mom and Dad tell me years ago, after Earl left?"

He turned to me, his hands on my shoulders. "I asked them not to. Why wreck *your* childhood memories? I never wanted to set foot on the farm again, but I sure as hell didn't want you to hate the place. And don't be pissed at Mom and Dad. It's in the past, where it should stay. I only told you now so you'd understand. I figured it might help you move on, help you understand that yes, bad things happen to good people. You and I are proof of that." He pulled me to him, and I inhaled Jacob's scent of burning wood and fresh air to tuck away in my heart.

Driving back down his tree-lined driveway, I understood why Jacob had chosen to surround himself with nature. It didn't judge or play favorites, didn't point fingers or assault. Nature could calm and comfort. The opposite of what we'd done for him.

I drove home in the dusk, able to take a deep breath again. Jacob was back in my life. One of the few people I now trusted.

Chapter 22

I arrived home Saturday night energized from my visit with Jacob, my enthusiasm tempered by shock and sorrow at the filthy truth he'd shared. Pria was bowling with some friends, and Luke had already put Ali and Codi to bed. I'd driven home in the dark, pushing my visit with Jacob late to squeeze in every second I could with him.

Luke sat in the living room, watching a basketball game, a bowl of popcorn on his lap. When I sat next to him and told him about what had happened to Jacob, he choked on a kernel.

"Holy hell! And nobody thought to tell you about it years ago?" Luke wiped his buttery hands on a napkin and set about cracking his knuckles at the news my brother had a more-than-valid reason for his tailspin.

I needed to call Dad, to put words to the feelings overtaking me, and to understand what the hell he'd been thinking when he'd sided with Earl instead of his own son. But I wouldn't make that call until I could be reasonable and listen. It might take days for that to happen.

Luke sighed. "I've been a jerk for assuming the worst about him."

I understood his need to reprimand himself. I'd done plenty of it today. "I wish he lived nearby. We have so much to catch up on."

"It would be nice to have Jacob closer. I hate leaving you for two weeks. I called Shawn today to make sure he'll be around in case you need help with something."

"I'll be fine. If I need help, I can call Barb, Maria, or Judith since they live close by. Or your girlfriend, Christina. Unless I need a big manly man for something."

"Ha-ha." Luke shook his head at my jab.

I thought of all the people I couldn't call for help—Luke's and my parents, Jacob, and Kara all lived too far away. Then there were people like Irene, right next door to us, yet someone who'd shunned us ever since the arrest. It didn't matter. The girls and I would be fine.

LUKE FLEW OUT FOR THE training in North Carolina the following morning, and our first week without him went by without a hitch. I skipped our bimonthly Wednesday night get-together, that one scheduled at a third grade teacher's home, since Pria worked at the grocery store that night and wouldn't be able to stay home with her sisters.

While my coworkers gathered to continue with the knitting project for needy children, I read a book I'd picked up at the library, *Outgrowing the Pain*, about adults abused as children.

And as I lay in bed that night, I thought of the children I'd taught over the years, children I'd observed who lived in a struggling family, had a disjointed home life, or needed help outside what I could give as a teacher. We did our best to be proactive but walked a fine line between overstepping our boundaries with families and involving outside help.

I always thought I was doing the best I could as a teacher. But I wondered if it was enough for me. People like Jacob—and Dastard, if I was being honest with myself—had needed help. Their actions cried for it. And neither had received it in time.

Allowing myself to understand my attacker's painful past only put me on a hamster wheel of guilt and understanding peppered with the endless question of "why" for everything.

We did our best to help children learn and meet their physical needs. But I could have done more for their emotional needs. I had needed help those past months to dissect my anger and anguish. And I was an adult, much better equipped than a child or teen.

I tucked those thoughts away for future consideration. For the moment, I needed to concentrate on myself and my family.

BY THE TIME I ARRIVED home from work Friday, my head hurt, my body ached, and I felt "off." We had nothing planned for the weekend other than Pria attending the high school girls' basketball playoffs with her friends. Early March often brought a final snowstorm for the season, coinciding with basketball's end. It would be a good weekend to stay home and rest. We'd received a lot of snow in mid-February, which meant a flooding risk to our rivers that spring.

My energy level hovered around zero. I took the easy way out and fed Ali and Codi macaroni and cheese for supper, lessening the guilt with sides of carrots and strawberries. Luke called at six like every other night since he'd left on Monday.

"Some of us from class are heading out for dinner at a sports bar soon," Luke said. "You doing okay? You sound beat."

"I'm fine. Just tired and feel like I'm coming down with something."

"I'll call you tomorrow morning. I hope the snowstorm misses you and you get some rest." Last night, we'd discussed Pria attending the playoffs. "Some of us are driving to Grandfather Mountain. They've got a mile-high swinging bridge. Should be a blast." There was irony in his voice. Luke feared very few things. Heights was one of them.

We said our goodbyes, and I summoned every ounce of energy to pop popcorn on the stove before snuggling on the couch with Ali and Codi to watch the *Cinderella* DVD Codi had gotten for Christmas. I skipped Codi's bath after giving her a good sniff test. *How dirty can she be this time of year, stuck inside?*

I napped on the couch after tucking them in, wishing I could go to bed myself. When a friend's parent dropped Pria off two hours later, I was watching *Forrest Gump*. Pria's cheeks were rosy from the cold.

"How did the girls do?" I asked.

"They won," Pria said as she shrugged out of her ski coat. "They play again tomorrow night. Can I go?"

"We'll see. Depends on the weather." The basketball playoffs were in a town thirty miles away. "Want to watch the rest of the movie with me?" I patted the couch.

Pria rolled her eyes. "Mom, you've watched this movie so much, you could recite it word for word. I'm going to bed." There was still popcorn in the bowl next to me, and Pria grabbed a handful before she headed upstairs.

She was right. And although the body aches and headache had improved somewhat, the exhaustion hadn't. I turned off the movie, cleaned up our dishes from supper, and let Percy, who'd been sleeping next to the couch, outside to our fenced-in backyard.

When he reappeared at the sliding glass door, I let him in and wiped his paws with the towel we kept nearby. His bed lay in the corner between the dining room and living room. As I trudged upstairs, I thought of how empty the house felt late at night without Luke there. Yes, the girls were in their bedrooms, but our bed was too big, too cold, and too lonely. It was tempting to let Percy sleep in our room.

As I slipped into our bed, wearing thick socks to keep my feet warm, I breathed in Luke's scent from his pillow and hugged it to my chest before falling asleep.

PRIA'S SCREAM AS SHE shook me awake nearly gave me a heart attack. "What? What?" I fought to claw my way out of a deep slumber. *What the hell's wrong? Is our house on fire?*

"Mom!" Pria repeated over and over. "How could you leave Percy outside in the freezing cold?" Pria had turned on the lamp on my nightstand, the light illuminating the anger pulling at her face.

I sat up. "Percy's outside?" My mind played catch-up.

"Yes! I heard him barking outside! Mom, he's so cold!" That was when I noticed the tears streaming down Pria's face.

"Is he downstairs?" I pulled on my bathrobe and followed her out of the bedroom and down the stairs.

"I wrapped him in a blanket. Will he be okay?" Pria had switched from being the reprimanding adult to a terrified child. She had already turned on the dining room light, and as I entered the room, Percy's low whine turned into a yowl, his tail wagging the plaid blanket around him back and forth.

"Oh, Percy!" I bent down and gathered him and the blanket in my arms and sat at the dining room table. His body shook as my eyes met Pria's damp ones. She stood next to me, both of us rubbing Percy's body. I had no explanation for how he'd ended up outside.

"I swear, I let him back in." Even I heard the doubt in my voice. But I remembered that I'd cleaned off his paws before I'd gone to bed. "Please get the hot water bottle from our bathroom cupboard upstairs, fill it up, and bring it here."

Pria nodded and ran up to our master bathroom, too scared to be angry with me. It was almost one a.m., and I'd gone to bed around ten. Percy had little hair and body fat on him. The high today, no, yesterday, had been thirty degrees. It was below freezing outside. I knew about animals from growing up on a farm, knew enough that a dog Percy's size, roughly thirty pounds, shouldn't be outside in such weather for over fifteen minutes.

Fifteen minutes, not three hours, Lily! My silent berating stopped as realization hit me. I studied Percy's shivering body before I put my ear to his chest. His heartbeat was steady and strong. His fur was cool to the touch, but he'd only been inside for a few minutes. Percy's pupils appeared normal, his breathing strong. I pulled back the blanket, touching the bottoms of his paws. He didn't whimper. Same when I checked his ears. He should have frostbite by then.

There is no way in hell this dog was outside for three hours.

Pria came back with the water bottle.

"Can you take him, please? I need to check a few things out."

Pria nodded. She gathered Percy with his blanket and settled him on her lap with the hot water bottle against his tummy.

"He doesn't have the signs of hypothermia. I think he's going to be okay." I could take his temperature, but I would need to use our thermometer since I didn't own one for animals. I held off, fairly certain Percy hadn't been outside very long.

"What do you mean?" Pria's brows furrowed.

"I went to bed shortly after you did. Did you hear barking for a while before you got up?"

She shrugged. "His barking woke me up. At first, I thought it was a dog somewhere else. But then I got up and stood by my window and realized it was coming from our backyard."

Pria's chin quivered as she hugged Percy to her chest. Her bedroom window faced the backyard. Our master bedroom faced the front yard.

"If Percy had been outside that entire time, you'd have heard him barking long before now. Do you remember if the sliding glass door was locked before you opened it?"

"I think so." She scrunched her nose. "But I can't remember. As soon as I realized it was Percy, I ran down here and opened the door."

"Let him down, please. I want to watch him walk." Percy had stopped shaking and was busy licking Pria's hands. I took out a doggie treat from the box. Before Pria could unwrap him, he jumped from her lap and made a beeline for the treat.

He was cold but okay. I gave Percy the treat and watched him walk around the dining room and kitchen. His limp was no worse than usual.

And as much as I was thankful he didn't have hypothermia, the relief was weighed down with worry and fear. My radar was on high alert as I walked to check our front door.

Locked. *If we didn't let Percy out, who did?* The dog had many talents, but opening the sliding glass door wasn't one of them.

It was after two o'clock when I crawled back into bed, Percy lying on the floor next to me. I would call the veterinarian's office in the morning just to make sure we didn't need to bring Percy in. Then I would call Luke and explain something I had no explanation for. Again.

Chapter 23

Sleep came in bursts, reminiscent of the months following the birth of our children, where I felt as if I'd skimmed past any REM cycle of sleep. My mind was too busy thinking of reasonable ways Percy could have gotten outside. *Maybe Ali or Codi let him out?* Neither were sleepwalkers, but it was a question I would ask when they woke up. Several times, I leaned over the edge of the bed to check on Percy. The dog slept better than I did.

With our home at the end of the street, and the small lake and woods bordering our yard, we had the privacy we craved. Nobody across the street from us thanks to the area surrounding the lake. Nobody to see what went on in our yard other than Irene next door. Irene's husband often worked out of town, and although I'd never have considered Irene a busybody before the attack, I sensed she often watched me and our family from the privacy of her home.

I liked Irene. I missed her. But I wouldn't ask her if she'd seen anything last night. And with the tall cedar fence around our backyard, she couldn't have seen what'd happened anyway. Giving up on sleep, I crawled out of bed, called the veterinarian's office at six o'clock, and left a message. The office opened from eight to noon on Saturdays. They would get back to me then.

I'd checked every window downstairs before Percy, Pria, and I went back to bed. Everything was locked, just as it had been before I'd gone to bed at ten. I was sitting at our kitchen table with a cup of hot green tea when Ali and Codi came downstairs. As they ate breakfast, I asked, "Did either of you wake up last night and let Percy outside?"

Codi looked at me, milk and Cheerios dribbling down her chin. "Nope."

Ali set her spoon down, instant worry furrowing her brows. She still ate Blueberry Frosted Mini-Wheats for breakfast every day but had made great strides in varying the number she began with. It was another step in breaking down her rigid life, and we were so proud of her efforts. "No, Mommy. It's too cold out for Percy."

"You're right, Ali. I just wanted to make sure neither of you had woken up during the night to let him out to go potty." It had never happened before, but there was a first for everything. "Did you hear him barking last night?" Their bedroom also faced the backyard.

Both shook their heads, and I let the subject drop. It hadn't snowed overnight, but now, in the gray morning, fat snowflakes fell in the swirling wind. "I'm going outside for a few minutes. I'll be right back. Pria's upstairs."

I put on winter boots, zipped up a ski jacket over my sleep T-shirt, then walked out into our front yard, burying my hands in the jacket pockets. My body still ached as if fighting off a bug. I trudged through the snow, making my way around our house to see if anything looked unusual. It wasn't until I reached the fence around our backyard that I spotted them.

Large boot prints in the snow led from the backyard gate toward the paved walking trail surrounding the small lake near us. The city shoveled the trails so once I reached the pavement, it was impossible to see where the footprints had come from. Back in our yard, it was harder to point out specific boot prints since the girls and Percy had beat down much of the snow in our front and back yard. It didn't matter. It was time to call Luke and Detective Boyle.

ALI AND CODI WATCHED cartoons on TV while I took my cell phone and went upstairs to our room. I didn't want them to overhear something that might put them on edge.

Luke answered his cell phone with a smile in his voice. "Hey, I was just about to call you." His cheeriness would be wiped away once I shared my news.

"Did you have fun last night?" It would be easier to tell him about the latest drama after we had a normal conversation. After Luke and I talked of his late night out with the other classmates from the training and of the high school girls' basketball win, I broke the news about Percy. "I've got a call in to the vet, but so far, he looks and acts normal. Well, as normal as he ever acts."

Percy found me in our bedroom as if he sensed I was talking about him. I petted his head while I continued. "There's no discoloration on his paws or ears."

Dead silence filled my ear, more deafening than if Luke had screamed. So far, he hadn't said a word once I told him about last night.

"Hello? You still there?"

I could hear him cracking his knuckles now, envisioned him pacing the hotel room, his cell phone sandwiched between his ear and shoulder. "Yep, I'm here." Another long pause. "So, how do *you* think Percy ended up outside?"

"Someone had to have let him out from our backyard." There was an edge to my words as if I'd sliced them off my tongue. I'd already told Luke about the footprints leading from the paved trail to the fence door. "I thought for sure I locked the back door after I let Percy in, but maybe the lock didn't catch. You know how sometimes ice builds up on the door frame and the lock doesn't connect." We both knew it, yet I felt as if he didn't consider that possibility.

"And why would someone do that, Lily?" The happiness that had laced his words when I first called was replaced by disbelief and mistrust. I all but felt it through the phone.

"How in the world would I know? Maybe it was high school kids pulling a prank." I didn't believe it, but it was the most plausible excuse. "You know, how teenagers toilet paper other teens' trees..." As if toilet papering a yard was similar to endangering a dog's life.

"Did you call Boyle yet?"

"He's next. I wanted to tell you first."

Luke exhaled a long sigh of frustration. "Okay. Well, let me know what he says."

We hung up a few minutes later. Before I could call the detective, our landline rang. It was Percy's veterinarian. After several questions, she gave me the thumbs-up on keeping him home. "Monitor him the next few days in case anything changes."

I promised to do that, and we hung up. She hadn't read me the riot act like Luke had. Although he hadn't said the words, I heard them all the same. He knew I didn't feel well yesterday when I'd come home from work. He hadn't asked if I'd taken something to make myself feel better, something to alter my judgment, but he no doubt wondered about it.

I hadn't taken so much as a Tylenol last night. Pria had spoken with me when she came home. She could back me up. But since Luke hadn't asked, I hadn't offered an alibi.

After speaking with the vet, I called Boyle's cell number.

He answered right away. "Lily." The one word in his deep, soothing voice took my blood pressure down an octave.

"I'm sorry to call you on the weekend, but you said I could call anytime." I stumbled over the apology.

"I meant it. No need to apologize. Everything okay?"

I gave him a summary of last night.

"I'm coming over. I'll be there in ten minutes."

"Thank you, Detective. I appreciate it." We hung up, and I changed out of my pajamas.

By the time he arrived, I had a pot of coffee ready for him and a green smoothie for me. "Let's have a look at the boot prints first," Boyle said as I met him at the front door.

I donned my boots and coat again and led him to the backyard where the prints began. He took out a camera.

"I don't see footprints leading *to* your backyard, only *from* the backyard," Boyle said as he snapped photos, his large boot next to the boot print. "I wear a size twelve boot. These are similar in size." He tucked the camera back in his coat pocket and looked around our yard.

"Any prints from there?" He pointed to the end of our road, the cul-de-sac several yards from the paved trail and lake.

"I didn't look anywhere else."

"Well, let's do it." Boyle nodded toward the street. We walked next to each other, studying the snow like crime scene dogs sniffing out a body.

On the other side of the cul-de-sac, we spotted footprints leading from the trail to the pavement. Boyle took more photos, again with his boot next to the print. We looked around as if the person would miraculously appear. It had been windy the past few days, and between that and our family's activity in the yard, it was conceivable we'd missed other signs.

Boyle crossed his arms over his heavy coat. "It's hard to see how they got from here to your backyard fence, but they could've walked up your driveway and then close to the shrubs, circling your house."

We walked up the plowed driveway—thanks to the man we'd hired to maintain our driveway and sidewalk while Luke was gone—then walked the edge of the shrubs to our backyard. It was conceivable that they'd taken that route. It was the most reasonable assumption. Any other alternative meant someone had been inside our home last night.

After Boyle and I went inside the kitchen, I poured him a cup of coffee. I sat across from him with a glass of green smoothie as he made notes of everything I'd told him. "We will park a sheriff deputy's SUV in your driveway until Luke gets back. It should deter whoever did this from coming back. I can also alert the deputy who patrols this area to make sure he patrols this street at night."

With our development outside of the city limits, the sheriff's department, instead of the city of Lakeview's police department, protected our area. I didn't care who watched out for us. I had proof that someone, or a group of people, was messing with us. I hadn't made those footprints, and I sure as hell hadn't left Percy outside.

He took a sip of coffee. "How've things been for Pria at school?"

"Better. I haven't heard of anyone harassing her in the past couple of months. Why? Do you think this was a teen prank?" I hadn't told him of my analogy to Luke.

"I sure as hell hope not. This is no prank, as you well know. I will, however, stop by the high school tomorrow and talk to the principal in case he has heard of any gossip about something like this at school. I'll let you know what I find out." He pointed at me with the black licorice from his pocket.

"Is there a time of day you don't eat that?" I nodded at the licorice.

"When I'm sleeping." He winked.

"I didn't think that ever happened." I laughed, a reaction that surprised me after the stress of the past several hours.

He stood to leave, and I followed him to the door. "I'll have someone drop off the SUV later this afternoon." Boyle took a bite of licorice and zipped his coat. I watched him walk back to his vehicle, thankful he believed me.

LUKE ARRIVED HOME LATE Friday night. In those five nights, I slept about fifteen hours. Nothing had happened, yet my nerves were on constant high alert. Boyle had turned nothing up after speaking with the high school principal, and nothing unusual had occurred around our area.

I stood in our living room and watched Luke pull into our driveway. I hated the damsel-in-distress notion that I needed a protector, yet the relief I felt at him coming home overpowered the happiness I felt at seeing him again. I was an independent woman. At least I used to be. Then I'd become someone afraid of her own shadow. He pulled into the garage. I opened the door from our kitchen, excited to welcome him home.

The garage was cold. As I stepped into his arms, Luke's embrace warmed me. "I'm so glad to be home," he murmured into my neck.

I pulled away and took in his bleary eyes. Between his mentally draining classes and his nights worrying about our family's safety, it had been a long couple of weeks.

He grabbed his suitcase and followed me into the kitchen. "I'm ready for a beer. Want anything?" Luke pulled out a Coors Light from the fridge, and I wondered if it was a test. We'd talked daily since last Saturday, and once I told him about Boyle's agreement that it had been someone outside our family who'd let Percy out, I felt trust reenter our conversations.

"I'll make a cup of hot tea."

We sat in the kitchen and rehashed the details of last Saturday night, including the lack of problems for Pria at school. Things were returning to normal for her, if there was such a thing.

Chapter 24

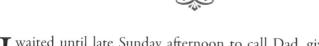

I waited until late Sunday afternoon to call Dad, giving me two nights to catch up on sleep after Luke had arrived home. I didn't want to be overtired and overly emotional when I called. Farm work was minimal in March, and Dad was often in the house by midafternoon until it was time to milk the cows again at night.

Mom answered their landline, and we visited awhile before I asked to speak with Dad. I had a beef with her, too, upset that she hadn't fought more for Jacob and hadn't done enough to fix things after Earl's evil deeds had come to light. Jacob had told me to let it go, but I couldn't until I spoke with Dad.

"Hello, sweetie." His voice, which normally calmed me, caused my heart to palpitate. "How's things with my perfect granddaughters?" Mom and Dad were softies with their granddaughters, likely the only grandchildren they would have.

"They're fine. We dodged a snowstorm here, and Pria has been watching the high school girls' basketball playoffs." I cleared my throat, closing my eyes as if it would center my thoughts. "Dad? I need to talk to you about something."

"Um, sure. What's up?" Caution etched his words.

"I talked to Jacob a couple of weeks ago, went to visit him." My hand covered my mouth for a second, hoping to control the words. "I know what happened now, Dad."

It was as if someone dropped an atomic bomb on our conversation. As difficult as confronting him was for me, I reminded myself that my call had blindsided Dad.

"Why didn't you believe Jacob? Why didn't you fight for him?" My voice broke, much as my heart did, thinking of my ignorance through Jacob's years of pain.

This was a conversation I'd hoped to have in person, but we wouldn't see Mom and Dad until Easter. I couldn't wait another six weeks or more.

"It's not your bridge to burn, Lily," Dad said. As if I hadn't been affected by it all.

"No, it was *yours* to fix, and you didn't. You turned your back on your son! Look what it did to Jacob, not to mention our entire family. You took him from my life, from Mom's life... because you didn't want to believe the truth!" I clutched a tissue, dabbing at my damp eyes.

When he spoke, his voice was hoarse. "Don't you think I know all of that? Don't you think I have beaten myself up a million times for not believing Jacob back then? Here's the thing. Earl was good. He'd set me up ahead of time, telling me things Jacob supposedly did or didn't do, making it sound like Jacob slacked off, not doing work for Earl so he could go hang out with his friends." Dad paused, and I swallowed a sob.

"By the time Jacob confessed what was happening, I was already pissed at him. I figured it was another excuse to get out of work, just as Earl said Jacob had done. Of course, Earl lied. I trusted the wrong person. It happens, Lily. I'm not proud of it."

There was a long pause before Dad continued. "Things were—they were different back then." Dad choked between his words as if they were so dry he couldn't get them out. "I know that's no excuse. And believe me, it kills me every time I have to go near the ground where the shed used to be." He blew his nose. "If there was a way to remove a chunk of earth, I'd do it."

"How could you and Mom not sense Jacob's pain?" It pulled at my heart to hear Dad's anguish, but it was nothing compared to my brother's years of trauma.

"You don't know how many times I wish I'd believed him. Back then, before the Catholic Church's sexual abuse and the Boy Scout sexual abuse came to light, we didn't understand 'trustworthy adults' weren't always trustworthy." Dad's voice quivered, both of us fighting back tears so we could get through this conversation in one piece.

"Hell, teenagers lie to their parents all the time. It wasn't the first time he lied to me about something. I know how stupid that sounds now." Dad's voice became a whisper as if he was talking to himself. "Who would make up that kind of excuse?"

I tried to empathize. It wasn't as if Jacob and I had been saints when we were young. Still, we wouldn't have lied about something as serious as rape.

"You know Earl was like a brother to me," he continued. "Who in the hell wants to believe the guy they considered family, one who'd worked alongside them for twenty years, would do that kind of sick shit to their son?"

I pinched the bridge of my nose, picturing Dad doing the same. "Yes, and Jacob is your son. Who in the hell wants to have to tell their dad that they were raped by a man the family trusted?" I felt like a bully, throwing punches at a man who'd already been beaten down. But if I didn't purge those words then, they would forever fester in my heart.

It was another hour before Dad and I hung up, saying "I love you" with a heavy coat of forgiveness. We all liked to believe what we wanted, what we hoped to be true. Nobody wanted to see the monster in front of them. Especially when it was someone they'd invited into their life.

INSTEAD OF OUR BIMONTHLY get-together for our charity, our group headed for dinner at Christina's restaurant of choice. Tomorrow, St. Patrick's Day, Christina would turn thirty-two. I had been thirty-two when Ali was born, a time in my life that now seemed like someone else's.

Christina had chosen a downtown restaurant known for its prime rib sandwiches. Barb, Judith, Maria, and I rode together, with Barb driving. Christina and two other early-thirties teachers met us at the restaurant.

Not a fan of prime rib, I chose salmon and paired it with a glass of pinot noir. After dinner, our server brought out a large slice of seven-layer chocolate cake for Christina, and we sang for her birthday. Afterward, some of the younger women pumped coins into the jukebox, and Maria and Judith walked over to meet a friend of Maria's daughter at another table.

I was on my way to the restroom when Brook came up behind me. "Hey there, Lily. It's good to see you out enjoying yourself." She hugged my shoulders. "I'm at the table over there." She pointed to a table a dozen feet away.

"I'll stop by in a minute. Duty calls first." I grinned, nodding to the restroom door.

"Sounds good." Brook headed back to her table.

I joined her a few minutes later. I kept an eye on our table, my coworkers coming and going as a few played pull tabs or stopped to visit with others. They would let me know when they were ready to leave.

"Have a seat." Brook nodded to the empty chair next to her. Brook's friends had gone off to play pool. "I talked to Doyle the other day. He told me about his recent visit to your home." She leaned forward. "Everything okay since then?"

"Yes. Everything's been good. At least, as of this second." I smiled at her question, feeling her support.

"Good. Remember, you can call me anytime too."

We visited for a few more minutes until I spotted my friends back at the table. "I'd better go. They're circling the wagons." Brook stood, and we embraced before I rejoined my friends.

"Maria won one hundred dollars on a pull tab!" Judith announced.

We all clapped at Maria's good fortune.

"The good-looking dude at the bar with the white shirt bought Christina a birthday drink. He wanted her phone number in exchange, but she drives a hard bargain." Barb grinned.

"Geez, I don't have anything exciting to report," I said, thankful for the lack of excitement in my life at the moment.

We collected our purses and coats, and it was after nine when Barb dropped me off at home. Luke looked up from the book he was reading on the sofa as I walked in the front door.

"You're in a good mood." He nodded at the bounce in my step.

"We had fun." I hung up my coat before walking to the kitchen, where I downed a glass of water. "I'm so thirsty. The salmon must've been saltier than I realized." I filled the glass again and drank it.

As soon as the water hit my stomach, it churned as if the salmon had come alive in the water. I braced my hands on the kitchen counter as a wave of nausea hit. Luke came up behind me, circling his arms around my waist.

"Ugh, please don't touch my stomach. I feel queasy."

He stepped to my side. "What did you eat?"

"Salmon."

"Did it taste like it was cooked well enough?"

"Yes." I took another deep breath. "I'm heading to bed."

"Good idea. I'll be up in a minute." Luke went into the living room to retrieve his book. I stood at the sink, wanting another glass of water yet leery of the aftereffect.

Holy shit! The Tasmanian Devil had taken over my body. My forehead and neck broke out in a clammy sweat, and my heart raced. I couldn't blame the one glass of wine I'd sipped over a three-hour period. I wanted to lie down on the kitchen floor with a barf bag.

Instead, I stumbled up our steps, catching myself before I tumbled backward.

Luke ran from the living room to support me from behind. "You okay?" I hated the wariness in his eyes.

"I'm fine. Just misjudged the step." I held onto the railing with one hand, my other clutching a glass of water. With Luke's help, I made it to our bedroom, set the water on the nightstand, gathered my pajamas, then headed into our bathroom. It hit me in the shower.

I was going to be sick. Like, vomit-from-my-toes-to-my-head sick. I'd gone from feeling good to what-the-hell-crawled-inside-me sick in less than thirty minutes.

My body exploded in a full-fledged sweat. I turned the shower water to cold, hoping to stop what I feared would erupt from me. My hand slid down the side of the shower, needing a support bar closer to the ground. I kneeled near the drain while everything I'd consumed over dinner came back up. I hovered above the drain, my eyes closed. No need to revisit the meal, which would only make me more nauseous.

"Hey, Lily!" Luke rapped on the shower glass door. "You okay? Can I help?" I didn't realize he'd come in the bathroom. I opened my eyes to see Luke's gray sweatpants through the fogged-up shower wall.

"Wait!" I shouted above the water before getting sick again. There was nothing he could do at this point. A few minutes later, I was freezing and relatively sure I had emptied my stomach. I stood back up, turned the water on hot, and finished my shower.

Luke enveloped me in a towel as I stepped out of the shower, steam surrounding us. He dried off my hair and body and pulled me to him, rubbing my arms and back. My muscles ached. Shaky and dizzy, I melted into his comfort.

"What did you have with your salmon, a poltergeist?"

I leaned back to look at him. "Yep, and let me tell you, the grilled salmon tastes putrid the second time around."

"That's it? What did you have to drink?"

"One glass of wine. And you know they only fill the glass halfway at the restaurant. I'm serious, Luke. I didn't feel the least bit tipsy. Or nauseous." I thought back. "Well, on the ride home, I sat in the back. I remember feeling a little light-headed but figured it was because Barb had the heat cranked up for Judith and Maria."

I stepped away to get my pajamas on. "I'm better now." I brushed my teeth and gargled several times before snuggling next to Luke in bed. The room spun if I closed my eyes.

Luke pulled me to him, wrapping his arm around me. Feeling sick was much more tolerable when you had someone to care for you.

Soon, Luke's steady breathing filled the quiet. Although I felt better, I couldn't turn my brain off, again wondering what had happened to me. Maybe my body would forever be sensitive to things after the attack. I'd rarely gotten sick before. But I felt off so often that nothing surprised me—or Luke—anymore.

Ah, Luke. My rock. My buoy when I felt like I was drowning. A man I always wanted beside me. While he slept, I thought of our honeymoon, the challenges it had brought, and the trust it'd fused between Luke and me.

We'd gone camping in the Wisconsin wilderness, where we'd had to rely on each other for the first time as a married couple. Seventeen years later, our resilience had been tested again, over and over.

Luke had been in charge of the camping equipment for our honeymoon, assuring me, "I've got this." My job was our food and drinks. Two hours away from my parents' farm, our drive ended after five miles on a potholed gravel road, our teeth rattling like dice as

Luke drove and I double-checked the road map to make sure we were in the right spot. The rugged campsite looked empty, with not a single soul anywhere.

Luke parked the truck. We picked out the most level spot next to a small creek, and he worked on setting up our tent. I unloaded our totes of towels, sleeping bags, food, and four-gallon jugs of water. When he finished, Luke unfolded two large air mattresses he'd packed.

"Aw, shit!" He looked all around as if someone had played a prank on him.

I walked over to him, carrying a tote. "What's wrong?"

He rummaged inside a duffel bag. "I can't find the foot pump for the air mattresses."

It had been a long day for us. "It's okay. I'm so tired, I could sleep on the ground. Isn't that what roughing it is all about?"

"We're not sleeping on the ground on our wedding night. This is 1993, not 1893. I'll manually blow them up." Frustration and exertion heated his neck and face.

My mouth hung open. "You shouldn't do that. You'll pass out."

"I'll be fine. I'll take my time. And drink water. And beer." Luke grinned.

I reached inside a cooler and took out a jug of water, poured a plastic cup full for each of us, then cracked open a beer for him. He chugged half of it down before settling in to blow up the first mattress. I hoisted the cooler with our food in it—beef jerky, peanuts, bread, peanut butter, fruit, potato chips, and other snacks—and made my way into the woods.

"Hey, where are you going with the food?" Luke asked. "Why put it so far away?"

"How close do you want the bear?" I grinned at him.

"Dammit. I hate that you're so nature savvy. This city boy has been trying to impress you, and I fear I'm failing miserably." He went back to blowing up the air mattresses, and I leaned in to kiss his cheek.

"I'll get us kindling for the campfire," I whispered into his flushed cheek.

After we finished our chores, we worked together on our campfire, determined to do it without the backup Bic lighters in the truck's glove compartment. We made a tepee out of the sticks, gathered dry leaves, then Luke went to work, using the bow drill he'd brought along.

"Wow! Impressive." My eyebrows rose. "See? You've got moves, city boy."

He rubbed his roughened hands together. "Thanks. Uncle Herb spent days teaching me how to use this. The man has patience."

We settled against two tree trunks, a drink in one hand and holding hands with the other, as we sweated in front of the fire.

For the next three days, we hiked through the woods, bathed in the narrow river, and never saw another living soul. By the end of our rough-around-the-edges honeymoon, it had proven our resilience many times over. We weren't quitters. Especially when it came to us.

Chapter 25

Paying bills was one of my jobs. I'd never missed a payment on anything—or so I thought. Our electric bill was due the fifteenth of every month, and it wasn't until I received a late notice in the mail on the twenty-second that I realized I'd not paid March's.

I swore we hadn't received one in the mail, and I tore through my file of bills at our desk that night. No March electric bill. It had probably gotten lost in the mail. I called the next morning, paid by credit card, and shrugged it off.

Two days later, Pria came home from school with her underwear in a knot. "Mom, you still owe the school for the softball league fee. I can't start practice next week until you pay." She whined like a two-year-old.

"Did you bring something home about it?" I didn't remember seeing the paperwork.

"No, they emailed you. Coach said the email went out a couple of weeks ago." Pria followed me to our home computer sitting on the desk, looking over my shoulder as I logged in as if she thought I would pull a fast one and delete something.

I scrolled through my inbox, searched for our school district's email address, and checked my spam folder, although it shouldn't have ended up there since I received emails regularly from our district. Nothing. "I must have deleted it by accident. I'll send a check with you tomorrow."

As I wrote out the check for Pria, I reminded myself to be more careful when I went through my emails and our mail. Clearly, my brain wasn't firing on all cylinders. Something I wouldn't admit to anyone.

Except Kara. And I would see her this weekend for a welcome getaway. A much-needed break from the nasty demon in my head blaming myself for every single thing that seemed to go wrong. I didn't feel I needed to visit Dr. Arlene again. She was another person on my emergency list, along with Detective Boyle and Brook. I appreciated them all but didn't want to need their services ever again. As if I could ward off my need for them, I spent half an hour each night playing either my flute or the piano, hoping the music would dance my problems away.

I'd quit swim lessons once I'd gone back to teaching and missed the endorphins. Soon, the weather would warm up, the streets would dry out, and I could attempt running again. Whether or not I ran, I wanted to restart swim lessons and enroll our children soon. Swimming could save our lives, and in the land of ten thousand lakes, I wanted to feel safe about embracing our area lakes.

THE LAST WEEKEND IN March, I left early Saturday morning and drove ninety miles north to visit Kara in Clear Creek. Her husband, Harry, was out of town for the weekend. Luke was more than happy to hang out at home with our daughters, and I guessed Pria was thrilled to have me out of the house for a couple of days.

We were back to butting heads off and on, and I considered it the lesser of two evils. I would take it over her treating me like china after the attack, back when she worried I would die. She would be sixteen soon. Her volatile hormones wouldn't last forever.

My time with Kara was too precious for us to do much but hang out in her living room and eat, drink, and talk. She caught me up on her life, how things were at her restaurant, Pizzorno's, how Harry's mother—diagnosed several years ago with schizophrenia—was faring, and what was new with some of her friends I'd met over the years.

Then we got down to the nitty-gritty of my life. We rehashed the latest concerns of lost mail, lost emails, feeling off or ill, and most concerning, the night someone had let Percy outside. I'd spoken to Kara on the phone since then, but often my family was within earshot and I would filter my words to avoid confessing what was going on in my mind.

"I swear, Kara, I think someone came into our house and let him out. Everything was locked except maybe the sliding glass door." I hugged one of her sofa pillows to my chest as we each curled up on recliners. "It creeps me out. Whoever was in our house could have come upstairs while we were sleeping!"

The top of our staircase was across from the girls' bedrooms. Ours was farther down the hall. I would never have heard the person.

"They had to have known Luke wasn't home, don't you think?" Kara shook her head. "Percy could've died! What if Pria hadn't heard him barking?"

We commiserated over the horrific possibilities of everything that could have gone wrong. I'd brought my getting-longer-by-the-day list of everything I'd sensed happened that I hadn't done, that I had no control over, and I handed it to Kara.

While Kara sipped her glass of cabernet, she studied my list even though she now knew of every situation. It helped to see the timeline in black and white.

After a few minutes, she looked up, her dark eyes locking with mine. "I have to ask this, so don't bitch slap me when I'm done. You are one thousand percent sure you had nothing to do with any of this? You didn't take a pill that you shouldn't have?" She tilted her head and studied my reaction.

Kara's directness didn't surprise or hurt me. I'd lied by omission to her last fall when I'd pretended I didn't crave to numb my life with opioids. She'd known the truth then. She deserved the truth now.

"I'm ninety-nine percent sure, and that's about as sure as I can get. If everyone had treated me and my family with respect and understanding after Dastard's arrest, I wouldn't question things so much. But a small part of the community is still being nasty, and I can't help but believe someone is still pissed off enough to try to make my life miserable."

Kara set my list and her wine glass down. "Maybe it's time for you to get the hell out of there." She leaned forward in her recliner. "Hey, your family would love Clear Creek."

I raised an eyebrow. "You know what? I've thought of that a lot. But Luke and I have preached to Pria about not taking the easy way out and facing things head-on. I wouldn't mind a fresh start, but with Pria in high school, we don't want to yank her out of there and make her start her junior year in a new place. Things have been tough enough for her already."

Later that evening, we met with Kara's friends for dinner and a movie. By the time I drove home on Sunday, I felt rested, recharged, and ready to take on life again.

APRIL SHOWERS WASHED away the remnants of snow. It also brought signs of spring, one of them being high school prom. Pria often did everything possible to avoid me or, if we spent over five minutes together, annoy me. Unless she wanted something. A junior boy she worked with at the grocery store had asked her to prom.

We'd met him a few times, and he seemed like a decent kid. Luke and I talked about whether Pria should go since it was only her sophomore year. If the past months of trauma hadn't affected her life, we would have said no, that she could wait until next year. But her life had been far from normal.

After Luke and I gave her permission, Pria asked to dress shop with Sylvie and Erin. I wanted most of her body parts covered and for the dress to cost less than her first year of college. When I insisted on being there, it killed her desire to have her friends go with us. But shopping with me was better than her not going to prom.

We went shopping the second Saturday in April, one of the few days she didn't have softball practice. Her first game would be next week. Pria was quiet as usual in the passenger seat as we headed to the mall late that morning.

I hummed a quirky Beatles song, "Yellow Submarine," one of their many odd songs that shuffled on repeat in my head. Their lyrics made little sense, much like my life. And humming calmed me.

Apparently, it didn't have the same effect on Pria. "Stop it! Your humming is so annoying."

I stopped midsong, not daring to finish so I wouldn't incur her wrath before our trip even began. I drove the last ten miles in silence.

We hit several stores in the mall, exchanging few words between us. I'd hoped our shopping excursion would be a chance for us to reconnect. Wishful thinking. We walked through the mall's concourse on our way to another store. Without realizing it, I rubbed my hand over the scar, hidden under my short hair, an action I found comforting. I caught Pria's sideways glance, and I pulled my hand away from my head. I never knew what might embarrass her those days.

Instead, her expression softened. She blinked several times, a telltale sign of her lying, but she said nothing. The only other reason she would blink was to fight back tears.

It lifted my spirits enough that hope put a bounce in my step. Yet with every dress I suggested in the next store, I received an "old lady," "butt-ugly," or "no way" response from her.

"At least I'm getting two words out of you at a time." I hoped to flip the switch from stressful to enjoyable. Luke and I had made sure Pria worked fewer hours at the grocery store with softball added to her schedule. Pria had tolerated my many moods over the past several months. I could handle hers.

She answered my comment with a small grin. I would take it.

"I'm going to sit down over there. When you find some to try on, let me know." I gave up on my suggestions, realizing it was easier to veto if needed. "Just remember, it needs to cover up the necessary body parts."

Pria had a small bust, her build similar to mine—petite and muscular. Several minutes later, she waved an armful of dresses at me as she headed to the dressing room. I got up and followed her. Every single dress she tried on looked good, but she shone in the coral-colored one. And the price tag didn't make me choke.

Pria was happy. So was I. In fact, we were so darn knee-slapping happy that we stopped for burgers on the way home. I couldn't remember the last time we had gone out to eat, just the two of us. It was something we needed to do more often. She was still my baby girl. And in two years, she would be off to college.

WHEN I CAME HOME FROM work the following Monday and checked our mail, my fingers grazed something cold and scaly. My hand recoiled, and I peered inside. Whoever was behind it should've known that farm girls aren't afraid of snakes—dead or alive. The dead garter snake didn't tick me off. But having our mail tampered with did. Barb had mentioned last week that her son and his fiancée had mailed their wedding invitations a few weeks ago. She asked if I was attending since we hadn't responded yet.

Her son was getting married in June, and as far as I knew, we hadn't received our invitation. "We never received it," I'd told her.

What I didn't tell her was that between the invitation, our March electric bill, and now the dead snake in our mailbox, I was certain someone was stealing some of our mail.

Messing with mail was a federal crime. I would have to prove that was the case and not a problem with my memory. I wanted to get a post office box. I suggested it to Luke that night.

He shook his head. "It'd be a hassle. The post office is nowhere near my work or yours. Most of the bills are on auto pay already, aren't they?"

"Yes, but that's not the point." I told him of the two recent mail items we hadn't received and the dead snake from today. "What else has gone missing that we don't know about?"

He ran a hand through his hair. "Who knows? Do whatever you want. It was a long day at work. I'm going to bed." Luke turned and headed upstairs, leaving me with a feeling I was making a mountain out of a molehill.

It all came down to trust, and I no longer trusted people to leave our mail alone. I thought of a recent phone conversation with Jacob. "I don't know who to trust anymore," I'd said.

"Trust nobody right now, unless they live hours away. It's taken me a long time to build up my trust in people again," Jacob had replied. "For you, be wary of anyone in your town. People you love, people who you think love *you*—they may not be trustworthy." He'd learned about trust the hard way. I would have to do the same.

Reconnecting with Jacob reminded me of the person I'd been in our youth. Tough. Resilient. Determined. I'd gone soft the past few years. Like a warrior donning their armor, it was time to step up and be that farm girl again. I not only had myself to fight for but my family as well.

Chapter 26

On Tuesday, I called and signed Ali and Codi up for beginner swimming lessons, and I signed up for advanced beginners. We would start our biweekly lessons the Tuesday after Easter, giving us enough of a jump before summer hit.

I also drove to the post office on my lunch break and opened a post office box for us. We could keep the mailbox for the time being, until I changed everything over to the PO box, but I would begin using that address for all our bills from now on.

I told Luke that night about our swim lessons and the new mailing address. "I think the swim lessons are a good idea. It's too bad Pria's so busy right now. She could use them. So could I. But the post office box?" He rolled his eyes. "I think you're overreacting."

We were in the backyard. Luke raked while I cleaned out a flower bed.

I took a calming breath before answering him. "You know something's going on, right? Someone let Percy out that night. Someone sent those creepy dismembered dolls last December. Someone called in orders and pretended to be me." My words picked up speed.

Luke and I stood a few feet away from each other, but the distance between us felt like miles. He pressed his lips together and gave me a small nod. I sensed he wanted to believe me. He should.

"And I think whoever is doing that is also messing with our mail."

Whenever I pictured the phantom person harassing us, the image of Ed from the grocery store came to mind. I hadn't seen him since our confrontation back in November, but I had no idea how many other "Eds" were out there, still blaming me instead of Dastard.

Luke walked over and placed his hands on my arms. "Yes, everything you said is probably true. But I also know that you missed the email about Pria's softball league, that you took pills last fall when you didn't remember taking them. That you did several things you didn't remember." He didn't need to say more.

I was still mortified about last fall, embarrassed at what I'd said to Erin about the size of a horse's penis when she'd called for Pria, and ashamed of every other thing Luke had told me about that I only had a vague recollection of.

"I'm worried about a possible underlying health problem." Luke leaned down to meet my eyes. "I'm not saying those things didn't happen, but I also wonder if there isn't some lingering issue from the attack that has affected your memory."

He reminded me of the several times where I didn't feel right, felt woozy or nauseous. "The doctors said you should have no long-term effects, but it might be worth checking. What do you think about getting some blood work done?"

"I've thought of that, maybe another CT scan too." I put my hand on his chest. "I swear, Luke, it isn't all me." *Please, God, it can't be all me.*

He pulled me in for a hug, and I inhaled the earthy scent of spring surrounding us, basking in the warmth of him and the sunshine.

I MADE A DOCTOR'S APPOINTMENT the next morning before the lines blurred in my day. It was an especially challenging start, with one of my students vomiting in our classroom, and by early afternoon it felt as if someone had split my head with an ax.

Words in the book ricocheted off each other as I struggled to read to the students. By recess, an anxious, nasty gremlin had crawled inside me. Barb and I stood next to each other on the playground, and I focused on holding myself together.

"You okay?" The fine lines around Barb's eyes deepened as she studied me.

I nodded, my lips pressed together.

"Maybe you took the wrong dose of a medication?" Barb poked in my business.

"I'm fine, Nosy Nelly. Don't be such a nagging mother clucker!" I walked away with my sharp tongue, my acidic words haunting me into the evening when the haze cleared. I apologized profusely to Barb the next day, accepting a forgiveness I didn't deserve.

THE TEMPERATURE HIT eighty degrees on Sunday, a perfect day for our annual family ritual of carrying our lightweight aluminum rowboat to the lake access near our house. The neighborhood lake was more like a large swamp, used mostly for canoeing. Two docks next to the access were used by anyone who wanted to tie up their nonmotorized watercraft.

Normally, Luke and I carried it, but today, Pria helped so I wouldn't injure my hands and shoulder. The air was warm, but the only family member brave enough to swim in the cold, murky water was Percy. And although we would never swim in the lake, I was glad I'd enrolled Ali, Codi, and myself in swim lessons. Maybe Pria would have time that summer for lessons. Possibly even Luke.

The following day, I had a CT scan done, along with blood work. I would get the results before we left for the farm on Friday for the long Easter weekend. My doctor reiterated the importance of plenty of rest, managing stress through exercise and music, a healthy diet—although she knew me well enough to know I had that covered—and if the results showed nothing unusual, to follow up with her in a few months.

When our group of coworkers met on Wednesday night to work on Easter baskets for children in need, Judith brought up the dog park in our neighborhood development. "I take my two collies there a lot now that the weather is nice again. I find it so peaceful."

"Good idea," I said. Percy had the freedom to run in our backyard, and we took him for walks. I was slowly working my way up to running again but not enough to give him a workout.

"I like to go when it's not busy, later in the morning on weekends," Judith said.

I made a mental note of it. We would take Percy with us to the farm that weekend, but after that, until I worked up to running a few miles again, Percy could run free at the dog park.

The doctor's office called me Thursday with the results from the CT scan and blood work. Everything appeared normal. I wasn't sure if that was good or bad news. I should've been happy with a clean bill of health, but it meant I had no excuse for whatever the hell was happening to me.

THE DRIVE DOWN THE familiar dirt road welcomed me with its intoxicating, comforting scent. *Dorothy was right. There really is no place like home.*

But I hadn't been home since my visit with Jacob and my candid phone conversation with Dad. My brother's painful past covered my old sunshiny view of the farm with a filthy film.

With school closed for Good Friday, Luke had taken the day off, and we arrived at the farm just in time for lunch. I helped Mom set the table, with sandwiches and potato salad for our meal, while Luke got the girls settled in Jacob's old bedroom.

After lunch, I followed Dad out to the pasture, where he'd been working on a broken gate. Dad continued to make repairs even though his back had never been the same since his surgery years ago. They had an offer on the farm. It would be their last summer there, and although I never thought I would want to say goodbye to the cherished home that'd helped make my childhood idyllic, the land was tainted.

The area where the mechanic's shed had burned down years ago was fifty yards from us. Grass and brush had grown over the charred ground, the remnants of the shed long gone. Dad and I talked little, focusing our conversation on the next phase of life for him and Mom instead of looking back at the emotional baggage from the past.

On Saturday morning, Dad and Luke took our daughters for a walk to a small creek where my brother and I used to fish. Mom stayed back to do some baking. They all understood I needed time alone to visit the site where my brother's life had been forever changed. It was a chunk of earth that I wished would be swallowed up in a sinkhole.

I headed to where the shed once stood and found a section of grass growing in the spring sunshine. I pulled off my socks and shoes and stood barefoot, my body one with the earth where Jacob had lost his innocence, his heart and soul. With my eyes closed, I mentally ripped Earl apart before he could ever lay a finger on my little brother.

The man I'd looked at as a favorite uncle in my youth was a monster. As I stood there, I wondered what had happened in Earl's past to make him do such a thing. Some people were "bad seeds," born evil to the core, but often, it was a domino effect from their upbringing.

We were lucky Earl hadn't messed Jacob's life up so much that my brother had turned and ruined someone else's. Jacob had lived a secluded life for twenty years, and I wondered if it was so nobody could get too close to him.

I stood in silence amid the budding trees. Spring brought the promise of a fresh start. Most of us got second chances in life, an opportunity to move on. But I couldn't do that until I had answers.

I slipped on my socks and shoes and made my way back to the house to help Mom with pies. It would be our last holiday at the farm. Mom and Dad's sale date was a month away, but per the purchase agreement, they would stay to help the new owner through the summer. At first, the sale of the farm had bothered me. I had fond memories of the cows, the scent of fresh-cut hay, and the sound of corn stalks fluttering in the breeze. But dirty secrets tarnished that once-precious plot of ground. It would never be home again.

OUR SWIM LESSONS WERE every Tuesday and Thursday after school, which worked well with Pria's softball game schedule of Mondays and Wednesdays. On the first Wednesday in May, we attended her first home game.

I wore shorts and a tank top for the first time since the attack. The scar on my shoulder had faded, a wound I allowed the public to view. Luke would arrive soon after work. Ali and Codi played on the swings at the playground near the bleachers with other young children.

Pria had made the varsity team. We'd been nervous about her playing with juniors and seniors who might still hold a grudge against our family. So far, so good. Their team's pitcher, a senior, was terrific. Tall and muscular, the teen threw a strike like a pro.

Pria had said the girl was also a talented basketball player who'd received sports scholarship offers from several colleges. She struck out two girls in the first inning. When she stepped up to bat, she hit a home run.

I couldn't help but compare her to Dastard. *This exceptional athlete being wooed by several colleges... how would her team react if some-*

one accused her of something, and they hauled her off to serve time? I wouldn't have guessed such a bright, rising star was capable of hurting another person. The football community must have viewed Dastard the same way. *We believe what we see over what someone else tells us.*

Nobody had seen him attack me, and if he hadn't admitted to at least being there, many people would never have believed me. They'd relied on blind faith. Blind trust.

I watched Pria's teammates as they smiled and cheered on their star player, reminding me of a popular song Mom liked from around the time I was born. The lyrics, by Joe South, talked of how smiling faces can hide the evil in people. Someone else in my life was hiding their evil behind a smile.

Ali's scream interrupted my thoughts. I scrambled from the bleachers as she ran toward me, pulling Codi behind her. Neither appeared injured, but Ali's panic-stricken face put me on high alert.

"What's wrong?"

"Codi almost got in someone's car, Mom!" Nerves shook Ali's body like a jackhammer.

"What car?" My parental antenna shot up as I scanned the nearby parking lot as if a car would illuminate with "suspicion" written all over it.

"It was a black car with an old lady. She drove away when I grabbed Codi." Ali let go of her sister's hand. Codi folded her arms across her chest, and her bottom lip jutted out.

A dozen or more black vehicles were among the half-full parking lot near the playground equipment, close to the ball field and bleachers. I took Codi's hand, along with a deep breath. "Can you tell me what happened?" I'd get the rest of Ali's side of it in a minute.

Codi blinked several times. "I didn't do anything wrong. You and Daddy tell us to be polite, especially to old people."

"You're right. Did this woman ask for help?" We'd warned our girls of "stranger danger," but Codi was young, too naïve to understand the line between stranger danger and etiquette.

"I was pumping super high on the swing. That lady in her car yelled that she needed my help, so I did. You said we're supposed to help people, Mommy."

"Can you show me where she was?" I held Codi's hand, reached out for Ali's, then led them toward the playground. A dozen or so other children were playing, and Codi pointed to the edge of the parking lot closest to the swings.

"There. She had her window down and yelled at me."

"Did she say your name? How did you know she was talking to you?" Maybe she wanted any child that answered her.

"She said, 'Hey, girl on the swing,' or something like that. I can't remember." Codi's chin quivered.

"You aren't in trouble, Codi. I'm not angry. I just need to find out what happened." I pulled her to me, reassuring both Codi and myself that she was okay. "What did she say when you got to the car?"

"She had some of those sparkly pink dress-up shoes she wanted me to try on. She told me I looked like the same age as her granddaughter and wanted to make sure they'd fit her."

My throat swelled, making it difficult to speak. "What did you do?"

"I opened the door so I could try the shoes on. Then Ali yelled." She gave Ali the stink eye.

Poor Ali. This would set her back for days.

"Ali did the right thing, didn't she?" I pulled her in for a hug. I would need their help to get up, but kneeling on the grass and comforting my daughters was worth the leg pain.

"What did you see, Ali?"

Her face was blotchy. I thumbed tears off her cheeks.

"I was on the monkey bars when I saw Codi going to the black car. I yelled at her, but she didn't listen." Ali's words tumbled out in a shaky voice. "Codi opened the car door. I screamed at her and ran over there. The car left before I got there so I didn't see the lady."

"What did she look like, Codi?" I couldn't imagine an old lady wanting to kidnap a child. What they considered "old" might be my age. "Did she look like your grandma's age?"

"She had long gray hair and a big floppy hat. And big sunglasses on too."

I tried to imagine how the person had appeared to Codi. It sounded like a disguise to me, which meant it could have been anyone behind the wheel. "Did you open the door, or did she?"

"I was trying to get the door open, and she reached over to help me. When Ali yelled at me, the lady shut the door and left. Are you gonna tell Daddy? I don't want to be in trouble."

"You aren't in trouble, sweetheart. Yes, we need to tell Daddy. We can all thank Ali for being so brave." I tightened my grip on them, thinking of how today might have ended in tragedy.

"Let's see if Daddy is here yet." I would tell him before I called Detective Boyle. I should have called 911 right away, but the person was long gone by the time the girls found me. Law enforcement would need more than a black car as a description. Good luck getting a better description from one of the children on the playground. The eldest was around Ali's age. I doubted a nine-year-old could identify the make of the vehicle.

Luke had arrived by the time we returned. He stood by some men at the other end of the bleachers, watching the game from behind the chain-link fence. I jogged there, Ali and Codi beside me, then pulled Luke aside to fill him in on the possible kidnapping attempt. A minute later, I had Detective Boyle on my cell phone.

"I'll be there in five," he said.

Pria's softball game was in the seventh inning by the time we'd finished speaking with Boyle and other law enforcement. They interviewed children and adults who might have witnessed the interaction.

"We'll write it up as a kidnapping attempt, but even if we found the person—which is unlikely—we have nothing solid telling us what their intention was," Boyle said.

Frustration put an edge on Luke's and my worry. Other than one seven-year-old boy on the slide, nobody had noticed Codi run to the car. The whole thing had probably only lasted a minute. At least it was on record, along with an endless list of threats that had no solid evidence. Neither Luke nor I slept much that night. I doubted poor Ali did either.

Chapter 27

The following Saturday, I drove to Pria's out-of-town softball tournament, which was near Kara's home. Luke, Ali, and Codi took Percy to the dog park that morning and had plans to visit Minnehaha Falls that afternoon.

Kara met me at the game. We sat in the shade under a large maple tree after Pria's first game and ate the packed picnic lunch Kara had brought from Pizzorno's. Over our Italian pasta salad, I told her about Codi's possible near abduction.

"Holy shit, Lily! You called the detective, right?"

"Yes. It's now added to the list of things I've reported with no solid evidence." I rubbed my forehead. "The good thing is, it reaffirms my belief that someone is out to destroy me and my family. That I'm not losing it. There haven't been any other kidnapping attempts in our area."

"You aren't losing it. Yes, you struggled last fall. Any of us would. But that has nothing to do with this. How have you been feeling? You said the CT scan and blood work showed nothing unusual?"

"Most of the time, I'm okay. Sometimes at school, I struggle to stay awake later in the afternoon. It feels like I can't concentrate. There have been nights where I can't fall asleep, worrying about stupid things, so I'm probably just overtired." I took a drink from my water bottle. "I'm not running much yet, but I'm making up for it with swimming."

Ali and Codi were enjoying their swim lessons, and I felt much stronger that spring than I had last December.

"Even though I'm sure someone is messing with our lives, I still sense Luke's disbelief once in a while." I swallowed my emotions with a bite of salad. "Dastard's attack was horrible. But the months since then are putting a strain on our marriage."

"Luke loves you. He's got to be as frustrated as you are about everything."

I pulled apart a breadstick and studied it. "Luke loves me, but he doesn't trust me one hundred percent like he used to. And I can't blame him. I used to think we had a perfect marriage. Now I know there's no such thing."

"You've got a solid foundation for this shit pile that's been stacked on your family. You'll get through it." Kara rubbed my shoulder.

"I hope so. I think about a teacher at my school that went through a divorce a few years ago. She'd talked to me about what went wrong in their marriage, that it wasn't cheating, drinking, or anything like that, but losing their teenager. Even after counseling, they couldn't move past it. I remember pushing her to take divorce out of their options." I took a bite of the breadstick, chewing over the memory of how clueless I'd been. "I thought every marriage was like ours, never considering how things would be for us if we faced challenges. Now I get it."

I drew strength from Kara's understanding eyes. Her mother-in-law's schizophrenia had put a strain on their first years of marriage until Harry's mother had gotten the help she needed. "Everyone has something going on. And there's nothing wrong with your mind. You have a stalker. Someone's out to sabotage you."

"Yes. And when Dastard is released from the correctional facility in August, I'm going to be there to watch him walk out."

"Are you kidding me? Why would you do that?" Kara's eyebrows shot up.

"Because I want to see who picks him up." There had to be a connection between him and the things that had happened to me and my family since he'd been behind bars.

I needed something concrete. And I needed closure.

THE FOLLOWING WEEKEND was the Minnesota fishing opener, an annual weekend away for several of the men from our neighborhood development, including Luke. Shawn owned a rustic cabin two hours north, the perfect place for the men to fish, talk big, drink beer, and unwind. Luke needed it more than ever.

He had been looking forward to the weekend for a long time, but he insisted on driving separately "just in case."

"In case of what?" I asked but received no answer. The unknown possibilities loomed over both of us, leaving us leery in the days leading up to the trip.

A few days before Luke was scheduled to leave, I struggled in the classroom after lunch, feeling as if I had cement running through my veins and fireworks exploding in my brain. It was all I could do to keep it together. Much of the afternoon was a blur to me.

All I wanted to do was sleep. Instead, I stirred spaghetti sauce on the stove after work, doing everything I could to make sure it didn't slosh out of the pan. I thought I was doing okay with it until an ear-piercing noise sliced the air.

What the hell is that? My head pulsated with the noise as if it would explode. There was a commotion around me, and I swore I yelled for everyone to keep quiet, although I wasn't sure that the words ever left my mouth. Instead of my voice, I heard Luke's.

Luke's home?

"Are you freaking kidding, Lily? What's going on here?" Luke yelled through a hazy cloud of smoke. I turned toward the door and watched him take a broom from Codi, who had been waving it at the ceiling.

Oh yes, our smoke detector. That's what the noise is. The thought crawled through my brain in a calming sort of way until Ali screamed.

"The house is on fire! The house is on fire!" Ali backed away from the smoke billowing through the kitchen.

Luke carried a chair over to the smoke detector then disarmed it.

Finally! So annoying. Now where was I? I turned back to the pan, which had a stinky burnt smell, and was about to stir the sauce again when Luke appeared next to me with a potholder.

He turned off the stove and slid the pan off the burner. "Seriously, Lily? You burned spaghetti sauce?" The look in his squinting eyes made me feel as if I'd just committed a crime.

"And you forgot Ali at her after-school skills class." He stomped off to the backyard, taking Codi and Ali with him, and leaving me holding a wooden spoon. I tossed it in the sink, poured myself a glass of water, and went upstairs to lie down.

I hadn't wanted to cook supper, anyway.

WHEN I WOKE UP, THE alarm clock read 6:43. For a moment, I thought I'd overslept. Then I realized it was p.m., not a.m. The house was quiet downstairs, and as I lay there watching sunshine dance across our ceiling, the previous hours came back to me.

Not clearly, but enough to know something bad had happened. I hadn't felt right at school—again, and I remembered cooking spaghetti. And the smoke alarm. *Did I forget to pick up Ali?*

I didn't want to go downstairs and face Luke. But delaying it wouldn't help. I found him and our daughters in the backyard. Pria wore her softball uniform, jogging my memory that she had an away game after school.

"Did you just get home?" I walked outside to the patio, where Pria and Luke sat. "How did the game go?"

Pria shot daggers at me with her eyes. "Yes, and fine. We won." By her attitude and Luke cracking his knuckles, I would bet that he'd filled her in on whatever had happened earlier. Ali and Codi played with Percy and their Hula-Hoops, coaxing him to jump through them.

As soon as I sat, Pria stood as if I would infect her. "I'm going to shower." She picked up her plate with remnants of a grilled hotdog, ketchup, corn, and Doritos crumbs.

I leaned across the patio table toward Luke. He leaned back and crossed his arms over his chest, pulling his gray T-shirt tighter over it.

"I'm sorry for whatever happened." I should've made a recording of those words I'd said too often since last fall. Half of the time, I had no idea what I was sorry about.

Luke raised an eyebrow. "*Whatever happened*? Do you remember any of it, Lily? Because I sure do. So do Ali and Codi." Steam all but blew out his nostrils.

Luke turned to our girls, still busy teaching Percy. "How about you two go in and get cleaned up? Ali, can you help Codi wash her feet in the tub? We'll skip a bath tonight."

They ran past us, Ali stopping to give me a questioning look. Luke shooed them inside.

I waited until the sliding glass door closed before relaying the little I remembered. He filled in the rest. "You forgot Ali at her after-school social skills class but, amazingly enough, remembered to pick Codi up from school." I usually picked up Codi on the days Ali had class so that she wouldn't ride the bus home alone. I didn't remember it though. In fact, the past several hours were murky.

"Ali's counselor called me at work, asking if I planned to pick her up. They were closing soon, and you weren't answering your cell phone. Then we walked in here with the kitchen full of smoke, poor Codi waving the broom at the smoke detector, and you stirring a sauce that had bubbled over the stove and burned."

He stood and paced behind me. "I threw out the sauce, which you'd forgotten to put hamburger in, grilled hot dogs for the girls, and called it good." Luke stopped next to my chair. "The thing is"—his voice turned from steely to a whisper—"what scares me the most is that none of it seemed to bother you. It was like you were in a trance."

My hand reached for his, thankful when he didn't pull it away. "I swear, I don't know what happened. I didn't take anything, if that's what you're wondering."

"Well, I can't leave you alone this weekend with the kids. I'm going to call Shawn and tell him I won't make it for fishing opener."

"Don't do that! I promise I'll be fine." It was a ridiculous promise with too many possible land mines. Even I knew that. The pressure in my head felt like it would burst at any moment, and tears fought to be released, egged on by Luke's rare anger.

"You could have burned our house down, Lily. And you scared the hell out of Codi and Ali. Something has to change." Weariness and frustration sliced each word, pushing the lever on a dam I'd fought like hell to keep shut.

The gravity of the situation pulled me under, begging me to drown. And I did. A full-blown cryfest that I'd buried deep inside pushed its way out, finally releasing the pent-up fear of the unknown person destroying every single cell of my family.

I needed to fix everything, but it was like putting a bandage over a gunshot wound. "M-maybe your mom could stay here this weekend?" I used a napkin from the stack on the patio table to blow my nose, willing to admit I needed a babysitter. My mom was busy that time of year at the farm, especially now as they went over things with the new buyer.

My chest heaved, and sobs peppered my words. I couldn't breathe as panic and anxiety squeezed the air out of me. It was the first time in our relationship that I cried and Luke didn't comfort me. "You n-need to get away this weekend." The last thing I wanted was guilt at keeping him from a much-needed break. I thumbed at the incessant tears covering my cheeks.

Luke pressed his lips together as if willing himself to stay angry with me. "We'll see." He walked into the house, leaving me alone as I tried to claw through my mess of a life.

A few minutes later, his cell phone beeped. He'd left it on the patio table. When it beeped again with an incoming text, I pulled it toward me.

"Hey, Luke, it's Christina. I'm so sorry to bother you. Can you call me when you have a chance? Thanks."

What in the hell? Why is Christina texting Luke?

I sat there and stewed, thinking of a hundred reasons why. I marched inside, holding his cell phone out as if it was a venomous snake, and found Luke in the kitchen, bent over the dishwasher.

"Why is Christina texting you to call her?" For once, Luke was on trial instead of me.

"Christina?"

"Yes, from my school. How many do you know? Plus, I recognize her cell number."

He stood and took the phone from me. "I've no clue. She's never texted me before. See?" He scrolled up above the text, showing no previous history.

"How did she get your number?" I felt like a prosecuting attorney, ready to nail him for a possible crime.

"You're the one who gave it to her. You gave it to Barb, Judith, and Maria, too, when I was in North Carolina. You insisted on doing it in case something happened." He set the phone on the counter with such force I thought it would break.

My attitude deflated, but my curiosity did not. "Aren't you going to call Christina?"

"Nope." Luke turned and left the kitchen. "I'm going for a drive." A minute later, he pulled out of our driveway, and my heart ached as Luke became an island instead of my life raft.

Chapter 28

Luke was back fifteen minutes later, his back ramrod straight as he walked toward me while I made a salad for myself in the kitchen. "Sorry. I just needed some time to think."

"It's okay, Luke. I get it." Oh boy, did I. Our life had become stifling, making every thought impossible without oxygen.

He pulled his phone from his shorts pocket. "I thought I should wait and text Christina when we're together. That way you can see whatever she wants." We stared at the text Christina had sent as if it had asked for our firstborn.

Luke typed: *Sorry, just saw this. What's up?*

Her response was immediate. *Can I call you, or is Lily around? Otherwise, I can call on my lunch break tomorrow. I need to talk to you about what happened at school today.*

We went from staring at Luke's cell phone screen to blinking at each other. "What happened at school?" Luke asked me.

I closed my eyes and concentrated on how I'd felt at school. That afternoon seemed like a week ago. "I felt tired and woozy again. You know how it happens at times—like my brain isn't functioning. It was like that today, only it seemed worse." I leaned against the kitchen counter. "Honestly, I barely remember coming home and starting the spaghetti sauce for supper. I think Codi colored at the kitchen table." My voice faded as I tried to focus on what'd happened in the hours between lunch at school and Luke's arrival home.

"I'm texting her that it's okay for her to call now. I've got nothing to hide from you, Lily, and maybe she can help us figure out what the hell happened to you today."

He typed out a text. *Now is good, if you're free.*

Within a few minutes, his cell phone rang. He didn't put it on speakerphone, but I stood close enough to hear Christina, holding my breath as if she'd tell a suspense story involving someone other than me.

"Hi, Luke. I've struggled with whether I should say anything to you." Christina sounded breathless. "Some of us at school are concerned about Lily's behavior. We're afraid she will get caught." She took a deep breath. "That's why I texted you. We weren't sure if something's going on with a medication Lily's taking or if you've noticed anything unusual at home."

Christina knew very little about my struggles the past several months. I didn't know her well enough yet, and Jacob's words of trusting nobody included her.

"Like what?" Luke asked.

"There have been some afternoons, when we meet each other in the hallway or visit between classes, where we get the feeling she's on something. It's not often. Just once in a while. Other teachers have noticed too. Barb and I talked about contacting you last time it happened, and Barb decided she'd reach out to you if it happened again. But she was gone today for a family funeral." Christina paused. "I'm sorry. Maybe I shouldn't have called, butting my nose into your business. But if someone reports Lily, she could get in trouble."

I knew what would happen if they did. It had happened to a fellow teacher at our school a few years ago. We could be tested for drugs, and if we refused, we would be put on paid leave until they settled the situation. I massaged the back of my neck, wishing the school year would end so I had time away from work to figure out what was happening.

"I appreciate you contacting me, and also, that nobody has reported Lily," Luke said.

"Judith drove Lily home in her car, and I followed in mine so I could pick Judith up. Then we stopped and picked up Codi at school. Lily didn't say anything to you?"

Luke and I gave each other an "ah-ha" look. That explained why Ali had been forgotten. I'd kept Ali's twice-a-week social skills class at a center three blocks from our school to myself.

I shook my head, thinking about them having to drive me home like some kind of drunk or addict. I was neither, yet there had been chunks of times when I hadn't been able to think for myself. And I would have to face those women tomorrow. Women who hadn't said anything to me about my behavior and felt sorry for me. I didn't want sympathy. I wanted answers.

"No, but we've had a busy night and haven't had time to talk yet," Luke answered Christina's question. We would have plenty to talk about after he hung up.

"I asked Lily if she took something this afternoon, and Barb said she asked her a month or so ago. Both times, Lily said she hadn't. We wondered if she might be on medication for anxiety or depression. Believe me, we aren't judging." Christina's voice held sympathy I didn't want or need.

"I understand, and I appreciate everyone's concern. Also, Christina, Lily read your text earlier. I need to tell her why you asked me to call you, okay?" Luke said.

"Of course. I understand. And please tell Lily I'd be glad to talk with her tomorrow about anything. I just thought you should know."

They said goodbye before Luke set the phone on the counter, and we stared at each other. "Let's talk about this later, once the girls are in bed, okay?" he said.

"Yes. But in the meantime, I'm calling your mom. I want you to go to Shawn's cabin on Friday. It would be nice to have Rita here."

After Ali and Codi went to bed and I continued to get the stink eye from Pria, I escaped to our bedroom and called Rita.

"I'd love to visit this weekend," Rita said. "A friend of mine in Minneapolis recently took her granddaughter to the play *Mary Poppins.* I'll see if I can get tickets for Codi, Ali, and me on Saturday. We'd be back early Saturday night so we can see Pria all dolled up for prom."

"You'd make Ali and Codi's day if you can nab tickets for that play." They could make it to Minneapolis in an hour, and if the play ran into the afternoon, they should get home in plenty of time to see Pria. "And Pria would love to have you here. They have a softball tournament out of town Saturday, so she's staying at her teammate Sylvie's this weekend, and they'll get ready at Sylvie's after they get home from the tournament. She promised they'll stop here for photos."

It had been another reason Luke hadn't thought he should go to Shawn's cabin. He would miss seeing Pria dressed up for her first prom. Whether he was there or not, we couldn't deny her this chance at a slice of normalcy after everything she'd been through. Luke could see photos and videos later. She would attend more proms in the future.

"I'll check online about the tickets and let you know. I'll be there Friday afternoon either way," Rita said.

Within an hour, I received a text message from Rita saying she purchased three tickets for Saturday's afternoon play. Luke and I discussed the upcoming weekend as we sat in bed that night. I felt almost normal again. The nap I'd taken earlier had helped.

"What will you do Saturday? Are you going to Pria's game?" He still wouldn't commit to leaving and wore an armor of distrust. I could all but feel the steel dividing us.

"Her game is almost two hours away, so I hadn't planned on it since I thought Ali and Codi would be with me." Every time I thought of the girls at a softball game, panic flashed a reminder of Codi walking to that woman's car last week.

Both Luke and I talked about being extra diligent with the girls after that. We'd always been cautious parents, but the incident brought it to a whole new level. Yet I'd put our children in danger over the past months. *Can I trust myself?* I'd thought so until recently. No wonder Luke was leery of leaving me alone with them for the weekend.

"There's a huge plant and shrub sale in town Saturday, and some of the women from school had invited me to go with them. I hadn't planned on it since I'd have been home with Ali and Codi. Maybe I'll do that. We'll only be gone a few hours."

Luke nodded as I studied his profile next to me. We leaned against pillows on our headboard, both of us wide awake with too many things weighing on our minds. Flecks of gray peppered his dark hair. The past ten months had done a number on both of us.

"I'll go, but I'll check in when I can. The cell service isn't good at Shawn's cabin, but better out on the lake."

I leaned over and kissed his cheek, stubble tickling my lips. "I'll be fine. Remember, Rita will be here." But as I lay there that night, unable to turn off my brain, I knew that even energetic Rita couldn't keep away whatever darkness continued to haunt my life.

I apologized to Christina and Judith the next morning before class began. "I'm not sure what happened to me. It's like my brain couldn't function. I think I'm just overtired." It was a feeble excuse, which they were gracious enough to accept.

Barb was back from an out-of-town funeral, and I pulled her aside so we could speak in private. I rehashed what had happened the day before. "You asked me before if I was taking anything, and I'm sorry I lied to you."

Barb's eyebrows shot up at my confession.

"It's just antianxiety meds. Nothing more. They shouldn't have anything to do with these episodes. Sometimes I don't sleep well. The stress of the past several months keeps me awake." I shrugged. "I don't know if that's it or not."

"Nobody is judging you, Lily, so please don't feel like we don't understand. Maybe summer vacation will push reset for you. You certainly deserve one," Barb said, hugging my shoulders.

I told her about Luke's mom coming for the weekend.

"So you can go with us on Saturday?" Barb asked. "We're going out for brunch first."

"Yes, I'd like that. Rita and the girls will leave about nine a.m. for Minneapolis and won't be back until around five."

My chest felt lighter after talking with Barb, Christina, and Judith. Nobody judged me except me.

BEFORE SUNSET, LUKE and the girls rode their bikes. Luke held Percy by his leash and pedaled alongside me as I jogged the streets of our neighborhood. For the past few weeks, I'd worked my way up to a few miles at a time at a snail's pace. Gone were the days I could run alone. If I went for a run, Luke was alongside me on his bike.

Running had been a part of my life since junior high. Even pregnant, I'd run until my sixth or seventh month in. And all those years, it had pumped endorphins through my body and held off any anxiety. I welcomed back my limited running, cautious with each step. Running alone before work each morning was one more thing in my life that had changed thanks to Dastard. Still, I would take any mile I could get.

LUKE LEFT EARLY FRIDAY morning as the girls and I got ready for school, still acting guarded toward me. His kiss before he left to follow Shawn's truck on the two-hour trip north felt like the kiss of a stranger. His insistence on driving separately instead of riding with Shawn and the others only reaffirmed his lack of trust in me.

Rita arrived after we got home from school on Friday. She'd made ravioli yesterday and kept a pan of it in a cooler on her way from Chicago. We heated it up for dinner, then Codi peppered the meal with funny stories about her kindergarten classmates.

Ali had forgiven me for Wednesday's mix-ups, and Codi barely batted an eye over the smoke alarm going off that day. I wasn't sure what would bother that girl but was thankful for her carefree attitude. It almost made up for Pria's acidic one.

I'd called Ali's after-school instructor yesterday to apologize for forgetting her, not bothering to mention the fact that I hadn't driven myself home from school that day.

Luke called from Shawn's cabin while Rita and I visited in the living room. I could hear the men laughing in the background, the crackling of a campfire, and the relaxation in Luke's voice. "We scouted out the lake today, found the spots where I'll catch all the fish," he said loud enough for the others to hear.

They reacted as expected, yelling back at Luke, teasing that he would catch the baby minnows while they caught the monsters. I held the phone between Rita and me so we could both hear. Luke's laughter and good mood lifted the weight of his mistrust I'd been carrying.

He called Saturday morning before Rita and the girls left for Minneapolis, speaking with all of us before they headed out fishing for the day.

Barb picked me up shortly after Rita, Ali, and Codi left. We met ten other women from school at Bobby's Breakfasts in downtown Lakeview.

"What a scorcher," Maria said, mopping her brow as we met her and Judith at the door.

For once, instead of stress, the weather became the reason I struggled to take a deep breath. I loved summer and sunshine, but in mid-May, our bodies hadn't yet acclimated after shivering all winter.

"I agree. Poor Pria and her team. They've got a softball tournament today," I said.

We all breathed a welcome sigh as we stepped inside the air-conditioned café.

Over a leisurely late breakfast, we talked about what we planned to buy at the large greenhouse outside of town. It was almost noon when Barb dropped me off at home, her SUV containing shrubs for her yard and two for ours, along with several annual plants for each of us.

It was too hot out to plant them, and after I unloaded my purchases, I headed into our air-conditioned house and took out the pitcher of iced green tea, downing two glasses. I had the afternoon to myself and pulled a book off the shelf. Reading for pleasure had become a rare treat.

I don't know how long I sat there staring at the same page, fighting fatigue. Maybe I just needed some fresh air. A walk to the lake access to get my feet wet in the lake sounded perfect. That was about as far as we ever went in the murky water. I poured another glass of green tea, put on a baseball cap, then walked the short distance to the access.

At the water's edge, I slipped off my sandals. The cool water lowered my body temperature several degrees as it sloshed around my ankles, much like the iced green tea was doing in my stomach. My eyelids drooped as if anchors weighed them down, the warmth of the sun and breeze adding to my fatigue.

Our boat, tethered to the nearby dock, rocked back and forth from the gentle waves. Without thinking, I crawled inside it, untied the boat, then used the heavy wood oars to push myself away from the dock.

That was the last thing I remembered. Until Luke's muffled screams jolted me.

Chapter 29

Luke's shouts penetrated the rocking cloud of blissful escape, forcing me out of a comfortable cocoon.

What did I do wrong now? I blinked several times, opening my eyes to the glare of sunshine. Warmth caressed the front of me while my head and back ached from something hard.

I sat up and looked around. I was in our rowboat in the middle of the lake, waves rocking the boat like a cradle, pummeling Luke's face as he fought to swim toward me. *What am I doing out here? And why is Luke swimming?* He splashed toward me, far from shore.

"Use the oar!" His shout was muffled by the waves.

I lifted the heavy wood oar and held it out for him to reach. My heart rose to my throat as I realized he was sinking. I stumbled around the boat, trying to find him, trying to concentrate. *Oh my God. He's going to drown!*

I did the only thing I could. I dove in.

The cold water jolted me. I opened my eyes to see if I could spot Luke. His white T-shirt was visible under the boat. It seemed like a million years before I reached for his still-buoyant body, pulling it toward me. I had Luke with one arm and held onto the edge of the boat with the other. As I broke the surface, I remembered screaming. Fear-infused screams. And of seeing people gathered at the small beach, shouting for me to "hang on."

Luke needed CPR. I had no clue how in the hell I was going to do that. *Think, Lily!*

I didn't have the strength to pull myself up into the boat, much less get Luke in there. Still clinging to the boat, I kept Luke above water, attempting to form a suction between our mouths for CPR breaths. I tried. Oh, God, how I tried. Anything to get him to breathe.

Ambulance lights whirled along the shoreline, illuminating a silhouette. Someone approached us on a paddleboard.

Our savior stepped from the paddleboard into our boat and pulled Luke's body inside the rowboat before helping me in. "They're inflating an airboat. Paramedics will be out here soon," he assured me.

Between us, we maneuvered the paddleboard under Luke, so he was flat on his back. He wasn't breathing, and in autopilot, I performed CPR breaths while pleading for him to wake the hell up.

What seemed like a hundred years later, paramedics arrived in an airboat.

Back at the beach, people bombarded me, asking where our girls were and how they could help. I wanted answers too. I wanted the paramedics to answer my relentless "Is Luke going to be okay?" question with a "Yes, he'll be fine." They didn't.

When the ambulance pulled away with Luke inside, I sat at his feet, wrapped in a blanket as a paramedic continued to administer CPR. And next to me, someone I'd never expected held my hand—our neighbor Irene.

The ambulance pulled up to our local hospital, where they whisked Luke inside on a gurney. Irene threaded her arm through mine and supported me as I staggered, shell-shocked, through the emergency doors. I must've been starring in a drama play. At any minute, the director would walk in and clap, shouting accolades at our astounding acting performances. The director never showed up. But others did.

A NURSE LED ME INTO a room, insisting I be checked over by a doctor after she took my vitals. When the young doctor arrived, I insisted I was okay and begged for him to let me get back to waiting and worrying about Luke. I was fine. My husband was not. My chest hurt. I welcomed the pain. It was the only thing that seemed real.

Irene sat alongside me, solid and dependable as she'd been before Dastard's arrest. We sat in silence, holding hands and staring into the vastness of the unknown hanging over the waiting room like a thunder cloud.

It seemed as if everyone showed up together. Rita, Ali, and Codi rushed in, the girls eerily quiet as they clutched their grandma's hands. Kara dashed in, Pria alongside her, their eyes wide with shock. My parents arrived soon afterward.

Irene stood and stepped aside so that Ali and Codi could sit next to me. I pulled them to me, inhaling their scent of jelly beans and fear. I had no clue who'd contacted everyone. I'd never made a single call. One by one, we gathered like the Whos down in Whoville in *How the Grinch Stole Christmas*. We joined hands, but we weren't singing. We were, however, praying. Even in my frantic state, I remembered prayers I'd learned as a child when our family would attend church, the rare occasions in winter when the farm demanded less of my parents' time.

At some point, Irene caught our group's attention. "My husband is on his way to pick me up, but I wanted to say something before I leave." She addressed my daughters, Kara, Rita, and my parents.

Irene folded her hands over her stomach. "First, I want to apologize for the way I've treated your family in the past year. I have no excuse for my behavior." Her eyes locked with mine before turning to look at Rita and Pria, who stood nearby. "I wanted all of you to hear what my husband and I witnessed, in case people spread rumors about Lily after today."

Rooted to the chair, I was eager to hear her version of the past few hours that were murky in my head. It was as if I'd missed the first half of a horror movie.

"I was trimming shrubs in our front yard when I watched you walk to the lake access, Lily. When you hopped inside your rowboat and pushed off from the dock, I thought of how you and Luke always take life jackets with you if you go in the boat and was surprised to see you row out without one."

She addressed our quiet circle of family again. "When Luke arrived home later, I heard him calling for Lily in the backyard. I was inside by then, and it wasn't until I heard him calling Lily's name down at the access that I stepped outside to see what was going on."

Luke should have been gone until tomorrow. If I was in any coherent frame of mind, I would call Shawn to see why Luke had come home early. Maybe later.

Irene continued, "When Luke jumped in the water and began swimming toward the boat, I remembered him telling me before that he'd never taken swim lessons. I ran inside, told my husband what was going on, and took my cell phone with me to the beach. When Luke started splashing in the water, his head going under the water, I dialed 911."

I felt nauseous. *Oh my God! What if she hadn't been there?*

"My husband ran to the beach with our paddleboard, the only thing we own that would get him there quick enough. He brought life jackets with him," Irene said. "I watched Lily lean over the boat with an oar, reaching out to Luke with it. When the waves pushed him under the boat, Lily dove in to save him."

Irene's words picked up speed. "I didn't think you could swim, either, but you pulled Luke out. Others showed up at the beach, and we shouted for you to hang on. You did." She dabbed at the corners of her eyes and came toward me with open arms. "I'm so sorry, Lily.

For everything." Irene's actions demolished the brick wall she'd built between us that past year.

I pulled back to look at her, gratitude swelling my throat. "Thank you for calling 911, riding to the hospital with me, and for telling us what happened." I didn't need to tell her I'd been in shock, didn't need to admit I had no clue what'd happened before I dove into the water.

Everyone else had been too far away when tragedy struck, yet she'd been there for me. Her husband had come to our rescue, and I hadn't even recognized him.

After Irene left, Pria studied me. I'd sensed her scorn entwined with pain. She'd probably assumed the worst of me—that I hadn't tried to save her dad. If so, I had Irene to thank for setting the record straight and for lessening my guilt that I could have done more.

While we waited, I remembered what Luke said after each of the girls' deliveries and after the attack. He'd wished he could have traded places with me because he couldn't stand to see me in such pain. Now I understood.

A doctor met with us to explain what concerns they had with Luke. She threw around words like pulmonary edema and brain hypoxia. They sailed right over my head. I wondered if this was what Luke experienced when they'd listed my injuries last summer.

"Is he going to be okay?" Fear riveted me to the polished flooring.

It happened so fast. In my fog of denial, I was surprised I'd noticed it—the sideways glance the doctor gave my parents, knowing they were down the line in the pecking order of potential grief. Her dark-brown eyes indicated Luke's chances. Not good.

I read the prognosis her glance conveyed, refusing to accept it. "No. You can't let him die!" I pulled on the doctor's white sleeve. "Please tell me what's happening to him!"

The doctor reached for my hand and led me to a chair in the waiting room. She took a seat next to me. "Luke's lungs have filled with water, and his brain has been denied oxygen. Luckily, not for long."

My parents led an anxious Ali and an unusually quiet Codi from the room. Kara followed behind them while Pria and Rita pulled their chairs next to me to listen to the doctor.

"Luke has severe brain hypoxia. We tested the amount of oxygen in his blood and did a CT scan to provide us with a 3D image of his head." She paused a few seconds to allow us to take it all in. "Various tests, everything from an echocardiogram to an electroencephalogram, or EEG, have been performed to test the electrical activity in his heart and brain."

Rita sat up straight. "What does this all mean? Brain damage?" We tried to come to terms with what'd happened, tried to grasp the reality of Luke's prognosis.

"It's a wait-and-see process. Possible seizures, brain damage, damage to his heart, bacterial pneumonia... it's too soon to tell right now." The doctor folded her hands. "He's alive thanks to quick action on everyone's part."

When I'd spotted Luke in the water, I'd struggled to function. I wasn't sure I had helped him at all.

Luke's dad, Louis, would arrive later that night, a night that had changed again for Pria, who now sat next to me in her dirty softball uniform. Pria missed prom that night. And I was still waiting for that damn director to yell "Cut!"

I FELT LIKE ONE OF the slaughtered pigs on our farm. I itched for an arsenal of mind-numbing drugs but refused to take that path again. Rita hadn't taken a single pill. Neither had our children, although Ali would need additional counseling in the coming weeks.

By the time Luke's father arrived from Chicago, the sun had dipped below the horizon outside the hospital windows. The doctors told us Luke was out of the coma, a reassuring sign. "Go home, get some rest, and we will see you back here in the morning. Luke needs your strength. You'll be of no help to him if you're worn out."

Kara had left for our house earlier with Ali and Codi. She'd treated them to McDonald's and was helping them get ready for bed when I walked in the door. I updated her on Luke's precarious state.

Kara pulled me in for a hug. "I can come back tomorrow if you need me."

"Thank you. Mom and Dad will stay here with the girls tomorrow. There's no point in Pria going to the hospital unless things change for the worse." I nixed that possibility as I walked Kara to the door. "I'll call you tomorrow."

Back in the kitchen, I put on a pot of decaf coffee. I remembered little after shopping at the greenhouse with my friends. When I'd gotten home, things had become blurry. As I cleaned off the kitchen table where my pitcher of green tea sat, now warm, I was fairly certain I hadn't drunk from the two glasses sitting next to the pitcher. I didn't have time to dwell on it.

Pria had ridden back to our house with my parents. A minute later, they walked in, followed by Luke's parents, carrying two bags of groceries. We would have a houseful for a while, and they'd had the foresight to stock up.

After I changed out of my crusty, dried clothes and into sweatpants and a T-shirt, my parents, my in-laws, Pria, and I gathered around our kitchen table. I wrapped myself back up in the blanket someone had handed me in the ambulance, possibly Irene. Within an hour, neighbors had dropped off bowls and trays of food, adding to the untouched snacks our parents had set out to replace the supper we'd all missed. In a handful of hours, news of our family's latest tragedy had spread across our neighborhood and community.

Agony skinned me, exposing every cell. Heartache tugged at Luke's parents' faces. Rita had driven an hour from Minneapolis with Ali and Codi, the Mary Poppins play interrupted by the news that her youngest child's life hung precariously by a thread. She'd kept it together for her grandkids. Luke had come from sturdy stock.

He'd been a rock for me this past year. It was time for me to be there for him.

Chapter 30

I never thought my swimming lessons would help me save someone's life. I'd never spent a great deal of time in lakes growing up, our summers too busy on the farm. Lessons were the one good thing from the attack. If I hadn't needed therapy, I wouldn't have been a strong enough swimmer to help save Luke.

Over the next few days at the hospital, I took notes about medical terminology like hypoxemia, bacterial pneumonia, decreased lung compliance, and ventilation-perfusion mismatch. I wished for a medical degree to sift through it all. The only thing keeping us afloat was the news that although Luke had a long road to recovery, at least he would recover.

We could weather anything as long as we clung to that lifeboat.

Every night, I curled my body around Luke's pillow. Breathing in the clean scent of his shampoo and aftershave made it easier to pretend he was there next to me. During the day, I pulled it together for the girls, although Pria emotionally barricaded herself from me. Apparently, Irene's testimony hadn't been enough to take me off Pria's "it's your fault Dad almost died" list.

Neighbors and friends delivered food to our home along with offers to have our daughters at their houses to give our girls—and me—a break. Most people ignored the recent rumor that I'd almost killed Luke instead of saving him and that do-good Luke didn't deserve what'd happened to him. As if I had deserved the attack. Thankfully, those people were few, and Irene was not one of them. She'd seen what happened firsthand.

Jacob had been so right. Bad things happened to good people. The people who continued to judge us didn't know the facts, didn't walk in our shoes, and didn't have a clue of how it could easily happen to them. People who looked at life much as I had until my own had spiraled.

With three weeks of school left, they found a substitute teacher for my class. I was in no emotional condition to teach. I'd let our daughters stay home those first few days when Luke's outcome looked precarious, volleying between our house and the hospital until they gave us the thumbs-up that he would pull through. Pria had finals coming up, Codi was content most anywhere, and Ali functioned best in the structured environment at school. I'd have loved some structure in my continually unraveling life.

My parents went back to the farm. The new owner would be arriving soon to work alongside them before taking it over. He'd been raised on a farm himself in a Wisconsin farming community, just a few hours from Mom and Dad's farm.

I sat at our kitchen table with Luke's parents, sharing a pot of coffee after the girls left for school.

"You know what I don't understand?" Louis crossed his arms. "Luke knows better than to swim that far without a life jacket. Where was his head when he jumped in without one?" He tsk-tsked.

He'd brought up the question circling inside my head the past few days. One I didn't want to share. The obvious follow-up question was why Luke had swum out to the boat. If I hadn't passed out, or whatever the hell happened to me in our rowboat, Luke wouldn't have needed to dive in to begin with.

But Louis was not one to back down from an uncomfortable topic.

"It doesn't matter now," Rita said, trying to defuse her husband. "All that matters is that Luke is going to be okay."

We hoped. He would survive. But "okay" was still up in the air.

Rita had spent enough time around me in the past year to see firsthand my up-and-down behavior. She'd been with me last weekend. I'd been fine Saturday morning before they left for the play in Minneapolis.

Of course, something had changed on Saturday. I stared at the two glasses in the sink. *Was something in the green tea?* Luke had never drunk it before. *Whose other glass was that?* Maybe I'd been so out of it that I'd used two glasses.

The lines had become so blurred in my life that nothing was certain. After Luke had told me of things I'd said and done under the influence last fall, I'd set myself up as an easy target. If someone was out to make me appear deranged, they'd done their job.

But I wasn't losing touch with reality. In fact, my mind had sharpened since Luke's near-drowning. It focused on everyone I'd been in contact with over the past year. I relied on Kara and Jacob for support from a distance, trusting them, along with Luke's and my parents, but nobody else. Only Kara and Jacob knew of my plan to witness Dastard's release in early August.

"I still think I should go with you," Kara had said when we'd spoken on the phone last week. "We can be Thelma and Louise."

"I was leaning toward Cagney and Lacey. I'm not sure I'm ready to kill anyone yet." We'd laughed, and for a moment, I believed I could get through anything with Kara by my side. The problem was, she wasn't always around. Some things I needed to tackle alone.

Rita and I tag-teamed hospital visits. I spent most of my time with Luke, who could now relay what he remembered from that day. Rain pelted his hospital room windows, and I wore a sweatshirt and jeans as I sat next to his bed. It didn't feel like May. It didn't feel like anything. One day blurred into the next, and if not for our daughters going to school that morning, I would have no clue what day it was.

Luke had lost weight over the past year after the attack, weight he couldn't afford to lose. In the past week, his face had grown even thinner.

"Tell me what you remember," I said, my hands warmed by the cup of hot tea a nurse had brought for me. Luke and I had spoken little up until then, saving his strength and energy.

"When we went back to Shawn's cabin for lunch, I tried calling your cell before we left the lake. You didn't answer, so I tried our landline." Dark circles rimmed Luke's eyes. "I had a gut feeling something wasn't right. Paranoid, I know." He attempted a smile. "When we headed back out on the lake an hour later, I still couldn't reach you, and I couldn't shake the fear something was wrong. You said you'd be home by noon."

He licked his lips, and I held a cup of water so Luke could drink from the straw. "Shawn dropped me off at the dock, and I drove home. When I arrived, I could tell you'd been there. The plants were there. Your green tea sat on the kitchen table, but you weren't around. I tried your cell phone again and heard it ringing on the couch, next to a book."

When I'd arrived home from the hospital that first night, I remembered seeing the book on our couch and vaguely recalled reading it earlier that day.

"It was hotter than Haiti, and I drank some of your tea—which isn't as godawful as I thought it would be—then I took a shower, unpacked... and that's it. I remember walking back outside to look for you and spotting our rowboat in the middle of the lake."

Luke closed his eyes as if reliving the moment, and I leaned in to catch each word and understand how our latest near-tragedy had unfolded. "My feet dragged like anchors as I tried jogging down to the access. As I stood on the sand, I noticed your legs dangling over the side of the rowboat. I yelled for you, but you didn't move."

He opened his eyes and focused on mine. "I may have shrieked like a girl when the water reached my crotch." Luke grinned at the memory. "Damn, doesn't that water ever warm up?"

I forced a smile back. None of us ever went past our knees in the muck.

"I got this hair-brained idea to swim out to you, figuring I'd dog paddle or float on my back if I got tired. With you not answering, I was afraid something happened to you." His eyes watered, and I thumbed away tears from my cheeks and his. I wondered how many tears we'd shed in the past year.

"A hundred yards into it, I questioned my decision. My body felt as heavy as an elephant, dragging me into the dark water. The dog paddle became impossible, and the waves pummeled my face."

"Oh, Luke." I clutched his hand to my heart.

"The last thing I remember is screaming for you to hold out the oar for me. And then I couldn't think. Everything went... dark. Like my mind shut down. Peacefulness took over, but I couldn't—" His words came out choked, fear of what might have been etched in his eyes. I understood that fear all too well. I pressed my cheek to Luke's, our tears commingling.

"Instead of me saving you, you saved me," he mumbled against my ear.

I pulled back. "No, Luke, we saved each other." And we would get through this together.

SIX WEEKS AFTER LUKE arrived home from the hospital, he was still in recovery and dealing with pain. We went for a slow walk one night in late June as Ali and Codi rode their bikes. Pria was at work. Luke and I held hands as we talked about our role reversal.

"I understand the phrase 'fighting for your life' now," Luke said. "When you wrestle with death, life takes on a whole new meaning."

We were well aware of how lucky we'd been to come out of our situations alive.

Dastard had robbed us of a third of our summer last year. The incoming summer wasn't much of an improvement. Luke was missing the busiest time of year at work. A medical leave wasn't exactly the vacation he'd had in mind.

After fighting his way back from cerebral hypoxia, leaving in its aftermath super-fun side effects like hallucinations, memory loss, and muscle spasms, he had improved from being a "vegetable" in the hospital to feeling like a "lazy ass" at home—his words, not mine.

On a sweltering afternoon the following week, Ali and Codi played at a neighbor's house with their daughters. Pria left for the beach with her friends, and Luke and I sat in the shade at our patio table, each with a glass of lemonade.

"We've had a helluva year, haven't we?" He reached for my hand. "I expected us to be one of those couples who grow old together and finish each other's sentences."

"A couple who dances so well together that people think we're one person," I added.

"We should probably take a few dance lessons first." Luke gave a lopsided grin.

We sat in silence for a minute.

"Why don't you drink your green tea anymore?" He nodded to my glass of lemonade. "Surprisingly enough, when I had a couple glasses of it, I didn't gag."

I studied my glass of lemonade as I chose my words. "Have you noticed that I haven't acted like I was drugged, that nothing odd has happened since your near-drowning?"

"I hadn't thought about it. Guess I've been a little self-absorbed." He winked. "What does that have to do with you drinking green tea?"

"You said you tried the tea the day you swam out to rescue me, right? There were two glasses with the near-empty pitcher of tea on our kitchen table when I got home from the hospital that night. I wondered if the other glass was yours."

"It was. I was thirsty and maybe a little dehydrated from drinking beer the night before. I poured myself a glass since it was sitting there. Figured I could use a little nutritional boost, so I drank two glasses of it."

He confirmed my suspicions. "I've wondered if the tea is what's affected my behavior. I'm the only one who drinks it, other than you that day. Once I stopped making it, I've felt normal again. And nothing strange has happened to our family since that day. I haven't misplaced anything or felt like I was being sabotaged. Nothing. No phone calls that I'm sure I haven't made." I paused to study his reaction, worried Luke would think I was scrambling for an excuse for my past behavior. "I think someone was out to sabotage me, possibly putting something in the tea. Maybe they've decided I've suffered enough after almost losing you."

Luke's eyebrows shot up. "If there was something wrong with the tea, it would explain my poor judgment that day and how sluggish I felt." He pressed his palm to his face. "Jesus, Lily. Is that how you felt all those times?"

I nodded. "Sometimes. It wasn't consistent. There were times when I felt out of it, as if I moved and talked in slow motion. Other times, I felt exhausted, drunk, or queasy. But I don't understand why the tea would have that effect on me now when it didn't before the attack. And I didn't feel odd every time I drank it."

"I've been a piece of shit for doubting you." He leaned over the table toward me. "Remember when you were in the hospital? You swore someone snuck into your room at night. What if that was real?"

His question dredged up my old accusations, ones that had sounded like paranoia last year. We'd both excused it as some feverish dream. But after the threats and possible drugging, it seemed more than possible. And terrifying.

"We know it wasn't Dalton—hasn't been him these past several months—but who else would do this? And is it more than one person?"

"If we understood the 'why' behind the attack, we might figure that out." It meant everything that Luke finally believed me. It was time to let him in on my plan. "When he is released in a few weeks, I'm going to the correctional facility to watch him walk free. Someone will have to be there to pick him up."

The victim's notification letter had arrived a few weeks ago with Dastard's upcoming release date of August fourth.

"I'll go with you," Luke said.

"No, I want to go alone. Kara offered, too—thought we'd be Thelma and Louise." We laughed at the idea. "I wasn't going to tell you about it, figuring you'll be back at work then. I have to do this, Luke. For my sanity."

He grinned. "Well, I'm all for your sanity. And I sure as hell hope I'm back to work by then. Hopefully, the doctor gives me the green light at my appointment this Friday."

I leaned in and kissed the man I'd nearly lost. "I hope you get the stamp of approval, too, so we can get back to living a somewhat normal life."

When we pulled back from the kiss, Luke's face held a wistful smile. We'd learned and lived a lifetime of wisdom and pain over the past year. There was no such thing as a life without hardships. The perfect life I'd thought we'd had was nothing more than a mirage. We'd weathered our storms and could only hope to sail smooth waters for a while. We deserved some smooth sailing.

Chapter 31

The first anniversary of the attack came and went. Luke and I spent the hot July day on our boat with our daughters, stopping to swim along the shoreline. After Luke's brush with drowning, we were all cautious with our time in the surrounding lakes. Pria had enrolled in swimming lessons with Ali, Codi, and me. Luke would take them when his body fully recovered, which would be months. The doctor gave him the go-ahead to get back to work, at least, and two months after nearly dying, Luke returned to his job.

During the weeks Luke worked and I waited for Dastard's release, I spent any free time I had researching options for an idea that had danced at the edges of my mind for several months, a new goal Luke and I discussed late into the evenings. The idea solidified when Mom and Dad wrote out a generous check to me—and one to Jacob—after the sale of the farm. Their gift of money would help me reach it.

I planned to make a career change. I'd always felt my impact on children in kindergarten was an important way to make a difference in their lives. It was. But I wanted to focus on children who had to deal with things that no child should have to live through. I couldn't change the world, couldn't make it fair. But I could help transform a child's life, one kid at a time.

On the first of August, I put in for a leave of absence from teaching and enrolled in classes to get my school counselor degree. I'd gotten my Master's for elementary education after Pria's birth. In September, I would begin a graduate school counseling program that included twenty-four credits of counseling-specific coursework. I would have a degree for a Tier 2 license by the following spring.

It was freeing to have had the time, energy, and brainpower to focus on that major life decision over the past month. It freed up my thoughts to focus on what would happen on the fourth. His release would take place tomorrow—after he'd served only two-thirds of his five hundred fifty days, which amounted to one year and a few days.

I LEFT OUR HOUSE BEFORE 6:30 a.m. on Thursday. His release could be as early as 8:01 a.m. I wondered what his life had been like inside those walls. He'd had a decent home with his foster family. Before the attack, he could've continued to live with them, play football, and be the star that led the high school team to a championship season. Instead, for whatever reason, one I would probably never know, he'd chosen to wreck those chances.

As of today, he would have a fresh start. I wished I'd been given a shorter sentence for my suffering. If I'd learned anything over the past year, it was this—life wasn't fair. It didn't play by the rules by freeing the victim as quickly as it releases the perpetrator.

Luke got ready for work as I prepared to leave. When I walked out of our bedroom, Pria stood in the hallway. "What are you doing up so early?"

For a second, I wondered if I was supposed to drive her to work at the grocery store. She'd turned sixteen and, in the chaos of our life, had just recently finished behind-the-wheel training.

She stepped toward me. "Please be careful, Mom." She wrapped her arms around my waist, and I wanted to cry. As much as Luke and I had been through, Pria had dealt with her own kind of hell. She knew of my trip to the correctional facility and, like Kara and Luke, had offered to go with me.

"I will." My words tangled with her long blond hair as she leaned her cheek against mine. "It's not like I'm going in there like Rambo."

Pria laughed, a sound so welcome to my ears that I tucked it inside my heart before driving away a few minutes later.

I WAITED AMID SEVERAL vehicles in our SUV. I had a decent view of the door in the back of the correctional facility where they released the prisoners. The circular razor wire above the impenetrable fences added to the claustrophobic image. Even with the spacious grounds, if I was incarcerated, I would never be able to forget the feeling of being trapped inside that fence.

I stood next to the vehicle, focusing on the side door through the binoculars I'd brought along. A middle-aged man was the first to walk out. Minutes later, another man walked free, met by his loved ones. The third time the door opened, I recognized the tall, young blond. My heart seized with painful memories. His hair had been cut, leaving the scar on his neck visible through my binoculars. He carried a box of personal items, his arms filled out with the physique of a man who'd taken advantage of the weight room in the facility.

I was so busy studying the differences in him that I forgot about looking for who would pick him up. Common sense told me it would be his foster family. He was eighteen and out of high school now. I hoped that it would be someone else, the missing piece to the puzzle.

I spotted a woman bustling toward him, her arms outstretched and flowing purple-flowered top billowing like bat wings. Her build was nothing like his foster mother's—tall, youthful, and thin. The older woman embraced him, her head not quite reaching his shoulders. The lump in my throat threatened to explode when she turned around.

I had no comforting arms around me. *I should've let Luke come with me!* In less than a heartbeat, I blinked the tears away, pushing my thoughts of my husband aside.

It can't be her. My eyes were playing tricks on me. I pulled the binoculars away, studying them as if they'd malfunctioned.

I wiped the moisture from my eyes to peer again through the binoculars, zeroing in on the face of the woman walking arm in arm with my attacker. My hand flew to cover my mouth. Shock flamed a fire in me as I broke out in a full-body sweat. Someone wailed. A muffled, haunting howl. Realizing the sound had come from me, I kept one hand over my mouth, my other arm wrapped around my stomach as if my body would fall apart if I didn't hold it together.

I needed to leave but was in no condition to drive. In an instant, memories pieced everything together, giving me an answer. That answer walked through the parking lot, ignorant of my existence. I'd allowed this person into our lives. The realization gutted me.

Judith! Holy hell! Although I'd hoped to find a connection to help make sense of our horrific past year, I'd had no clue what to expect other than a possible disgruntled football fan. Nowhere in my imagination did I think it would be a coworker old enough to be my mother.

My legs trembled. I reached for the car door frame to keep myself from crumbling. I wished I had let Luke or Kara come with me. Someone to verify that my eyes weren't playing tricks on me now. To prop me up so I wouldn't disintegrate into a puddle of disbelief.

Focus, Lily, focus! I pushed myself away from our SUV so I had a better view and squatted behind another vehicle, rooted to the hot asphalt. Judith's car passed the row where I'd parked, clueless of my bird's-eye view as she drove my attacker to his freedom.

Once they were gone, I reached for my cell phone with shaking hands, took several calming breaths, then called Luke. He answered on the first ring.

"You'll never guess who picked up Dastard," I whispered as if anyone else in the parking lot cared. I relayed what I'd witnessed.

"Holy shit! Are you okay?"

"Hell no! I can't believe Judith has anything to do with all of this. Do you suppose they're related?" My thoughts flipped through the past year, from the day Barb had introduced Judith to me at school to the last time I'd seen her—the morning Luke almost died.

"Can you Google her name and his? I can't wait until I get home. I have to know. Her last name is Johnson. Too common in Minnesota." I pulled myself up from squatting, my knees aching with the adrenaline wearing off. "Still, *something* should show up connecting them. I'll call Detective Boyle later, but I don't want to jump the gun until we have more information." I wouldn't stop digging until I got all the answers I needed.

"Let's meet for lunch. That way, we can talk about it away from the girls," Luke said.

"Good idea." We agreed to meet at a quiet café in downtown Lakeview at eleven thirty for an early lunch.

I took several deep breaths so I wasn't a complete mess while driving. Dastard walking out a free man hadn't closed the door on that chapter of my life. It had kicked it wide open.

WHILE I WAITED FOR Luke to arrive, I sat in my vehicle with the air conditioning on and called Kara to relay the news.

"When you get home, you'll have to look at your list of all the crap that happened to you and see if you can connect Judith to any of those things," Kara said. "Listen, Louise, you need to think back to every single time she was at your house and every time she had access to your life at school."

"I'm not Louise. You're Louise," I blurted as if that was an important key to our conversation.

"You are not. If I'm going to help you with this, I get Brad Pitt. It's the least you can give me."

I groaned. "Fine, you can have him." I had Luke—the only man I ever wanted.

As I promised to keep Kara updated, my husband pulled up in his work truck. We headed inside the café toward a corner booth in the back. We didn't want anyone to overhear our conversation.

"I didn't find anything yet," Luke said after we'd ordered. "I did a couple of Google searches, but it's busier than hell at work. Someone cut one of our cable lines outside of town, so most of our crew is out of the office doing repairs."

"That's okay. I've been thinking about the things I know about Judith—or at least what she's told me. Her husband died, but I'm not sure how long ago, and I think she just had one daughter, who died of drugs. I'm guessing that was many years ago." I shrugged, realizing she could've easily lied.

Our server placed a dinner salad in front of me, and I pushed it aside. Luke ignored his cheeseburger, neither of us feeling hungry.

"I bet that's why she applied for the job at your school. But what's the motive to be around you when she's connected to Dalton?" He leaned across the booth as if I might whisper words to enlighten him.

"Those are a few of the questions I've asked myself during the drive back from Faribault. Did Judith plan to befriend me? And is she related to him?" We spent Luke's lunch hour dissecting every possibility until he had to get back to work.

"I'll try to leave work early so I can help you with research." He leaned in and kissed me before we walked back to our vehicles. His work was only a few miles from downtown, and I would be home in less than ten minutes.

I turned on my vehicle and cranked on the air conditioning. "We can call Detective Boyle after you get home."

Luke reached for my hand. "I just have to say this." His face was mere inches from mine, still thinner than usual after his brush with death. "I'm sorry for every single damn thing that's happened to you since the day he attacked you. Sorry for every time I second-guessed you."

I leaned my forehead against his, closing my eyes. "You weren't alone in the 'is Lily losing it?' camp. I second-guessed myself too."

As I drove home, I called and left a message on Jacob's cell phone as I'd promised him I would do. He planned to call me back when he got off work later, but for the moment, he would at least know who'd picked Dalton up.

I called Kara again from our driveway, not wanting our daughters to hear the conversation, finishing our speculation before I went inside to do research. "Do you suppose she became your frenemy to gaslight you?"

I chuckled at Kara's terminology of my relationship with Judith. "No doubt. But like Dastard, I don't understand why."

"Do you think..." Kara paused.

"That I shouldn't have let her into my life?" Guilt had eaten at me on the long drive from the Faribault Correctional Facility to Lakeview. I'd let this woman into our house. Let her spend time with our girls.

"Not that. I'm wondering if Judith had a hand in Dastard's attack or if she came into the picture *because* of the attack," Kara said. "You know, the whole chicken-or-the-egg thing."

I pulled into our garage and turned off the vehicle. "Guess we'll find out soon enough, right? Pria will keep Ali and Codi busy so I can Google Judith's name." I'd never have guessed a year after the attack, I would still have to rely on Boyle and Brook. "I've got to go. I'll keep you updated after we talk to Boyle."

We said our goodbyes, and I walked into our home, where Judith had been a guest several times. I forced a smile before stepping into our backyard, where Ali and Codi jumped on the trampoline. Pria stretched out on a lawn chair in the sun. She shot me a questioning look.

"Judith picked up Dalton," I mouthed before walking over to the trampoline.

Pria's mouth hung open for several seconds, her brain probably overloaded with questions for me.

The girls stayed in our backyard while I slipped inside and fired up the computer. Before I typed anything, my cell phone rang. It was Jacob.

"You're off of work already?" It wasn't even one o'clock.

"Nope. I'm on my lunch break and got your voice mail. Mother clucker! You mean to tell me an old grandma has been the one messing with you?"

"It sounds crazy, doesn't it? But it would explain a few things. I work with Judith. I've befriended her thanks to Maria, my long-time educational assistant. Judith's been in our home several times."

"I hope they lock her up," Jacob grumbled.

"Me too. But everything that's happened is so vague. I'm not sure you can arrest someone for those little things, other than mail tampering. And I can't prove any of it."

We hashed it over for a few more minutes before he had to get back to work. "Love ya, sis. I'll call you later, okay?"

It wasn't until after we'd hung up that something Jacob said registered. *Grandma.* Was Judith his grandma? She said she'd had one daughter. I'd assumed the daughter had been Judith's only child. I'd also assumed that the daughter had died young because Judith said she'd lost her to drugs. But drug addiction had no age limit. If Dastard was Judith's grandson, a dead addict mother would explain why he'd ended up in foster care.

But that didn't make sense. Dalton Digg's mother was still alive. She'd come barreling into town to take him away after I'd named him as my attacker.

Boyle would help clear things up. I texted him, asking if we could call him once Luke arrived home from work. In my text, I gave him a few details of my trip to Faribault and of Judith, describing her as a woman old enough to be my mother who had befriended me and worked alongside me at school.

Boyle's response came almost immediately. *Am I on Candid Camera? Are you pulling my hairy leg? Who'd guess an old Q-Tip would be so vindictive?* I pictured him pacing, chewing on black licorice.

I laughed at his calling Judith a Q-Tip, his description for old, white-haired people. Judith had some gray hair sprinkled in with her red, not a true "Q-Tip" yet.

I typed him another message. *It's not your fault. Who would imagine a grandma would stalk me?* I'd never felt "stalked" around Judith. I wished my radar had alerted me to danger.

I'll do some research and wait to hear from you, Boyle texted.

I sat back down at the computer and Googled Dastard's full name, something I'd never bothered to do before. An obituary came up for a Davis Johnson. I clicked the link and found the connection I'd been looking for. The obituary was from early last August, a few weeks after the attack. It listed Judith Johnson as Davis's wife of forty-two years, his daughter, Angela Digg, and grandson, Dalton Digg.

Oh my god! I called Luke's cell phone and relayed what I'd found.

"I'm finishing up at work right now. I'll be home in fifteen minutes."

I called Mom, rehashing the day's events and discoveries, and either Luke or I would call Rita later. I'd spoken of Judith and my other coworkers several times to Rita and Mom, and Mom was stunned beyond words as I laid out events where I was now certain Judith had messed with me and my family.

There were a few different obituaries with similar information about Judith and her deceased husband, and I read them while waiting for Luke to arrive home. I'd assumed Judith had always lived in Lakeview. Instead, they had lived in a small town twenty miles away, which meant Judith had moved to Lakeview within the last year. Probably about the time she'd landed the part-time job at my school.

What a coincidence. What a scheming, lying monster.

Chapter 32

Pria brought Ali and Codi to her bedroom—a rare invitation for them—and they played card games on the bed. Downstairs, Luke and I sat in the living room, huddled over our laptop.

I recapped my research. "Remember when Brook and Boyle said Dastard often stayed at his grandparents' home in a nearby town? That he helped his grandma care for his sick grandpa? Judith is that grandma."

Luke nodded. "When they arrested him, he was staying with his grandparents. His foster parents hadn't seen the scratches you'd left on him. But Judith would have."

"And she didn't go to the police about it," I added.

By the time we called Detective Boyle, putting him on speakerphone so we could both hear, we had more questions than answers. It all led back to "why."

"Okay, so let's get down to the underbelly," Boyle said. "I did some poking around on my end after your text this afternoon. Judith's husband was in the hospital when Dalton attacked you, but he never told his foster parents that. So when he stayed with Judith those few days after the attack, they figured he was still helping with his grandpa."

I laid out everything for Boyle. Judith had been in our home. She'd known from class that I was the only one in our family who drank the green tea and smoothies. She'd even had access to my computer and food at school. "The first time I felt woozy was after Luke and I went away for the night back in February. Judith came to visit Maria, who'd stayed at our house with the girls for the weekend."

"That's too coincidental. It may be hard to prove. Unless..."

Luke and I leaned into the phone, both on full alert as we listened to Boyle's plan.

LUKE AND I DROVE TO Detective Boyle's office the following Saturday morning, in plenty of time for me to get set up with a recording device. Boyle led the way down a narrow hall to his office. We took a seat, and he went over the simple recording instructions. "Super easy."

"I hope so." My knees knocked like mallets banging on a xylophone.

"You control the conversation so she doesn't derail it right off the track." The detective winked at me before ushering us out the door and to his vehicle. The show was about to begin.

We counted on Judith's routine of going to our development's dog park around ten in the morning, when she and her collies usually had the place to themselves. If she wasn't there, we had other options. The plan was to get her alone, get her talking.

"I don't know how you're holding it together." Luke squeezed my hand. We sat in the back seat of Detective Boyle's unmarked SUV.

"Who said I'm holding it together?" I forced a smile. My guts churned like a washing machine with an agitator stuck in overdrive. I'd eaten nothing that morning except a banana.

Detective Boyle planned to drop me off a block from the dog park, and then he and Luke would find a spot nearby where they had an unobstructed view of me with Judith.

It was a beautiful, crisp early August morning. After a gentle overnight rain, the temperature had dropped, reenergizing the flowers. It reminded me of the day I'd come home from the hospital.

Everything had seemed so hopeful then. I'd thought the worst was over.

Instead, a year later, I would finally face my nemesis. One of them anyway.

After Boyle parked the vehicle, I turned on the small recorder, took a drink from my water bottle, then kissed Luke.

"Please be careful," he whispered, clutching my hand.

"She doesn't know I'm showing up. It's not like she's sitting at the dog park with a knife or gun." Then again, I didn't know the real Judith at all.

I'd thought of taking Percy with me, but I had too much on my mind to navigate him right now. My legs wobbled as I stepped out of the car. Boyle rolled down the windows, and Luke moved to the passenger seat in front. They gave me two thumbs up.

I'd recited what I would say to Judith so often that I could have written it word for word. I quietly hummed "Ob-La-Di, Ob-La-Da" as I walked toward Judith, her back to me. Her dogs barked as I approached, giving me away.

Judith's head whipped around as I opened the gate, her eyes as big as the sun when she spotted me. We hadn't seen each other since mid-May when Luke had nearly died, but our daughters sometimes saw Judith when they took Percy to the dog park. She pushed herself up as she clutched her stomach. "Lily! What a pleasant surprise!"

I'd wondered how she'd play out our meeting. Such a convincing actress could have made it in Hollywood.

Not anymore. I held the script she'd yet to read.

"How good to see you." Judith's hand made its way from her stomach to cover the distance between us.

My body flinched at the idea of her touching me. I took a step back.

"Did you bring Percy with you?"

"No, I didn't. And yes, I bet it's a surprise to see me. Not so pleasant for you, though, is it?" I walked to the bench and sat, patting the place next to me where she'd sat before I interrupted her peaceful morning.

"Please, Judith, sit back down. We've got a lot of catching up to do." My voice was void of emotion. *I should be the one going to Hollywood.* "After all, I haven't seen you since the day Luke almost drowned."

Her lips quivered at that comment. She clutched the beige cardigan around her stomach like a security blanket before she slowly sat back down, her pupils bouncing around like ping-pong balls. Even if she tried to flee, age was on my side. I let her squirm for a minute.

"I hear you have a grandson living with you. You, who implied you had no living family." The need to complete the unsolved puzzle fueled my courage.

As if she'd been holding a vat of lies for way too long, Judith sighed, her pale lips fluttering as the air escaped her lungs. "How did you find out?" Her shoulders slumped.

"I drove to the Faribault Correctional Facility two days ago when he was released. I was there when you rushed to greet him and lead him back to your car." I steadied my voice.

Judith studied her dogs as if they were more important than our earth-shattering conversation.

"The pieces fit together." I didn't want to touch this woman who had wrecked my life, but I deserved her attention instead of her dogs. I reached for her face, a face I used to trust, and turned it toward mine. "Look at me—at the woman whose life you and your grandson destroyed!" *Get a grip, or she'll take control.* "Why did Dalton attack me? I deserve the truth."

Judith's thin lips pursed. Her sweater had a large pocket on each side of her hips. Her hands fidgeted before she reached into her left pocket and pulled out a small tan wallet.

Is she going to offer me money? No amount could wipe out what happened. Instead, she opened it and pulled out faded wallet-sized photos.

I recognized one photo as her deceased husband, the one used for his obituary. The second was of a young woman with elbow-length blond hair, full lips, and pale eyes that held so much anger I was surprised the camera hadn't exploded. The woman stood behind a young Dalton, her thin hands grasping his small shoulders. His blond hair was uncombed, his plaid shirt wrinkled. He wore such a pinched expression it was obvious he'd been crying.

"Why are you showing me this picture? This is Dalton when he was young. And your daughter, I assume?"

Judith nodded, studying my reaction. I sensed Dalton wasn't the reason Judith had handed me the photo. I'd been so busy focusing on the pain and anger seeped in the photo, it took a minute to register the woman's face. She looked a lot like me when I'd had long hair. Like I'd looked the day he'd attacked me.

"Because your daughter looks like I did?" I couldn't pretend to understand Judith's way of thinking. Then something clicked in the spinning wheel of my thoughts, a warning to heed. I didn't have time to process it as Judith dug in her wallet again.

She pulled out another photo of her daughter in her teens, a Polaroid that'd been trimmed to fit inside a wallet. The faded image exploded like colorful fireworks in my head. Her daughter was smiling up at a young man in a navy-and-tan-striped V-neck sweater. It had been almost twenty years, but I recognized the sweater. And the man wearing it.

Judith received the reaction she wanted as my eyebrows shot up and I gasped.

Nowhere in my script of our conversation had I imagined I would be speechless. Yet I fumbled to form syllables, to ask questions. I fought to ground my thoughts, replacing shock with attitude.

"So, that's your daughter and Luke? Dalton's mother? Is that supposed to be justification for his actions? For yours?" My fingernails dug into my palms. I took as deep a breath as I dared without looking like a person fighting off lightheadedness, which I was.

Judith harrumphed and yanked the photos from me. "You stole Luke from my Angie and from *his* son. Her life fell apart after they broke up. Angie and Dalton would have had a good life with Luke if you hadn't wormed your way in." Anger sharpened her words.

His son? Dalton wasn't Luke's son! Angie must've been the woman Luke had told me about, who was already pregnant before they'd begun dating his senior year of college. The time frame fit. So did his description of Angie—similar looks as me but unhinged and living in a fantasy world.

I eyed Judith. The apple hadn't fallen far from the tree. "Luke is not Dalton's father."

There was no way Luke would have fathered a child and not taken responsibility for it. He was responsible and cared about others, helping others. I knew my husband, but Judith didn't.

"Because of you, Angie struggled to find a decent man to be a father to Dalton. She married a man who turned her into a druggie. She couldn't take care of herself, much less Dalton. She let her father and me raise Dalton, showing up off and on to hit us up for money with the threat she'd take Dalton away." Judith withdrew a tissue from her pocket and blew her nose.

"Dalton's life was torture when he lived with Angie." Judith's shaky hand pressed another tissue to her eyes. Although I had a fair idea of what Dalton's life had been like, I hadn't expected such insight. Anger at his mother, and the court system that had let him down, crept into my heart.

"How did he end up back here in foster care instead of living with you?" *Oh, Lily, why do you care? This isn't what you came to ask!*

"Dalton came to live with us again when he was ten, and things improved for him. Then my husband had a stroke. He already suffered from heart disease. I couldn't care for both my husband and Dalton, who needed a lot of emotional care. I had breast cancer the year before and was in recovery myself. Angie showed up after being absent from our lives for two years. Dalton was twelve. Her eyes were clear, her tremors gone. She appeared to be clean." Judith shuddered. "I let him leave with her, wanting to believe things were good with Angie. It lasted less than six months. Dalton showed up at our house one day. He'd walked ten miles from her apartment to ask for our help. She had left him to fend for himself for over a week before he realized his mother wasn't coming back."

She turned toward me, pointing to her left ear. "Angie's 'friends' abused him. One cut him from his left ear down his neck. When he was five, another one burned his cigarettes into Dalton's stomach." Judith wrinkled her nose at me. "You used those marks against him when you identified him." She tsk-tsked me as if I was a naughty girl for ratting him out.

"Dalton finally had a decent life until *you* wrecked it by accusing him. As if it wasn't enough that you took his father from him!" Her body vibrated as she jabbed me with her finger.

"Luke *isn't* his father. Is that why Dalton attacked me? Because he thinks that? We'd seen each other for months on the running trails. What made him decide to attack me that day?"

Judith gazed at her dogs running carefree, oblivious to the drama encasing their owner. She turned to me. "I spotted the anniversary photo of you and Luke in the paper the week before. I recognized Luke and realized you were the woman who stole him from Angie and Dalton's lives. And that you lived in Lakeview." The woman I'd worked alongside for months sneered at me. "I pointed you out to Dalton as the woman who ruined his mother and his childhood."

Shock shot through my heart like a lightning bolt as the knowledge of her actions hit me. I slapped Judith across the face. I'd never hit a person before. Never believed I could. But hearing her ridiculous reasoning made me realize we are all capable of anything.

Judith blinked several times, no doubt stunned at my behavior. I sure as hell was. She shut up, and I redirected our conversation back to *my* life. "So *you* instigated the attack?"

Judith rubbed her cheek where my hand had reddened her skin. "I had no idea he encountered you while out running. It's not my fault. I think seeing you again, knowing who you were, pushed him to snap."

"He more than snapped. He could have killed me, and you continued the poison, not only destroying me but my family as well." My palms itched to slap her again.

"Well, you destroyed Dalton's future by putting him behind bars. You ruined his football career. You took him away from me. My baby." Judith's chin wobbled.

She's off her rocker! As tempting as it was to ask what world she lived in, I needed to focus on the reason I was there. "You messed with my emails at school, didn't you? You wanted to make me appear as if I couldn't do my job." I wanted it recorded. "And took our mail, left the dismembered dolls for our girls, and placed calls pretending to be me."

Her wicked smirk reminded me of the evil cat, Lucifer, in *Cinderella*. "Maybe. And perhaps I borrowed your keys from your purse to move your car and made a duplicate of your house key so I could make myself at home while you were gone." Judith's eyes sparkled as if I should be impressed by her scheming. "I may have visited you in the hospital late at night, reminding you how easily I could snuff you out of this world."

Another puzzle piece clicked into place. To know that it hadn't been a figment of my imagination boosted my determination to confront her lies. "From the beginning, you tried to make me appear unstable. To get me back for 'ruining' your daughter's life?" I refused to add Dalton to the scenario. Luke had had nothing to do with his birth. "I didn't even know Luke when he broke up with your *pregnant* daughter." It was clear she wanted to blame someone for everything that had gone wrong with her family.

I picked up steam. Our conversation was far from over. "You're twisted, Judith. You even let Percy out that freezing night. He could have died!"

Judith grunted, evidently unbothered despite having two dogs of her own. I shuddered to think of the cold-hearted woman lurking in our home while we slept.

"What did you put in my food or tea?"

She folded her arms over her chest. "Oh, a bit of this and that. Sometimes my husband's leftover painkillers, sometimes alcohol or Ambien." Her mouth twitched as if stifling a grin.

"Not only did you mess with my health, but you also endangered our children's lives!"

She scoffed as if she had a conscience. "I would never hurt your children, Lily. You told me that nobody in your family drank your green smoothies or green tea. Your kids told me the same thing. Sometimes I had access to your lunch at school, other times when I'd visit your house. Occasionally, I'd put something in your drink if a group of us got together."

I would have laughed if I wasn't so horrified by her ignorance. "You let me drive under the influence. Let me teach and care for my children drugged. You endangered so many people's lives besides just mine." Anger pushed my words out through gritted teeth. "What about the softball game? You tried to get Codi in your car at the playground. You don't consider that endangering my children? What would you have done to Codi if she'd gotten in your car?"

"Don't be silly. I wouldn't have driven off with her." She all but scolded me.

"How did you get my personal information to reorder my pills? How did you know we typically ordered pizza from the Pizza Pad? How did you know Luke's coworker is allergic to nuts?" *Did she follow us everywhere?*

"Disguises. When I lost my hair from chemo treatment years ago, I ordered several wigs in various hair colors and styles to cheer me up. It's easy to blend in when people don't pay attention." Judith folded her arms over her chest. "And just so you know, you talk too loud when giving out your personal information. That's your fault, not mine."

"How dare you blame *me* for your behavior." What a twisted world her mind lived in.

"Don't you judge me as if *you'd* never seek retaliation for a loved one." Judith leaned toward me, her eyes wild. "Angie said Luke is Dalton's father. You took him from her without an ounce of guilt. You deserve everything that's happened." Her pale lips were damp with lies.

"I would never—"

"Vengeance is in all of us. Others will understand my motives—others who haven't had a perfect life handed to them like you have!" Spittle flew from her mouth. "People who have lost loved ones killed by a drunk driver. People ridiculed by a teacher, a parent, a spouse, beating down their self-worth. People molested by a babysitter or a family member. People whose lives were ruined. Vengeance lies within them."

Jacob's confession of attacking Earl flashed through my brain. My family hadn't sensed Earl's evil, just as I hadn't with Judith. I asked the one question I wasn't sure I wanted the answer to.

"What did you put in the tea the day Luke almost drowned?"

Judith pulled back so fast it was like I'd hit her with a stun gun. "I never meant to hurt Luke. He was supposed to be gone all weekend!" She huffed. "I wanted him to leave you so he, Angie, and Dalton could be together again."

A boulder of guilt weighed in the pit of my stomach. I'd let my guard down so much that I'd allowed her to mess with not only me but my family as well. In trying to destroy me, Judith had nearly killed Luke.

Chapter 33

If Luke had been clear-headed, he'd have worn a life jacket before attempting to swim that distance. If not for our neighbor's quick actions, he'd have drowned.

But Judith hadn't meant to hurt Luke. It was me, always me. "You wanted to kill me, not Luke."

She shook her head, causing the loose skin on her cheeks to jiggle. "No! I mean, yes—I wanted you to feel what it was like to lose everything. I thought if Luke got sick of your behavior, he'd go back to Angie—and Dalton."

Judith grasped my arm, but I yanked it away.

"Luke must've remembered that Angie grew up in a town near Lakeview, the same town I lived in until last year. When I spotted his picture in the newspaper last summer, I took it as a sign that he had been looking for Angie. He must have wondered about his baby. Angie said he'd loved her back then. He could love her again. Angie and Dalton deserve happiness. You took it away!"

"Your daughter's drug problems, her poor choices... those aren't Luke's fault." I wouldn't get into Dalton not being his child. I had to believe that Luke had told me the truth. "Even if I died tomorrow, Luke would want nothing to do with Angie. She's a train wreck!"

Judith sneered. "*You* have been a train wreck. Yet he stuck with you."

I couldn't argue with that, but that was thanks to her and Dastard's actions. Judith was a wolf in sheep's clothing, and I'd allowed that wolf into my family's life. So many emotions invaded me. Sympathy for Dalton and the horrible upbringing he'd had. Even empathy for Judith and her daughter. But anger blanketed it all. Anger at what we'd endured the past year. At how easily my husband could have died.

Years ago, Luke and I had written up a bucket list of places we wanted to travel to, concerts to attend, and daring things we wanted to try like parasailing and rock climbing. Judith had almost destroyed our dreams and future together.

Without another word, I pushed myself up from the bench and walked away as Judith's pleading words for me to understand rebounded off my back.

Apologies wouldn't wipe out the last god-awful year for Luke, me, and our daughters.

I tried to dissect the fine line that separated right from wrong, justice from forgiveness, and accidental from intentional. I'd needed the truth, and I'd gotten it.

If I'd learned anything over the past year, it was to not judge. I would let the court system do that. Tears fought their way up my throat. I swallowed them. It was not the time to melt into a hot mess. Luke and Detective Boyle were waiting for me.

Luke. *Dammit, Luke. This is all because of you!* I leaned against an oak tree out of Judith's view and closed my eyes. Tears trickled down my cheeks. Dastard had beaten me to within an inch of my life because of Luke's bad date choice before we'd met. In the last year, I'd come up with a dozen possible reasons why he attacked me. Luke dating his mother hadn't been one of them. I wondered if Luke even realized who Dastard's mother was. I would find out soon enough.

I rounded the corner of the tree-lined street, and there stood Luke and Boyle, leaning against a fence.

"What're you doing here?" They were supposed to wait for me in Boyle's car.

Luke walked toward me, his arms open wide.

I'd dried my tears but hadn't tamed the turmoil inside me. "You and I need to talk. Later." Not in front of Boyle. Our conversation would have to wait until Luke and I were alone.

"You okay?" Boyle asked me as he monitored Judith, still sitting on the bench.

"Hell no." I turned to him. "You two have no idea what I just heard." I cast a look at Luke, his eyes etched with concern.

"Actually, we know." Boyle nodded to where the small recorder was hidden on me. "There's a microphone and transmitter in the recorder. When I heard Judith's twisted views on vengeance, I figured I better hustle my flat ass here, in case she came after you."

"You were listening?" So Luke had heard everything.

"Did you think I'd leave you alone? She could've tried to strangle you," Boyle said.

As shocked as I was, I couldn't help but laugh. "She's not that type of criminal." At least, I didn't think she was. But I'd been so wrong about her. "Plus, she's a lot older than me."

"There's no age limit on evil," Boyle said. "I'll wait here for backup. Someone will drop you two off at the sheriff's department."

"What? You're arresting Judith now?"

"Hell yes." Boyle popped a peppermint in his mouth. "I'll meet you back at my office." He pointed to an SUV that pulled up several feet away, blocked from Judith's view. "They'll take you to my office, get you some of our bitter coffee." Boyle turned his focus back to Judith.

The sheriff's department was a few miles from the dog park. I held on to the anger festering inside me, waiting until Luke and I sat alone in Boyle's office. I glared at Luke. "Okay, you heard Judith. What do you have to say about Angie?"

His eyes looked like a sad puppy dog, begging for forgiveness. "Angie's last name was Johnson when we dated. How was I to know she was Dalton's mother? His last name is Digg."

Luke was right. Besides, the connection between Angie and Judith hadn't been obvious either. They shared the last name of Johnson with hundreds in Minnesota.

"I'm so sorry, Lily. And no, in case you're wondering, Dalton is not my child. I told you—she was pregnant before I even met her. My old college friends can verify that."

I waved his words away. If I didn't trust him enough by now, I never would. "Let's talk about this later."

Soon, Boyle joined us. "Okey dokey, we've got a recording to listen to. And donuts. I promised Luke." He winked. "There's a law that you can't listen to a confession without donuts and bitter coffee."

I wasn't sure my stomach could handle a donut. But it was a celebration of sorts. We had Judith's confession. I had answers. And in my heart, I understood Luke was not to blame. Neither was I.

KARA, EVER HELPFUL, arrived Sunday morning, raring to go back-to-school shopping with our daughters. I handed Pria my credit card, and after they drove away, Luke and I settled in at our patio table, both of us tired from a long day yesterday. I'd called Kara last night, asking for her help in getting the girls out of the house so Luke and I could talk things over.

"Okay, let's hear it."

Luke clutched my hands. "What's the thing you've always said you like best about me?"

"Your kind heart." It was a simple answer.

He took a deep breath before starting. "White lies. Everyone tells them, right? We say them to protect someone's feelings from getting hurt. This is one I told to Angie shortly after you and I met in August of '92. She wouldn't listen to the truth, so I felt like I had no choice. I hadn't considered her delusional personality, her precarious grip on reality."

I nodded for him to continue.

"Remember when we took a day off of work that August—you from waitressing and me from my aunt and uncle's farm? I had just landed my first 'adult' job after college and needed work pants and shirts."

"Yes. I think we went to that mall near your old apartment, where most of the college students shopped."

"Yep. You'd left the department store to go to the restroom while I looked through dress shirts. A minute later, something bumped into me. I turned around, and Angie was there, pushing one of those small baby strollers back and forth, its little wheels bumping into my heels."

My eyebrows rose at that piece of news.

"I hadn't seen Angie since we'd broken up several months earlier. She was thinner than before, especially for just having a baby. I'd peeked into the stroller. A tiny baby slept, wrapped in a light-blue baby blanket. 'Long time no see,' she'd said. 'Is that your girlfriend?' She'd seen you leave for the restroom." He closed his eyes for a second as if picturing the scene. "I told her yes, you were my girlfriend. I didn't tell her your name, remembering that if you fed her information, she ran with it and twisted the hell out of it."

"What did she say?" I asked.

"She asked if you were the reason I'd broken up with her." Luke shook his head, his mouth downturned. "She was a mess. Her blond hair hung like a dirty mop, her jeans so encrusted with grime they could have walked away on their own, and she wore a stretched-out, stained tank top. She'd been dealt an unplanned pregnancy and had the gumption to go through with it and keep the baby." Luke's voice faded to a whisper. "I felt sorry for her."

After another pause, he continued. "I'd heard through the grapevine that she'd had the baby, but didn't know she'd kept him. I knew you'd be back in a minute and did *not* want to introduce you to

Angie. I'd reminded her why we broke up—the reason was front and center in the stroller." He cracked his knuckles, and his leg bounced under the patio table.

"Angie clung to my arm. She started rambling about how good we'd been together and all the fun we'd had. Then she said, 'It could work for us! My son has a dimple like yours. You could pass for his birth father. We wouldn't have to tell anyone. We could be a family.' I yanked my arm away, not wanting to get pulled into her twisted dream world."

I shook my head at Angie's convoluted plan. Unlike Luke, Dalton had blond hair and fair skin. "Other than green eyes—and okay, the dimple, too—he'd never pass for your son."

"I know, but reasoning didn't work with her. And she must have led her mom to believe that I was Dalton's dad. We'd barely dated. It was never serious. But to her, I was the answer to the situation she was in." Luke stood and paced. "She begged me. She stood so close that I could smell her—she stank like a wet dog, making my stomach roil. I felt bad for her and the situation she was in. I was a sucker. Angie probably remembered that about me."

I hated that what I loved most about Luke had been used as a weapon against him.

He ran his fingers through his hair. "It was awful, Lily. She wouldn't leave me alone!"

My heart ached for him as I pictured the scene he described. Luke would have wanted to make Angie feel better. "She kept bugging me, asking if I still loved her, as if I ever had to begin with. Then she started yelling, 'Say it. Tell me you love me and that it's her fault we aren't together' over and over. All I could think about was you coming back, and how I might make her so angry that she'd take it out on her baby."

Luke downed several gulps of water from his glass. "I caved. I told her, 'You're right. I broke up with you to be with her. I'm sorry, but I've got to go.' I said goodbye and almost ran down the store aisle toward the women's restroom. I didn't peer back until I rounded the corner. She was right where I'd left her, her hands white-knuckling the stroller handles."

He leaned down and took my face in his hands, his palms warm against my cheeks. "I was so ignorant, thinking I'd said the right thing. Thinking I'd dodged a bullet. I didn't. That bullet lay in wait for eighteen years until it found us."

"I remember that day. You were fine when I left for the bathroom, and when I walked out, you were waiting there for me and pulled me out toward the exit, saying you didn't feel like shopping anymore. I'd thought you were upset with me about something. You were so quiet on the ride back to the farm."

"I should have told you then what happened. I figured I'd never see Angie again, never thought about the harm in my white lie. I should've offered Angie help instead of worrying about hurting her feelings."

Instead, the lie had become a hot ember, smoldering for years until Judith spotted our anniversary photo and Luke's name. All it had taken was a little fanning for the ember to burst into an inferno.

I put my arms around his neck. "Your compassion and empathy are what I love about you—things it's taken me years to embrace myself. I've learned firsthand how easy it is to stumble when life trips you." I leaned in and kissed him. "Feel better now?"

Luke leaned his forehead against mine and nodded.

"Me too." The weight that had felt like a hippo sitting on my chest over the past year disintegrated, allowing me to take a deep breath again.

Chapter 34

I called Jacob on Sunday night, relaying the details of my conversation with Judith.

"Holy shit!" Jacob waited until I was through the long-winded replay of events.

"The worst thing was listening to her calm reasoning as if everything they had done made perfect sense to her. As if everyone with a shitty life deserved to wreck someone else's." I winced, thinking of how that was what Earl had probably done to Jacob.

"You and Luke talk it out? Does he do that?" It broke my heart that Luke and Jacob barely knew each other. Jacob hadn't experienced Luke's kind heart, his love for his family, his honesty and empathy.

"Yes. And now we're kicking it to the curb. It's in the past where it belongs."

"When I was in my heavy drinking days, I dated any woman that had a pulse," Jacob said. "I cringe thinking about any of them coming back to mess with my life now. Not that I was any great prize back then. I was screwed up. Most of the women I got together with were too."

I closed my eyes, reflecting on our carefree youth. Back when Jacob and I believed all we had to do was work hard and everything would turn out fine.

"It's good you're letting go of your shit pile of a year," Jacob said. "You'll feel better."

"Listen to you. You haven't let it go with Dad. You quit our family, Jacob. *For twenty years.*" My nose tingled with unshed tears. "You need to do the same with Dad."

There was silence on his end for so long that I looked at the phone to make sure our connection hadn't dropped.

"Fine," he said at last. "And you need to confront them about giving you the twisted idea that only the weak stumble."

"I didn't think you were listening when I confessed that." I smiled for the first time in days. "Mom and Dad are going to need our help to move from the farm soon. We'll make a family party out of it. A big 'let's purge the past' party." It wasn't a question. I was the older sibling, and I hadn't been able to boss him around for twenty years.

Regret was too big a pill for us to choke on for the rest of our lives.

THE LAST WEEKEND IN August, our family made one last trip to my parents' farm to help them move. So did Jacob. It was the first time we had all been together in years. Our first night there, Jacob and Dad went for a drive. I don't know where they went or what they talked about, but I swear, when they arrived home, the lines on Dad's face had softened, and Jacob's posture had relaxed.

For three days, we packed, unpacked, and helped Mom and Dad settle into their new, smaller home. During that time, I addressed the lesson I'd thought my parents had tried to instill in me from childhood. I started with Dad as we loaded boxes in the back of his pickup.

He set down a box and turned to me. "Aw, Lily. I can't believe that's what you've thought all these years." He hoisted himself to sit on the open tailgate, and I did the same.

"Yes, I may have said, 'People fail because they don't try hard enough,' referring to your grade school classmate's family, but in their case, they lost the farm because her dad gambled all their money away. He had an addiction, something that can happen to any of us. I probably didn't choose the right words back then, but I didn't want you to worry about us losing the farm." He nudged me and smiled. "Guess I didn't realize you were hanging on every word."

I approached Mom that night as we packed kitchen items, reciting my childhood memory of us in the garden. Back then, I'd asked her why some garden plants failed to thrive. She'd said, "Only the weak fail."

"Poor girl." Mom pulled me in for a hug. "I wanted you to understand that everything we plant doesn't always produce. That's just the way life is. We're all weak, Lily, because we're human. Nobody's perfect."

I knew that, but it had taken too many years to be okay with living it.

BETWEEN COLLEGE CLASSES, studying, and substitute teaching, September taxed my brain. I welcomed the challenge, glad to think clearly again. My class schedule filled three days a week, allowing me to fill in as a substitute teacher.

The first week back to school, I stopped in at my old school and visited with some of the teachers during lunch break. Maria pulled me aside, apologizing over and over for bringing Judith into my life.

"It's not your fault." I hugged the soft-spoken woman who'd been my sidekick and Barb's for every year I'd taught at the grade school.

"But it is. When my son-in-law met Judith and told me about how she was looking for part-time work and loved children, I'd taken that first step and called her. I encouraged her to apply to our school.

If I hadn't called her, she wouldn't have been in your classroom." Maria shook her head as if she hadn't scolded herself enough already.

"Listen, Maria, I think Judith targeted your son-in-law. You said he met her at the hospital while his mother was in surgery and Judith's husband was in critical care, right?"

Maria nodded.

"By then, Dalton had attacked me. Judith knew who I was, where I taught, and likely traced you to your son-in-law at the hospital. You couldn't have stopped her from worming her way into my classroom if you tried." I held Maria's warm hand in mine.

She dabbed at her dark eyes. "But I invited her into your home, into your circle of friends. Oh, I'll never forgive myself." She clutched a hanky over her ample chest.

"I befriended her too. Believe me. She did a superb job of deceiving us." I hugged her shoulders.

I would miss teaching at the school and the eager and energetic children. But I could see my old coworkers off and on as I shadowed the school counselor at the grade school between my college classes. It wouldn't be the same. But nothing stayed the same in life, and maybe that was okay.

Pria had gotten her driver's license, and so far, her junior year was going well. It was almost as if the past year hadn't happened. Almost. But I'd changed—physically and mentally.

If not for the past year, I wouldn't have mended my relationship with Jacob. I wouldn't have felt the pull to pursue my counseling degree. Luke and I wouldn't have dug our heels in to fight for the marriage we'd once taken for granted. And Judith—at sixty-five—wouldn't be sitting in jail. She'd taken a plea bargain, accepting charges of harassment versus felony charges for drugging, stalking, and several other crimes they'd brought to the table.

"Just think, she will spend most of the next year sitting in jail. Funny, Dalton is a free man, and his grandma is behind bars," Luke said after Boyle shared the news with us yesterday.

Luke grilled burgers in our backyard while I set a salad and grilled potatoes on the patio table. "Funny, and sad. I used to think we had a perfect life. Now I know nobody's life is perfect—that most people have invisible wounds. And I'm thankful we survived to share more of our imperfect lives."

The girls had been back at school for three weeks, and it was a rare night with no practice or soccer game for Pria. We'd decided to celebrate our family's opportunity for a do-over, and Ali, who'd done a stellar job rolling with the punches of the last year, had insisted we make a cake. Luke pulled me in for a kiss just as the sliding glass door opened, and our daughters walked out, balancing the chocolate-layer cake and plates between them.

Luke and I broke apart to pull them in for a family embrace—our imperfect children who completed our imperfect lives.

Acknowledgments

Picture Elaine from *Seinfeld* crazy dancing, and you'll envision my reaction after I received "the call" from Lynn McNamee at Red Adept Publishing. Thank you, Lynn and the RAP team, for bringing Lily's story to readers. Content editor Angie Lovell's expertise helped me smooth out story wrinkles with recommendations like changing the story from three points of view to one. And line editor Marirose Smith's wisdom helped tame my grammar and punctuation.

Writing a book often feels isolating. That's where the Women's Fiction Writers Association comes in. When COVID-19 hit, a WFWA writing Zoom group formed thanks to Michele Montgomery. We prop each other up and cheer each other on across the miles as we create stories. The WFWA connected me with my critique partners, Kerry Morgan and Lynne Marino, who gave helpful feedback in the early drafts of this book. Also, much thanks to other authors outside of the WFWA who have shared their wisdom along the way.

This book would've been a hot mess without insight from professionals. For medical research, many thanks to Dr. Shawn Roberts, Dr. Kara Maucieri, and Dr. Arlene O'Connor. For legal and detective research, Brook Mallak and Craig Katzenberger. In the education field, Laura Paulson and Tim Edinger. For insight on correctional facilities, Warden Kathy Halverson. Any factual errors are mine.

Books without readers would be like me without chocolate. Authors count on librarians, book bloggers, and booklovers on social media who help connect books and readers—people like Susan Peterson, Kristy Barrett, Tonni Callan, Suzanne Leopold, Linda Zagon, Suzy Missirlian, Barbara Kahn, Cindy Roesel, Tamara Welch, Kate Rock, Tina Hogan, Dawnny Ruby, Denise Birt, Stephanie Ward, Jennifer Bryan-Vawser, Annie McDonnell, Kayleigh Wilkes, and all the dedicated readers who share their love of books... too many to list here!

Thank you to my husband, Don, for putting up with my writing angst and the many hours this book took me away from doing "fun" things like cooking and cleaning. Thanks to my girlfriends and family, who have been so supportive of my writing journey. And thank you to the Jacobs family for giving me some of my best childhood memories from summers spent on their farm.

Readers often ask where I get my story ideas. This one came from people who appear to have a perfect life and have had anything but. We never know what invisible wounds others might carry, and I used the lyrics to Joe South's "Walk a Mile in My Shoes" as the backbone for this story. This book is dedicated to my dear friend Donna, a mother of four sons who always said if she'd had a daughter, she would have named her Lily. When Donna passed away, I knew I'd write a story about a woman named Lily—a woman with invisible wounds.

If you enjoyed Lily's story, I hope you'll recommend it to your friends and take a moment to leave a review. They help not only the author but fellow booklovers as well. Please follow me on social media to get updates on book news!

Don't miss out!

Visit the website below and you can sign up to receive emails whenever Jill Hannah Anderson publishes a new book. There's no charge and no obligation.

https://books2read.com/r/B-A-ZTQR-AEKVB

BOOKS 2 READ

Connecting independent readers to independent writers.

Did you love *A Life Unraveled*? Then you should read *One Little Word*[1] by Audra McElyea!

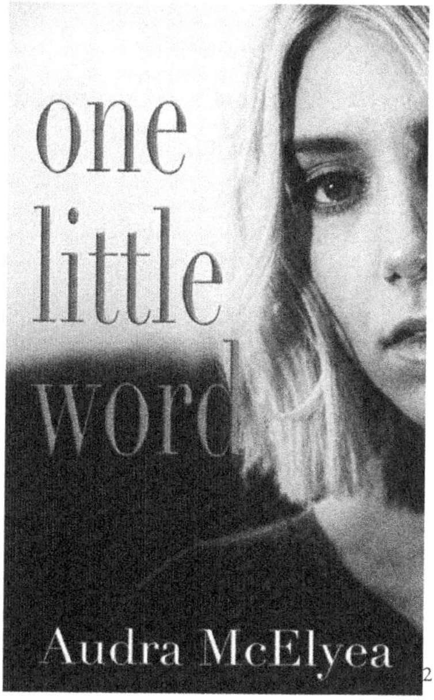

[2]

Allegra Hudson was murdered.

An anonymous "source" drops the note into recently widowed Madeleine Barton's lap exactly when she needs it most. As a new single mother, she is struggling to make ends meet as a freelance reporter, and covering the mysterious death of local bestselling author Allegra Hudson could be the career-launching story of her dreams.

Working with Allegra's grieving husband, Connor, Madeleine plunges down the rabbit hole of the writer's privileged life. The deeper she digs, the more dirt she finds: a conniving best friend, a stalker ex-boyfriend, and a marriage in shambles. The closer Madeleine gets to the truth, the murkier the waters become.

---

1. https://books2read.com/u/47QMoN

2. https://books2read.com/u/47QMoN

Her source's looming presence and constant meddling in her investigation paired with her growing bond with Connor over their shared grief have blinded her to the facts, but nothing explains why Allegra Hudson's life feels so familiar. Only one thing is certain: Madeleine can trust no one.

One Little Word is a deliciously clever game of cat-and-mouse with a completely unexpected twist.

Read more at audramcelyea.com.

About the Author

Jill Hannah Anderson writes stories about "strong women in tough situations." Jill is a member of the Women's Fiction Writers Association (WFWA) and wrote part-time for ten years for a Minnesota women's magazine.

Jill lives on a lake in Minnesota with her husband in their rarely empty nest. When she isn't writing or reading, you'll find her running, curling, biking, crazy dancing, and spending time with their adult children and sixteen grandkids. She loves to connect with book clubs!

Read more at www.jillhannahanderson.com.

Red Adept Publishing

Unlocking New Worlds

About the Publisher

Dear Reader,

We hope you enjoyed this book. Please consider leaving a review on your favorite book site.

Visit https://RedAdeptPublishing.com to see our entire catalogue.

Don't forget to subscribe to our monthly newsletter to be notified of future releases and special sales.

Made in the USA
Monee, IL
31 May 2023

34826450R00174